Too Sharp

Tara Sharp Book Three

d

Too Sharp

Marianne Delacourt

deadlines

by *deadlines*

www.twelfthplanetpress.com

This edition published by Deadlines, March 2017
First published in Australia in 2010 by Allen & Unwin.
Copyright © 2010 by Marianne Delacourt

National Library of Australia Cataloguing-in-Publication entry

Creator: Delacourt, Marianne, author.
Title: Too sharp / Marianne de Pierres.
ISBN: 9781922101334 (paperback)
Series: Delacourt, Marianne. Tara Sharp; 3.
Subjects: Private investigators--Fiction.
 Telepathy--Fiction.
 Music trade--Fiction.
A823.4

To Kylie T.

for teaching me what it means to smile through adversity.

Chapter 1

Wal let me into his flat above the empty antique shop. He cast a furtive look into the night then quickly closed the door and locked it.

A little shiver tap-danced along my spine. My security chief was confident he could handle himself in any situation. It came from having been a roadie for some hardcore bands and a misspent youth developing an unhealthy obsession with weapons. Wal didn't lock doors unless something bad was going on.

Had I been followed? Was there a sniper on the roof across the road? Someone hiding in the rosebushes along the fence? A stream of scenarios flashed through my mind, none of them good.

'Got your text. 'S'up?' I said, glancing at the window as if someone might suddenly rappel through it.

My paranoia was accentuated by a bunch of different things. For a start, there was the crime lord, Johnny Viaspa, who wanted the worst for me. And the wealthy businessman, Bolo Ignatius, who would happily see me locked up. And the hit man who was locked up—because of me.

On top of that stuff was my psychic ability, which let me read auras and body language. That kind of affliction … er, gift … left a girl a little sensitive to all the nasty things in life. For example, on my way to Wal's, I'd stopped at the petrol station to fill up my beloved 1970s Monaro, Mona. The guy behind the mound of lollies and lottery tickets on the counter had a stark white aura that glowed like a halo. In my experience, white auras meant health problems. I tried to ignore it, but then I spotted a dark mole on his wrist.

'You should get that checked,' I said before I could stop myself.

'You should mind your own business,' he said, scowling at me.

I left, embarrassed. That kind of thing happened all the time. People thought I was either nosy or kooky, neither of which made for good first impressions.

'Keep away from the window,' said Wal now as I walked across the room and peered out.

'Sniper?' I asked.

He gave me a funny look. 'Nope. Glass is cracked. You touch it, it'll shatter.'

I sighed and reined in my imagination, feeling foolish. 'How did that happen?'

'Someone tried to break in last night.'

Aha! My imagination was vindicated. I gave Wal a stare. His aura was busy; sparking and sputtering around him like he was about to short circuit. Something was definitely going on.

And normally he favoured the bogan Russian mafioso look—tight black jeans, black shirt, black cigarettes with gold filters—but today he was all Australian in faded, baggy denims and a singlet. I didn't know how old he was but the skin on his arms and shoulders was scarred and spotted. He had a naturally brawny physique and long red hair that came from his Irish ancestors. The snarl, though, was all his.

'Problem?'

'Nothing I can't handle,' he said.

'Then why am I here?' I usually called Wal to help me, not the other way around. He'd started as my part-time security chief a few months back when narcolepsy had forced him to quit the band life. These days he was living on the pension, the bit of cash I was able to send his way, and my rich Aunt Liv. It seemed to be enough to keep him in cigarettes and ammunition. I sure as hell never asked about the latter.

'Got this mate who's in a spot,' he said.

'And?'

He slunk across to his tiny kitchenette and put a pan of water on to boil. Looked like I was getting a cuppa whether I wanted it or not.

'Sugar?' he asked as he took a chipped mug from the

cupboard. 'Milk?'

This had me even more worried. Wal didn't make tea.

'One sugar and raincheck on the milk,' I said as he sniffed at the carton he'd pulled from his tiny bar fridge. 'Tell me what you want.'

He didn't answer, but carried on going through the tea ritual. In fact, not until I was sitting on his Liv-donated overstuffed armchair with a scalding cup of black tea in my hand did he even look at me.

'Stuart—my mate—he's a music promoter in Brisbane,' he said finally.

'And?'

'We go back. He was a roadie with me, though he was younger; started managing a garage band a few years ago. One thing led to the next and he turned to promoting a year back. We keep in touch.'

I didn't ask what that meant. With Wal it's always better to know less.

He took a sip from his cup. His was rum, though, not tea.

Something about this Stuart guy was really bothering him and I waited for him to get it off his chest—not that he seemed to be in any great hurry to do so. I watched him for telltale signs of dozing off, but his narcolepsy had been better since Liv had made him promise to take his meds (and promised to pay for them). Not sure that the rum was a good idea but that wasn't really my business—at least, when he was off duty it wasn't.

'He's a bulldog once he gets his teeth into something,' Wal went on. 'Never known a bloke to be so dogged. Stuck at the business for a year with nothing much happening and now he's finally landed a big act.'

'Great!'

'Would be,' said Wal, glowering. 'But some prick's trying to squeeze him out.'

'How so?'

'Venues aren't returning his calls, equipment places won't hire to him.'

I didn't say anything. No point in asking what he wanted me to do. He'd get to it.

'Thing is, there's a few big guys on the block and he can't pick where it's coming from. If he could, maybe he could deal with it.'

'Uh-huh.'

'So I said I was working for someone who'd be able to help him. Said you was good.'

'Wal, you're killing me with compliments.'

He shot me a narrow-eyed look. 'Can't talk like a woman to him, boss. Blokes don't get that. I said you was good, he knows what that means.'

I pulled a face. 'Joking. You want me to chat to him?'

His frown lifted. 'Would ya, boss? It'd mean a lot.'

'Don't know if I'll be able to help.' I took a sip of the tea. 'Not to be rude, Wal, but can he pay?'

'Mates rates.' Wal framed it as a given.

I sighed. I couldn't really afford mates rates right now, but how could I refuse Wal a favour when he'd worked for me for nothing on some jobs? Besides, he could torture me in a million different ways.

'Okay. But that means your cut will be less.'

My little joke. He didn't get paid unless I did, and that wasn't often enough for either of us. That's why I was still living in my parents' garage, putting up with my mother trying to matchmake me with wealthy losers.

Aaaah, mother dear; Joanna Sharp, heiress of highbrow and super-snoot. I loved her. I did! But we were different animals. In fact, she confided in me once that she thought they'd mixed up babies at the hospital when I was born. Her little joke. She laughed in her twinkly, silvery, refined way when she said it. But I never found it all that funny. I also figured that dark thoughts would get me nowhere fast, and life was full of enough landmines without stepping on one deliberately. So I let it go. She still drove me insane though.

'I'll get him to call you, then,' said Wal, knocking back the remainder of his rum.

'Fine,' I said. 'Tomorrow. I've got a date tonight.'

'Huh?' His eyebrows rose. 'Which bloke?'

I gave him my most quelling look. Which bloke indeed! 'Ed.'

'Poor sod.'

'What do you mean?' I asked, and immediately

wished I hadn't. Wal told it like he saw it, with no real consideration for feelings.

'Doesn't know if he's coming or going with you.'

'Ed and I are in the early stages of a friendship,' I said primly.

He shrugged. 'Well, don't string him on too long on account of that rich fella.'

'I have to get going,' I said huffily, putting my tea down on the table.

He saw me out, unperturbed by my stiff manner. 'See ya later, boss. Thanks.'

The door locked behind me.

Once I was back in my car and on the road, I calmed down a little. Wal didn't often comment on my personal life—never, actually. Maybe I should take his comments under advisement.

Truth was, I had a Clayton's love life: the kind you have when you don't have one. First there was Eduardo, my date, a sweet, gorgeous model and former country boy I'd rescued from a bunch of marauding gym ladies. Since then we'd been dating on and off. He found my work hard to stomach and I found his stomach … hard!

I turned off Stirling Highway at the Jarrad Street traffic lights.

The Ed thing should have been perfect for a girl whose life was in a state of flux, but there was this other guy I couldn't get out of my head. It wasn't because, as Wal said, he was rich. In fact, I found the whole rich thing a tad tiresome because it brought with it a coke-addicted wife and way too much baggage. Thing was, there was this kind of electricity between Nick Tozzi and me. Truly! Not the kind of electricity you read about in romance books but the real kind. When we touched, my aura gave me a hundred-volt shock. I got all tongue-tied and quivery and … well … messy. It was embarrassing. I tried to stay away from him but we had history. I saved him from losing his business and he … well … saved my life.

Now it'd gotten complicated. We'd talked about it a little; agreed that we were attracted to each other but that it didn't have to mean anything in the grand scheme. He'd gone away happy and was trying to sort out his marriage. I'd come away more confused than ever. I mean, I liked Eduardo a lot. Really a lot! And found him smoking hot. But this 'thing' with Nick Tozzi kept stopping me from committing.

So right now, before my date with Ed, I was on my way to a Smitty and Bok therapy session. My two best friends weren't ones to hold back on the subject of my love life, and even I knew it had reached the point where I needed intervention.

I pulled up outside Bok's apartment block and sat for a moment to summon my courage. This is necessary, I told myself. I need help.

My last relationship had ended worse than badly because The Bastard ran off with our housemate and my furniture. That, combined with the whole I-can-read-auras thing, left me pretty wary of starting over. It was hard to feel good about someone when their aura was telling you they were hot for the girl next to you.

I did a quick check in the rear-view mirror. Make-up still intact (Bok hated it when I didn't wear lippy). Hair scraped back in a ponytail—must remember to brush it out before I met up with Ed later.

Okay. Let's do this.

I key-locked Mona—no central locking on a 1980s Monaro—and caught the lift to Bok's apartment.

Smitty opened the door with a glass of champagne in hand. 'Darling, hurry in and start drinking before I drain the well dry.'

'Smitts?' Her normally flawless complexion was blotchy and her cute nose red and runny. My frightfully decent and usually immaculate bestie was looking a mess.

She hiccoughed, sniffed and then screwed up her face. 'Henny and I had an awful fight.'

I put my arms around her and she fell against me, her head in line with my armpit. I steered her backwards inside and let the door close behind me.

Bok came out of his bedroom with his phone to his ear. He took one look at us and the champagne bottle upside down in the ice bucket and told whoever he was talking to he'd call them back.

'Smitts,' he said. 'You murdered a whole bottle of Bolly while I was on the phone.'

The only reply he got was a heartfelt sob.

Bok and I exchanged looks as I gently lowered Smitty onto the couch. My t-shirt was getting snotty and tear-wet so I tried to ease her away, but she clung to me like a limpet with separation issues.

'Come on, Smitts. How long have you two been together?' I asked, knowing the answer full well. Smitty, Henry and I had been through school and uni together. They'd been a couple forever. And a great couple at that. Three gorgeous kids, no mortgage (on account of him being a well-heeled doctor) and an out-of-control dog named Fridge. They had everything I thought I wanted … except moments like these.

'Jane Smith, stop being a drama queen. What's a little disagreement between the perfect couple?' Bok's lame attempt at stern just caused further sobs.

In the twenty-plus years I'd known Smitty she'd only cried like this once before, and that was when her mum passed away.

'Hey there, Smitts. No one's died.' Then a terrible thought assailed me. 'Is Claire alright?' Hen and Smitts' eldest suffered from Crohn's disease, and had been in hospital on and off all her life.

Smitts actually stopped crying for a moment and raised her head. I took the opportunity to extract myself from her embrace.

'No, Claire's fine,' she said. 'As fine as a nearly sixteen-year-old can be.' Sniff.

'Then what's wrong with you and Hen?'

'I think…' She paused as if having trouble getting her tongue to pronounce the words. 'I think Henny is having an affair.'

Bok and I were silent for a full minute before Bok disappeared into the kitchen and returned with another bottle of champagne. A cheaper bottle. I'd planned to drive to my date with Ed, but something told me tonight wasn't going to go according to plan.

'He can't be,' I said after a large swig of sparkly goodness.

'He thinks you're a Goddess, darling,' added Bok.

Smitty looked unconvinced.

I finished my glass and poured another, ignoring Bok's withering frown. 'Okay, let's examine the evidence. Lay it on us.'

Smitty reached into her purse and withdrew a dainty handkerchief. After a less than delicate blow of her nose, she took a breath.

'I took his suit jacket to the dry cleaners. They found something in the pocket, so they pinned it to the front in an envelope. I don't read his email or anything, you know that,' she said. 'But…'

'But?'

'I didn't know what it was, so I opened it.'

'Smitts, you're killing us,' I said. 'Get to it.'

'It had Belle Bussey's name and phone number on it.' She curled up into a ball, hugging one of Bok's silk-covered pillows.

'Is that it?' asked Bok. 'You're having a crack-up about that?' He stared at the crumpled pillow like he wanted to wrest it from her grasp and possibly hit her on the head with it. Bok was not the patient type.

Nor was I. In fact, we weren't the greatest pair to help with heartbreak, but I knew Belle Bussey and Bok didn't. I understood why Smitty was in the foetal position on the couch.

'Honey, I'm going to make you something stronger. I'll be back in a jiff.' I turned to Bok. 'Unlock the booze cupboard,' I ordered.

He preceded me into the kitchen and planted his back to the pantry, arms crossed.

Bok was gorgeous. Long, silky black hair and a beautiful face gifted from his mixed Asian-Latino heritage. Girls went mad for him. So, did guys. He enjoyed the attention from both.

Right now, he was gifting me with his most stubborn look.

'You do not get any more of my booze until you tell me what's going on,' he said.

Being a magazine editor who entertained visiting models, clients and industry people, Bok always kept the booze cupboard well stocked. He also shifted the hiding spot for the key on a regular basis, in case I found it. Not that I was a big drinker or anything but there are … occasions that require certain measures—of the spirit kind. Now was one.

'Belle Bussey caught the same bus as us but she was a year older and went to another school. The father owned a bank. According to JoBob, the mother was connected to the Swedish royals, though I doubt it. Nothing naturally blonde about her.'

Bok looked thoughtful. 'You mean Spanders Bank?'

'Yeah, that's it. Anyway, Belle had it bad for Henny. When we finished school, she offered to take him to Europe for summer hols.'

'And he didn't go?'

'What? And leave Smitts here alone? Our girl was something else when we were teens. I mean … she still is.'

'Yes, she's always had the Grace Kelly look going on,' he agreed. 'So this Belle Bussey is a would-be ex-flame. If he didn't go for it back then, why would he go for it now?'

'Well, the summer we finished high school, Henny and Smitts had a huge fight. Can't remember what about but it was epic. They didn't speak for nearly two months.'

'Don't tell me. He slept with Belle.'

I rolled my eyes. 'You got it. But it gets worse. Belle proposed to him.'

'Shut up!' said Bok, his eyes widening. 'So, what did bachelor boy do after she got down on bended knee?'

'What any normal eighteen-year-old would do—he ran a mile. All the way back to Smitts.'

'Did she welcome him with open arms?'

13

I remembered Smitty's agonising. 'Not one bit. She made him work for it, but the deal-breaker was Belle. He had to promise never to make contact with her again. Ever!'

'Oh.' Bok produced the key from his jeans pocket. 'In that case, there're some vodka on the bottom rack. Or we could crack a bottle of bourbon.'

I gave the pantry a quick squiz. Above the shelves of booze was a single shelf with two different breakfast cereals, six tins of salmon, a box of ginseng tea bags, an open packet of water crackers and some Tim Tams.

'Remind me not to come here for dinner,' I said, grabbing the bourbon. 'Got any Coke?'

'Dry ginger ale?'

'Sounds good. I'll get the glasses.'

I returned to our foetal friend and plonked the grog and glasses down. 'Okay,' I said. 'He's up to speed.'

She uncurled, took a glass and held it out. As I poured, Bok appeared with the mixer and a plate of brie and stale crackers. We huddled in and got to it.

'Could be a bunch of explanations, Smitty,' I said. 'Give him the benefit.'

She shook her head. 'We had a deal. Never her. Never again. I can't believe it.'

'Tara is right, Smitts. There could be a good reason. Henny isn't stupid. He knows what would happen.'

'Maybe he's sabotaging our marriage. Maybe he wanted me to find out. Have I got too fat? Am I terribly boring?' Her lips quivered and she took a gulp of bourbon. 'It's the pearls, isn't it? He always said he hated women in pearls because they reminded him of his mother. I wore pearls to the Maynards' wedding.'

'No, Smitty, it's not the pearls.' I sighed and topped up her glass, and my own. It was going to be a long night.

We talked back and forth for an hour or so, Bok and me defending Henny while Smitty vacillated between blaming herself and him.

When Bok's art deco clock chimed 8PM, I got out my phone to send Ed a text. crisis talks. cn u pick me up @ boks. drunk t

Smitty bumped my elbow and I pressed send.

'Whatcha doing?' she asked, squinting at the screen.

'S'posed to be meeting Ed.'

'Oh my God!' Her shriek had me plugging my fingers in my ears. 'How selfish of me!'

'Calm down,' I said, unplugging. 'He'll come and get—'

My phone beeped a reply. My car is in garage. Another time.

'Ooooorrr NOT,' I finished lamely.

'Nooo,' moaned Smitts, rocking from side to side in the grip of alcoholic dramatis. 'I've ruined your date.' She'd never been able to hold her liquor as well as Bok and me.

'Shall I slap her sober?' whispered Bok from behind his hand.

I sighed and shook my head. 'Put the kettle on.'

Bok nodded and weaved a slightly erratic path to the kitchen. As he disappeared, Smitts grabbed my hand and hauled me close. Suddenly she appeared sober.

'T, you have to do something for me.'

'What?' I asked, feeling slightly annoyed by Ed blowing me off.

'I want you to spy on Hen.'

Chapter 2

'You're kidding me!' I croaked.

'I want him followed. I want proof.'

'I can't do that. After you and Bok, he's one of my oldest friends. Smitts, don't ask me—'

'Tara Sharp,' she said in her most clipped and proper voice. 'Do you love me?'

'Smitts, please—'

'Do you?'

I rubbed my forehead, feeling a headache coming on, one that wouldn't go away any time soon. 'But I can't, he'd see me.'

'Then put one of the others on him. I want my husband tailed.'

'Wal can't—'

'Not the Russian mafioso. No ... what about that young girl?'

'Cass?'

'She works for you, doesn't she?'

'Um… I guess so.' There was no stopping Smitty once she'd made a decision.

'I'll pay you, of course.'

'Smitts, I don't think it's a good idea.'

'Shhh. Shush! ShhhhSH!' She waved her finger at me. Maybe she wasn't so sober after all. 'Don't you dare tell anyone. Even Bok. Client privilege.'

I took the cushion she'd been clutching and banged it against my head. 'Arggh. This isn't fair!'

'What's not fair?' Bok was back with a tray of coffee and tea and some fancily wrapped chocolates. I took a mug and sipped away so that I didn't have to answer. The tea scalded my tongue but it was better than admitting to Bok that I'd just agreed to spy on Henry.

'To husbands who cheat,' declared Smitts, knocking back the last of her bourbon. She crossed her arms and fell back into the couch, her hair covering her face. Before I could take another sip of my tea, her jaw sagged a little and she fell asleep.

'Thank God,' said Bok. 'I was considering Valium.'

'We'd better ring Henny.'

'To say what?' Bok was short on sympathy sometimes. Other times he was overflowing with it. You could just never tell.

'The truth … kinda.'

I decided Bok's impatience with Smitts' meltdown might have its roots somewhere in the fact that he hadn't had a partner in a few years. No one who'd lasted more than a couple of months, anyway. I didn't exactly have the best track record either, which had left me with some trust issues, and was partly why I was so miffed at Ed giving me the flick. I contemplated calling a taxi and just turning up on his doorstep, but first I needed to sort Smitty out.

Scrolling through my contacts list, I pulled up Henry's mobile number. He answered quickly, sounding anxious.

'Tara?'

'Hi, darling,' I said lightly. 'Look, Bok's had a bit of a crisis and Smitts and I have been counselling him heavily. Poor Smitty darling's gotten all worn out and fallen asleep on us.'

'She's drunk,' he said flatly.

'Well … yes. But all for a good cause.'

'Matter of opinion,' he grumbled. 'I'll come and get her.'

'Look, Henny, she's out cold. Why don't you leave her here tonight? Bok will bring her home first thing. Besides, Bok needs someone here. He's in a bad way.'

Bok rolled his eyes and made throat-cutting gestures. His normally fresh blue aura darkened to cobalt with annoyance.

'Why. Lost his favourite handbag?'

The jibe was unlike Henry, who really was a decent bloke. Bitchy cracks like that weren't his style. Still, that didn't mean… I refused to believe… 'Claire has physio at 9AM,' he said. 'Make sure she's back in time.'

'Scout's honour,' I promised.

'In which lifetime were you ever a bloody boy scout, Tara Sharp?' He hung up.

'Ow,' I winced.

'Should have taken her home.'

'Not like this,' I said. 'She might have said something she'd regret.'

Bok sighed this time. 'You're right.'

He smoothed back Smitty's hair then fetched a blanket from his bedroom. He tucked it around her and eased her back into a more comfortable position on her side.

'She's always so calm and perfect,' said Bok. 'I'm not used to seeing her like this.'

'Henny and her kids are her entire world.'

'But it's not true. He'd never cheat.'

'No,' I agreed. 'He wouldn't.'

We both stared at our sleeping friend, keeping any other thoughts to ourselves. Henny and Smitts were the centre of our universe; all that was good, all that we aspired to. All that we weren't. Any kind of rift between them was likely to rip our universe apart.

I made a decision right then. I was going to get Cass to follow him. But if it turned out Smitty was right, I wasn't going to tell her. I'd go straight to Henny and knock his head until he got some sense. Yes, that's what I'd do. If there was a problem, I'd fix it.

I smiled at Bok, who was lost in his own musings. 'I'll grab an Uber.'

He nodded absently. 'I should get to bed. Early start

tomorrow.'

I kissed him on the forehead. 'Leave some water on the table for her and the bathroom light on.'

Another distracted nod.

I walked to the front door and glanced back. Two bottles of champagne and a bottle of bourbon sat empty on the coffee table among the broken crackers and scrapings of brie.

Maybe I wasn't as sober as I thought I was.

I took the lift down to the foyer and dithered over what to do. The smart thing would be to cab straight home, but I had a sudden desire to walk. The evening air was fresh but not cold—a hint of summer on the way. And the nearby gardens were wafting the scent of early-flowering gardenias at me. Walking to my place would take nearly an hour, while Ed's was only fifteen minutes away. I hadn't exactly been invited over, but maybe a surprise visit was just the thing to break the ice between us. I figured it was time to at least press the flesh with him.

Taking a right turn, I began to wind my way down Queenslea Drive past Bethesda Hospital and Christ Church Grammar. The school's night lights showed enough of the grounds to give me a giggle at times past. Christ Church boys always liked to party back in my day.

Before long I was almost at the Stirling Highway lights and the church. The memory that evoked was entirely different. Nick Tozzi had parked in the church driveway the night he'd rescued me from Johnny Viaspa's front fence. I'd been snooping and slipped. Next thing I knew I was hanging onto one of the wrought-iron palings, swinging my bum above Viaspa's dog.

Tozzi, being nearly seven-foot-tall and an ex-NBA basketballer, had been able to lift me bodily off the fence and whisk me to safety in his Lambo—but not before parking right here and giving me a serious talking to.

Aaah, Tozzi... What was it about that man that just wouldn't go away? He was married, in love with his wife—sort of—and altogether too used to getting his own way for my liking. But he also had a great sense of humour and a goofy side that showed itself from time to time. Most of all, I loved his warm and sticky aura, which flowed around his body with the consistency of caramel topping. Sometimes, though, that aura would go hard and send sparks flaring off mine like flint and steel. On those days, I'd learned to run and hide.

Oh, Nick. If only you were single and not so rich...

'Tara?'

I was so mired in maudlin thoughts that now my daydream was talking to me.

'Tara!'

This time the voice was growly and insistent and jerked me out of my bourbon-induced reverie. I swung around to face the street and saw a car pulled up at the kerb next to me with the window down; a Porsche Cayenne that was all too familiar.

'How did you do that?' I gasped.

'Do what?' asked Nick Tozzi.

'Appear when I was talking to you!'

I could barely see his face in the gloom but I knew he was scowling at me. 'You're not making sense. Why are you walking? Has your car broken down?'

'Er … no. Jus' needed some air.'

'You're drunk.'

'No!'

'Yes.'

'Not!'

'You shouldn't be wandering the streets alone.'

'It's Claremont, for chrissakes. What's going to happen to me? Gonna be attacked by an oc-to-gen-gen-ar-ian?' I stumbled over the last word, spitting it out in half a dozen syllables.

'Remember the Birnies. And the Claremont serial killer. You're very stupid sometimes, Tara, for a girl who's been through … stuff.'

He was right. The last few months I had been through stuff. A lot of it to do with him. Why, oh why, couldn't I get him out of my head? Tozzi and I were never going to be a couple.

Then I thought of the best, happiest couple I knew—Smitts and Henny—and an unstoppable gush of self-pity welled. I jammed my fists to my eyes to stop it.

'Tara?' Tozzi sounded alarmed. 'That wasn't meant as an insult. I mean… I just…'

The car door slammed and a warm sensation flooded

me. Nick was standing a breath away from me and his magnificent aura enveloped me in concern. I wanted to wallow in it but that would have looked pretty damn weird. So I settled for hugging myself and soaking up his settling vibes. I could never ignore Nick's aura, no matter what I did. The tears slowly subsided and I felt myself sobering up.

'It's alright,' I said. 'Had a bit of a personal crisis in the family tonight. Smitty needed some … help.'

'Jane Smith? It's usually the other way around, isn't it?'

'Friends help each other.'

'Indeed,' he said. 'So let me give you a lift home. I mean … if that's where you were going.'

I thought about Eduardo. I couldn't really ask Tozzi to drop me there.

''Preciate that,' I mumbled. 'But I'm fine.'

His hand dropped onto my shoulder. 'Actually, you're not fine and I insist. My mother would never forgive me if I left you alone here in the dark.'

Nick's mother terrified me. All four feet eleven inches of her.

I felt myself weakening. Ed might not welcome me lobbing on his doorstep in the wee hours, and I could score a ride home in Tozzi's Cayenne. It was late and the beginnings of a nasty hangover were creeping up on me.

'Well, I'd hate to upset Eireen…' I said. 'Okay. But only if we can stop and get a burger.' Bok's brie hadn't exactly filled the hollows of my cavernous stomach.

He sighed. 'Is everything a deal with you?'

'Only with people who think they know what's best for me.'

'Get in,' he said, clearly exasperated.

I ambled around to the passenger side, got in and buckled up. The inside of the car reeked of perfume—not mine.

'Smells nice in here,' I said innocently.

Tozzi shot me a sideways look and started the car. I made a note to remember the scent for the next time I ran into his wife. Call me suspicious, but if Tozzi had a girlfriend, I wanted to know.

He drove in silence after that until he pulled into the burger bar off the highway.

'What do you want?' he asked.

'Bacon and cheeseburger, no onion,' I said. 'And a vanilla milkshake.'

'A milkshake?'

'Calcium. Prevents hangovers.'

He rolled his eyes and got out of the car.

Nick Tozzi was the richest person I knew. It would have been easy to sit there and let him pay, but my stubborn self wouldn't let my lazy-self off the hook. I threw open my door and stumbled over to stand in the line with him.

'What are you doing?' he demanded.

'You didn't take the money.' I fished around in my lovely Miu Miu bag—a present from Bok. 'Here.'

His lip curled at the sticky two-dollar coins I placed in

his palm. 'I don't—'

'Yes, you do,' I said, cutting him off.

Feeling very pleased with myself, I returned to the car. My mouth was watering from the delicious burned bacon smell coming from the burger van. I sat forward in my seat and peered through the windscreen, wishing it was daylight so I could see the ocean.

Suddenly, my eyes were blinded by a series of flashes.

'Wha-a—?' I gargled.

'Hey! What the hell do you think you're doing?' That was Tozzi, but I couldn't see him because of the shapes still whirling in front of my eyes.

I heard a door slam and a car roared away.

'Tara?'

'Nick? What was that?' My vision began to clear and I saw he was at my window.

'Bloody journos,' he hissed through clenched teeth.

'Why would they take a picture of me in your… Oh…' I trailed off.

'How the hell am I going to explain this to Antonia?'

The distress in his voice made me feel awful. Tozzi was trying so hard to save his marriage. She didn't deserve him in my opinion. He didn't deserve this, though.

'I'm so sorry. Look, just tell her the truth. I'll tell her if you like.'

'Bad idea,' he said quickly.

The burger guy called our number and Tozzi stomped off to fetch the food.

I thought about the last time I'd seen Antonia. She'd been snorting a line of coke with Johnny Viaspa in the backroom of a nightclub. I'd never told Nick because … well, it really was none of my business. Prior to that, we'd met on two other occasions—one time she'd turned on the snobbery, the other she'd turned on the waterworks. Either way, I found her the epitome of annoying. Tozzi was right—talking to her wasn't such a good idea.

He folded his enormous self into the specially modified driver's seat, handed me my milkshake, and dropped a paper bag in my lap. 'Let's get out of here.'

There were only about a dozen people at the van but they were all looking in our direction. It only took a dozen people to start a rumour that would spread through Perth in a day. Small city, big networks.

Tozzi drove a way down the sea road and pulled into one of the little car parks south of the Cottesloe groyne. JoBob used to bring me swimming down here as a kid when the main beaches were crowded. There was just enough clear water to wallow about in before you hit rock.

I slurped some vanilla-flavoured milk and fished around in the paper bag. 'There's only one serve of chips,' I told Tozzi as I passed him his burger.

'Yours—I'm trying to keep my weight down,' he said, and took a gigantic bite of his steak and egg.

'Me too!' I chowed down just as quickly on the bacon and cheese.

When he finished his mouthful, he chuckled. 'Toni's friends eat celery sticks and diet pills, you know,' he said. 'I always feel like a glutton around them.'

'That's because you are,' I said cheerfully. 'But in a good way.'

He took another chomp and the burger disappeared. The man could eat. Given he was seven feet tall, that wasn't surprising.

With a cursory wipe of his hands on the paper serviette from the bag he settled back to watch me.

'So what's concerning the lovely Jane Smith?' he asked.

'Since when are you interested in my friends?'

'Since I learned that they're the ones charged with keeping you out of trouble.'

'Your faith in me is underwhelming,' I said, pulling a face at him and stuffing some chips in my mouth. 'How's big business?'

Tozzi owned a sporting goods chain. Despite shite with the economy, I heard along the vine that he was doing all right. In hard times people fell back to watching sport and drinking at home. And Tozzi had some decent contracts with football, basketball and cricket teams.

'Can't complain.'

'And my favourite car?'

'I sold the Lambo.'

'You what?! How could you?'

'Had an offer too good to refuse. Besides, I've got a

hankering for something else.'

'What?'

'I'll surprise you one day. So what's been happening with you? You got work?'

'Can't complain,' I lied. 'Heading to Brisbane for a job soon, as a matter of fact.' I wasn't going to tell him there was no firm deal yet. It wasn't like we saw each other every day.

'Interstate? Your reputation is growing.'

I stared at him suspiciously to see if he was being facetious but I couldn't detect a smirk. 'I'm good at what I do,' I said.

'You are. And what's the job?'

'Client privilege.'

'Fair enough.'

'You know that I know how to keep my mouth shut, Nick.'

We shared a moment of silence filled with awkward memories. The man had saved my life and I'd saved his business from going under. Like it or not, we were tied to each other by the past and certain secrets.

'No trouble from Viaspa?' he asked.

'No. And I plan to be out of town for a while, so that will help.'

'Oh? How long?'

'It depends on how the job pans out. How's your wife?'

He sighed, and I wasn't sure if it was about me

being out of town or about her. 'Things have been okay. I mean… I think she's clean. But I just keep worrying that she's not.'

'You want me to suss her out? I can do that, you know. I can tell if people are using.'

'No!'

'It would be a freebie.'

'No, Tara!'

'Okay. Settle, petal.' I didn't push it any further. She wasn't clean but I felt like I couldn't tell him that unless he directly asked me. And clearly he wasn't asking. At least his refusal gave me a clear conscience. I'd offered.

'Sorry … look … you finished? I'll drop you home.'

He started the car and drove me back to Lilac Street much more quickly than he had to. Luckily there were no cops about.

I stole a quick glance at his profile, which had turned stern and forbidding, and guessed that light banter was over for the evening.

'Thanks for the ride, Nick,' I said softly when he pulled up next to the letterbox. 'See you around.'

He grabbed my arm as I went to get out. 'Tara, I…'

'You what?'

'I take marriage seriously. I want mine to work.'

'You don't have to convince me, Nick,' I said, shaking his hand off. 'You just need to do a better job on yourself.'

I got out of the car and scooted down the side path before he could reply.

Chapter 3

Baby let me love you down…

It took me a while to realise that Usher and I weren't on a dinner date and that he hadn't just burst into song at our table. When I did, I groped around for the only other place Usher could be singing—my ringtone. I checked my display and saw it was a number I didn't recognise.

That required a glass of water, a scrub of my face and a good throat-clearing cough before I called back. Seven AM. Who rang so early? I hit call back and waited.

'Reverb Promotions,' said a man's voice.

'Tara Sharp here. Did you just ring me?'

'Tara Sharp—you're Wal's … err … associate?'

How had Wal described our relationship? I wondered. 'Yeah, that's right.'

'Look, Tara, I've got some stuff going on. This has gotta stay on the down low. You dig?'

'And you are?'

'Stuart Cooper.'

31

'Before we discuss your "stuff", Mr Cooper, perhaps we should discuss my terms,' I said, a little primly.

'Terms? Yeah, yeah, sure.'

'I'd need airfare, accommodation and a daily retainer if you want me to do some looking around for you. Or I have an hourly rate, if you'd prefer.'

'Airfare, yeah, yeah. Accommodation, sweet, sweet. Wal said you'd give me a deal on the retainer.'

I hesitated for a second. I preferred three hundred and fifty dollars per day but instinct told me this guy wouldn't have it, and I'd promised Wal mates rates. 'Two hundred and fifty per day plus expenses.'

'Two hundred and fifty?!'

'I'm good at what I do, Mr Cooper.'

'Yeah, yeah. Sure, sure. Look, that's a deal. Give me your email. I'll send through a ticket.'

'Don't you want to discuss the job first?'

''Course, 'course. Need a set of eyes on the ground over here. Got a big act about to touch down soon and my venues are flaking off bookings like they got sunburn. I need to find out why.'

'Who's your act?'

'Slim Sledge.'

'Seriously?'

'Hope to die.'

'Don't mean to be rude, Stuart, but I would have expected Slim Sledge to be touring with one of the big guys.'

'Yeah, yeah. Thing is—entre nous—he's high maintenance. Mushroom brought him out three years ago, and, among other things, he forked his minder.'

'You mean with cutlery?'

'Yeah. Silver. Listen, can you come today?'

'Umm … today. Uh, sure.'

'Great, great. I'll be in touch with a flight time.'

I gave him my email address for the e-ticket and he hung up, leaving me both irritated and bewildered. It was the most rushed interview with a client yet. And I knew that if he continued to repeat the first word of every sentence when we were face to face, I would likely smack him.

My phone rang again before I could take that thought any further.

'Tara?'

'Hoshi?'

'You have a job?'

'How did you know that?'

'You should cancel.'

'Excuse me?'

'I dreamed something bad.'

'What? About me?'

'Yes. You're surrounded by cars and then you die.'

'That's it?'

'Yes.'

I paused. 'You been on the sake or something?'

'Don't take the job.'

'I have to. I need the money. And I promised Wal.'

I heard a distinct harrumph. 'Don't expect me to come to your funeral.' He disconnected and left me staring at my phone's display.

I hadn't had one of those days in a while, but this was shaping up to be one.

Hoshi Hara taught me everything I knew about reading auras. He'd also helped me turn my affliction into a semi-paying job. I owed him a lot and I listened when he spoke. He was on the weird side of odd, had a spiteful sense of humour and was married to the scariest woman I'd ever met (aside from Eireen Tozzi), but he was seldom wrong. If he said I was in danger, then I probably was. Sadly, that was nothing new.

I climbed out of bed, grabbed my towel from the floor and headed out the door. Living in the garage in the back garden of your parents' home meant forgoing certain luxuries. The toilet and shower were only a step or two away, but it was a bitch when it rained.

Still, the water was hot and I returned in better spirits and proceeded to rummage for clothes and food. Eventually, I unearthed a clean shirt and some knickers and pulled on yesterday's jeans. I padded around in bare feet collecting strewn undies into a basket ready to carry up to JoBob's.

A quick look in the fridge told me there was no point in lingering here. The milk was a week old and the olives had shrivelled and fallen off the pizza crusts, which now resembled baked play dough.

By now Dad would be up and reading the paper. Hopefully Joanna would still be in bed. I headed outside, around the pool and let myself in the back door. Dad was not, as I expected, in his chair reading, but was struggling with sticky tape and paper at the kitchen bench. I saw the pink ribbon and the little cakes on the wrapping paper and my heart sank to my heels. 'It's Mum's birthday?'

Dad looked up at me. 'Did you forget?'

'No,' I gulped. 'Not at all.'

He raised two disbelieving eyebrows. 'Do you want to put your name on my card?'

'Could I?'

Still fiddling with the tape, he nodded at the pen.

'Can I do that?'

'Your contribution?' he said mildly.

I scribbled in the card and took the parcel from him. 'I've been busy, Dad. I'm sorry. I've got a job in Brisbane. Heading over there later today.'

'Brisbane? How long will you be away?'

'I'm not sure yet. I'll let you know when I get there.'

'Are they paying your expenses?'

'I wouldn't be going otherwise.' I finished with the tape.

'You will be careful, Tara Sharp, won't you?'

My father only used my name like that when he wanted to get my attention. I glanced up and he was hovering. Though heading into his late sixties and a little less

35

muscular than he used to be, my dad was still a decent-looking man with a full head of hair and a pleasant face. No wonder Joanna had lassoed him.

'I'll be fine, Dad. Big girl now.' I grinned.

'The bigger you get, the bigger the trouble,' he countered.

'Trouble? What trouble?' My mother was standing at the kitchen door wearing a yellow and blue kimono that Aunt Liv had given her, with just the tiniest hint of black lingerie underneath. Her hair was epically mussed.

Joanna never appeared outside her bedroom less than immaculate. I bit my lip to stop a gasp escaping and sent my dad a look of deep admiration. Looked like he'd given her a birthday present already.

He walked over and put the kettle on, ignoring me.

'Happy birthday, Mum.' I slid the envelope on top of the parcel and passed it to her, glancing a kiss on her cheek.

'Tara, how sweet of you. I didn't expect you to remember.'

Ugh. 'Of course I remembered.' I retreated to where Dad stood by the kettle and shooed him away. 'I'll make the tea and toast and bring it out to the pool.'

He nodded and took Joanna by the arm. 'Our daughter is making us breakfast,' he said gravely.

They both chuckled and Joanna kissed him on the cheek. Then they strolled outside.

Vom-it. My parents didn't do public displays of

affection. Nor did they project afterglow.

As I buttered and jammed the toast and tinkled my teaspoon into Russian Caravan tea, sugar and some Royal Doulton mugs, I told myself to stop being childish. My parents were entitled to celebrate their relationship.

With those stern words in mind, I carted the tray out to the wrought-iron table and chairs set alongside the pool. We watched Joanna open her present while we sipped.

For one long, horrible moment I thought Dad—we—had bought her a computer game and then I saw the Apple logo.

An iPad. OMG!

'What fun,' cooed Joanna.

'You'll be able to store all your recipes on it,' said Dad.

She leaned over and kissed him again. 'You're such a thoughtful man, Bob. And thank you too, Tara,' she added. 'I expect you're the one who chose it.'

I was saved from answering by the pool gate creaking open. Cass traipsed through it, dressed in black and carrying a bouquet of orange and pink gerberas. They were a colourful contrast to her drab shift, bovver boots and eye-punch make-up. Joanna had adopted my stray teen friend when they discovered a mutual love of cooking. But even Dear Mother couldn't take the Goth out of the girl.

Cass had been staying a few nights with a friend she'd made at her new deli job, giving us a break from each other. My flat was too small for roomies but I couldn't toss her out on the street, which was where she'd likely end up, having nowhere else to go. It wasn't a long-term solution, but the fact I was going to Brisbane would buy us a bit more time.

'Happy birthday, Mrs Sharp,' she said, smiling sweetly as she handed over the bouquet.

'Cassandra, how charming. Thank you.'

I had to hand it to my mother—she might be a terrible snob, but once she decided you were family, you could run naked through the streets of Euccy Grove and still have her approval.

Unless, of course, you were her daughter. In that case, you could never win it.

'I also got you this.' Cass produced a little plastic card from her sleeve.

Joanna took it and peered at it.

'It's an iTunes card. You can buy apps for your iPad with it.'

'Ohhh... I see. How marvellous!'

'Nice call, Cass,' I agreed. 'Glad you're here, actually. I'm going to Brisbane today for a job. Can you look after the flat while I'm away?'

Cass's face lit up. She was inclined to be sullen but when she smiled, the sun grew dim. 'You sure?'

I nodded. 'You've got your key. Just check in with Mum and Dad while I'm away.'

'Working in Queensland? You will make sure you don't wear thongs everywhere, won't you, dear?' chimed in Joanna. 'Queenslanders do like to dress down.'

Heaven forbid I dressed down! 'Yes, Mother,' I said automatically. 'Must run now. Have to wash and pack.'

'Of course, dear. Pop in and say goodbye before you go.'

I gave JoBob fleeting hugs and tapped Cass on the head before escaping to do my laundry.

Gotta love dirty clothes.

Chapter 4

When I got back to my flat my phone was ringing. 'Tara, it's Stuart Cooper. Got you booked on a three o'clock flight today. Ticket's in your email. I'll pick you up at the other end. Ping me through a photo.'

My heart beat a little faster. I was really going. 'Will do! How's the weather there?'

'Beautiful one day. Perfect the next.'

I recognised the Queensland tourist slogan and grinned. 'Can't wait!'

'Flight gets in around ten. We'll go straight to one of the bookings, so wear club gear.'

'Fine. See you soon.'

I hung up, relieved that he'd stopped repeating himself. Maybe he only did it when he was nervous—the way some people blink. I pulled my suitcase out from under my bed and began stuffing in clothes. I'd pick up my clean undies from the dryer on the way out.

Then I grabbed my newest LBD off my clothes rack.

It was a Bok photo shoot cast-off: a beautiful, light Saba bohemian-style dress, simple in design with tuck detailing. You could dress it up or down, make it classy or clubby. I slipped some metallic bracelets onto my arm and unearthed my suede cut-out heels. The mirror was pretty damn pleased with me.

'Brissie,' I told it, 'here we come!'

The drive to the airport was uneventful and I booked Mona into long term parking. Cooper could cover the costs of that, as I didn't fancy leaving my most prized possession parked alone outside Lilac Street.

After check-in, I grabbed the new Tana French novel from the NewsLink store and settled at my gate lounge to wait. First, I googled Slim on my phone and began browsing the latest articles. He'd been in rehab three times, lived in a fortress in LA, had lost a family member in a gang-related shooting, a big sports fan. His mum was a member of the Black Panthers and his dad was in the military—parents divorced way back. I imagined what the conversation at the dinner table must have been like when he was a kid. Yikes!

According to Wikipedia, he'd won two Grammys and shipped thirty-five million units (albums, I guessed). The last few years, though, he'd become too hot to handle due to personal problems.

It was impossible to believe a promoter as small-time as

Wal's mate Cooper had picked up such an enormous act, even if he was blacklisted by the big guys. My antennae began to quiver. Something wasn't right here.

I shifted my search to Cooper but there wasn't much to find. I found his website and endorsements from some local acts plus one decent international blues singer and the latest travelling production of the Tongan fire walkers. Other than that, it was all back-of-house stuff. He was registered on the Australian Promoters Association which gave him some legitimacy and probably access to free legal advice. I hoped I wouldn't have to go there with him. Lawyer-speak gave me indigestion.

Somehow all that didn't add up to a world class recommendation. I made a mental note to ring Wal and grill him a bit more after I'd met Cooper.

It was an age since I'd had the time to sit and read, so I tucked my phone away and opened the book. It took a tap on the shoulder from the gate steward to let me know the plane was about to close its doors. Full of apologies, I hurtled down the walkway and into my seat. The Airbus had two aisles and I was on one side against the window. My seat companion, a big, muscled guy, levered out of his seat to let me in.

Before we'd even begun to taxi I remembered why I hated air travel. No leg room. Scrunched like a handkerchief, I peered around, looking for a spare seat.

No luck. But I saw someone who sent my heart lurching sideways: Johnny Viaspa was in the centre column two rows behind me. I shrank back behind my seat companion and was suddenly grateful of his size.

What was Johnny Viaspa doing on my plane to Brisbane? Why hadn't I seen him in the transit lounge?

A second sneak glance confirmed it was him, dressed in a tight black business shirt and pants and spilling his jaundiced-yellow aura onto the people next to him.

I sagged back again and tried to calm my panicked breathing. Five hours in a confined space with the only man on the planet who wanted me dead. He'd tried it once and failed, and I figured it would only be a matter of time until he tried again. Nick Tozzi and I had crossed him and I didn't for a moment imagine he was the sort to forget.

'Everything alright?'

I gave the man mountain next to me a startled look. His beard, tattooed fingers, faded denim and the gold filling in his front tooth said biker.

'Umm... I ... ummm...'

'Tight squeeze, eh? Fuc—I mean, freakin' airlines keep makin' their seats smaller.' He was sweating profusely and his largely purple aura was beset by troubled swirling browns.

'To tell you the truth, it's been a while since I've flown,' I said.

'Me too. Goin' to a funeral. Promised the lads I'd do it.'

'Sorry to hear that.' I tried to decipher the emblem on

his finger tats without staring but his hands were clasped tightly.

'He was an arsehole. Got what he deserved. But a man's gotta do the right thing. See him off.'

I nodded sympathetically.

'You get nervous goin' up or down?' he asked. Sweat slid down his face and dripped onto his shirt collar.

'Um … both,' I lied, hoping it might calm him a bit. 'Hate it. Makes my ears pop.'

'Dontcha worry about it. She'll be right.'

'Cheers,' I said.

I picked up Tana French and dived into it again, trying to block out what was about to be the flight from hell. But as we picked up speed towards our take-off, my seat started to shake.

I risked a glance at the biker and saw he was rocking as far forward as his seatbelt would stretch. His hands were two giant fists pressed against the seat in front and, above his beard, his face was pasty white. People near us were looking at him. Fearing that one of them might be Johnny Viaspa, I opened my mouth. 'What's your name?'

The plane began to accelerate as the pilot poured on the power.

'Erp?' he replied, glazed-eyed and vomity-looking.

'Your name?'

'Big … Nuts.'

'You're kidding.'

He turned his head stiffly and met my gaze.

Nope. He wasn't kidding.

'Er, Big Nuts, I'm scared.'

One paw unlatched from the other and he grabbed my right hand in a killer grip. My fingers began to go numb as we approached lift-off and I lost feeling in my wrist when we hit the first few bumps. By the time we reached cruising altitude, I was wondering if my arm was still attached to my shoulder.

The upside was that I'd had an eyeful of the tattoo and Big Nuts had stopped shaking.

He released my hand when the seatbelt sign went off and I subtly pinched feeling back into it.

'You sure are a scared one...' he said.

'Tara,' I said. 'I sure am.'

'When does the booze cart come around?'

'Soon, I expect.'

'Too long,' he said, and pressed the call button.

The flight attendant eventually became convinced she should serve him now when he threatened to go and get it himself.

A bunch of little whisky bottles later, his colour had returned and brought with it a desire to chat. I heard all about his pit bull terrier, Maxine, and how he'd been a roadie for a while.

'You wouldn't happen to know Wallace Grominsky?' I asked.

'Grom? You know Grom?' Frowning, he twisted his

bulk towards me, which was no mean feat.

'Yes,' I said, suddenly wishing I hadn't asked.

But his frown transformed into an enormous grin. 'I figured that ugly little prick was dead.'

'Definitely not dead,' I said.

'Whas 'e doin'?'

'He … um … works for me.'

Big Nuts' eyes popped.

'I run an investigation business,' I explained.

'No shit?'

'None,' I said solemnly.

'Little prick knows his stuff.' He lowered his voice and gave me a wink. 'Does he still like to play with hardware?'

I rolled my eyes. 'Wouldn't know.'

He laughed. 'Say, you gotta business card?'

I could have lied and said no, but he was already pressing his own into my hand, and my Joanna Sharp upbringing required that I reciprocate.

While he slipped mine into his shirt pocket, I peeked at his. It had the same emblem as appeared on his knuckles and read:

> Bon Jovi Ames
> Sergeant-at-arms
> West Coast Cheaters (Bay Creek division)

Jeez! Bon Jovi Ames? Really? Parents have a lot to answer for. But that didn't detract from the fact that Big Nuts didn't just look like a biker, he was the real deal.

Last press I'd seen on the West Coast Cheaters was an epic brawl outside a club in Fremantle that included thirty uniformed cops and stun sticks; a riot by Perth standards.

I pressed the button for the flight attendant and ordered two mini bottles of white wine.

By the time the plane landed, Big Nuts and I had got pretty loose, swapping injury stories. Weirdly, I suddenly felt less scared of Johnny Viaspa. I'd held Big Nuts' hand and we'd exchanged business cards. That made us friends, right?

As we disembarked, I took care to stay in the shadow of his considerable bulk. That worked right up until I'd retrieved my luggage. Viaspa was on the other side of the conveyor belt, deep in conversation with a man wearing the same uniform of sunglasses and black dress shirt and pants.

As I peeped at him from behind Big Nuts, I heard the biker hiss.

'Bon?' I couldn't call him the other bit. I just couldn't.

'Snake's arsehole.' He was staring over at Viaspa and his mate with the kind of expression you might wear if you'd bitten into a burger and found out it was rat, not beef.

'You know them?'

He flicked a look over his shoulder at me. 'You?'

'One of them. Can I just hang behind you until he leaves?'

He gave me another look, nodded and fished his

phone out of his pocket. His conversation was short and cryptic, but it must have been something to do with Viaspa and the other guy because he used the word snake several times.

After he hung up, he turned towards me. 'He's gone.'

'Thanks, Bon.' I stuck out my hand and we shook formally. He was taller than me, and at least forty kilos heavier, and it made my teeth rattle.

'Watch out for snakes, Tara Sharp,' he said.

'Back atcha,' I said.

Relieved the flight was over, I headed out the double doors into the balmy Brisbane night, wondering where my ride was.

As I pulled out my phone and switched it on, I caught sight of Viaspa's back ahead of me. On the other side of the road, a man of medium build with a round face, wearing a crumpled shirt and jeans, was holding up a sign.

Viaspa glanced across at him casually then froze in his tracks. The man was unaware that Viaspa was staring at him with such interest and continued to wave his placard.

Shit! The sign said TARA SHARP in giant capitals.

Chapter 5

I slunk back behind a group of people standing by a large column-shaped ashtray, just as Viaspa swivelled in my direction.

With trembling fingers, I sent Stuart Cooper a text. Please put down the sign. I'll meet you outside Virgin arrivals. Will explain then.

I back-pedalled into the terminal and threaded my way to another exit and on down to the Virgin terminal. A few minutes later, Cooper turned up panting and looking a little bewildered.

I tapped him on the shoulder and stuck out my hand. 'Hi, I'm Tara. Look, sorry for the run-around but I like to stay below the radar when I'm on a job. You waving a sign with my name on it is … problematic.'

It sounded a tad OTT but Stuart seemed to accept it. 'Sure. Apologies. Let's get out of here.'

We paid the short term parking and were soon blasting along a well-lit highway in a tired old Holden Camry with

Cooper talking quicker than I could blink.

The gist of it was that the owner of a club called Little Paolo's had called Cooper earlier in the day to come in and talk about the booking for Slim's tour. Apparently, it was one of the main live venues left in Fortitude Valley and crucial to the tour's success. If Slim didn't do Paolo's he might as well kiss the whole Queensland leg of the comeback adios.

'When does Slim arrive?' I asked.

'Tomorrow. That's why I wanted you here quick. Got an independent publicist working for me as well and she's lined up a bunch of radio and some TV. I'll get you to tag along on most of the promo.'

I nodded. That sounded fair. 'So what outcomes are you looking for from me, Stuart?' 'Outcomes' was a term I'd picked up from Bok, who'd been doing his staff performance reviews these last few weeks. Being clear on outcomes is important, T, he told me. Then everyone has their eye on the same ball.

'Outcome, outcome? Yeah, yeah? Well, I want this tour to go okay… Truth is, my whole business hangs on this, Tara. I'm one of the little guys. We don't get this kind of chance too often. If it works out for me, I become a player. It doesn't work out, I'm on the dole. Dig?'

'I feel for you on that,' I said carefully. 'But I can't guarantee your future.'

'Sure, sure,' he said. 'Just want you to know the stakes. Want you to find who's trying to squeeze me out.'

'You got any ideas on that yourself?' I pulled my phone out.

'You gonna take notes?'

'You alright with that? Client confidentiality applies. No one sees them but me, but I need to keep a handle on the details.'

He stuck his tongue in his cheek and rolled it around for a bit. 'You delete them afterwards.'

'If you want,' I said. 'Apart from your contact numbers.'

He thought about it for a moment or two. 'Fine, fine. The way I'm figuring it, there're two guys who really want me to crash. Actually, there're probably more, but these ones have got more cause than the others. First is a guy called Andreas Giannoukakis—Easy A Productions. He brought Slim Sledge out last time he toured and took a big hit when Slim forked his minder and had to cancel most of his dates. Andreas is pissed with me on a whole number of levels.'

I raised an eyebrow and glanced sideways. 'Care to expand on that?'

His mouth was pursing and un-pursing like he was working to spit out an olive pit. 'I was engaged to his niece, Sofia Zachariou.' His shoulders slumped a little.

'Lemme guess … you jilted her at the altar?'

'Nah, nothing like that.'

'What then?'

'Her papa checked my credit rating.'

'She dumped you because you weren't earning enough money?' How last century. I tried to keep the sympathy out of my tone and stay matter-of-fact, but truth was I was feeling a bit sorry for the guy already.

'No, no. Sofia's the sweetest girl in the world.' His voice grew thick. 'She'd never do that. But she does what her family says. That's her way. Gotta respect her for it.'

In the glow of the flashing-past streetlights, his body language didn't show the same conviction as his words. In fact, he looked like he was having an attack of appendicitis. Time to change the subject. After seeing Viaspa at the airport, I wasn't really in the mood for Stuart's emotional baggage.

'Who else then?' I asked.

'Joel Aprile.'

'OTB Records?' Even I knew of Aprile. He'd ascended the ranks to become the biggest Aussie promoter and label in the last few years. Joel Aprile was a legend with some serious family money behind him. In the last few years he'd brought out Adele, Rihanna, and a bunch of other big acts. The notion that Cooper might be going up against him over Slim Sledge made me want to tell him to stop the car so I could run to the toilet.

Instead, I crossed my legs and looked out as we headed up a huge bridge to cross a wide river. What a view! All twinkling lights and river reflections wrapped up in a warm breeze. Strangely, I felt immediately comfortable.

'Gateway Bridge is the best thing that ever happened

to this city,' Cooper remarked into the silence. 'Used to be you had to drive through the CBD. Traffic was a bitch.' He waved over at the rainbow-lit skyscrapers that surely marked the heart of Brisbane.

'Nice,' I responded.

'We're a city of bridges really.'

I saw what he meant as I peered downriver. The man-made constructions lent the city an exotic night appeal. Fairyland of a type.

'Anyway, as I was saying, I worked for Joel for a few months when I first came east. Learned a lot and then moved on.'

'He pissed off with you about that?'

'Kinda. One of his clients came with me when I started out on my own. Joel thinks I poached him but I didn't.'

'You think stealing one of his clients is enough that he's trying to put you out of business?'

'Well, like I said, I didn't steal him. It was the client's idea. He chased me when I left. And yes, I do. Aprile doesn't forgive easily, and he's pretty big on loyalty.'

'Did you explain to him what happened?'

'You don't tell Joel squat. Joel knows. That's it. I could have refused to take on the client, I suppose...'

'But you didn't.'

He shrugged and nosed the car over two lanes to take an exit.

'Where does this go?' I asked, reading the exit signs.

'Paolo's is in the Valley,' he said.

'Fortitude Valley?'

'Yeah. Bris-Vegas's answer to Kings Cross,' he said with a laugh.

'Bris-Vegas? Sounds like a bit of an overstatement.'

'That's the point,' he said. 'But don't make fun of it. We love our city.'

I got that. Really I did. I loved Perth as well. But I couldn't tell if he was winding me up or not about the 'Bris-Vegas' thing, so I contented myself with adding more notes onto my phone while he negotiated increasingly thick traffic. Finally, he pulled into a multi-storey car park called McWhirters.

He tugged the keys out of the ignition and stared at me. 'Are you as good as Wal says you are?'

'Yes,' I said simply. 'But you have to let me do things my way.'

I thought of Nick Tozzi then, and how he was always trying to make me more responsible. And my ex-fiancé Garth Wilmot, who just shook his head in despair over the way I lived my life. Come to think of it, the only guy I knew who liked some of my more eccentric habits was Ed. Admittedly I'd crossed the line once or twice with him as well. Like the time we nearly got arrested outside a chop shop, and the time I'd ruined his swimsuit photo shoot and then…

I pulled myself away from dwelling on my failures and concentrated on my job. We were now walking along a street that was busy despite the late hour. Some of the shops were still open and there was music blasting from club doorways as we passed. The air stuck to my skin and suddenly I was possessed with a desire to go dancing and drinking.

Concentrate, I told myself sternly.

We headed right into a mall teeming with people. It was hard to tell if they were waiting to get into the Irish pub or the row of restaurants. Or perhaps they were just hanging out. It seemed like a place to do that.

Sandwiched between the Naked Dance Studio and an Oporto chicken joint was Little Paolo's. It had a narrow shopfront but once we went inside and up a flight of narrow stairs it turned out to be quite large. Three separate dance floors by the look of it and a stage on one of them. The stage was empty but the dance floor was filled with people dancing to a hip-hop medley.

Stuart nodded and waved at people as we threaded through the throng and over to one corner of the stage. A short set of stairs led up the side to a door and the bouncer there let us in without a response to Cooper's 'How they hanging, man?'

As soon as the door shut behind us the music cancelled out. Stuart walked along the corridor a little way, knocked on an open door to the left and entered.

I admired the sound-proofing, but that was about all. Little Paolo's office smelled of stale pizza and bourbon, and every space that wasn't covered with CDs, piles of paper and electrical cords was thick with dust.

'Stuart, you skinny little bastard. Was wondering when you'd show.'

The greeting came from a man sitting behind a wide, cluttered desk. I mean, a mountainous man. Possibly the biggest man I'd ever seen—pushing one-sixty kilos with a bright white ring around his brown aura that told me he was nursing more than one health condition. He had dark cropped hair, sharp eyes and a face that was as puffy as a donut.

He held a giant packet of gummy bears in one hand and cradled a phone receiver into the folds of his neck.

'Paolo Tamp, this is Tara Sharp. My ... er ... sister's girlfriend.'

Say what?

'Maybe Tara would like to step outside and enjoy the club while we do our business,' said Paolo. His voice was deep and breathy like the Smoking Man in the old X-Files series. Only Paolo didn't look like a smoker. No time for that when you had gummy bears.

''S'cool, Paolo,' said Stuart. 'She's working for me right now. I'm looking to build my female client base.'

Paolo looked me up and down. His aura darkened a little as his brain ticked over, sizing me up and fitting me into his mind map.

I was also working, observing the hilt of a large baton peeping out from underneath a pile of papers on his desk, and the empty cartridge box in his wastepaper bin. Looked like Little Paolo had some stuff going on.

'Fine,' he said. 'Sit.'

Stuart offered me the only other chair in the office and leaned against the wall. He looked nervous now. 'Can we talk about the booking? You said there was a problem.'

Paolo laced his fingers together and leaned his forehead against his thumbs. We listened to him breathe for a second or two before he replied.

'I'm not sure we're the right fit for Slim Sledge, Cooper. He's trouble—we all know that. And I got different kinds of kids coming in here these days. They want doof-doof and electro. They just don't dig the live vibe anymore. It's too real,' he said.

Stuart paled. 'That's crap, Paolo. You're playing an R&B medley out there now. The dance floor's packed.'

Paolo's aura took on a light brown tint. I guessed that if he was healthier then the colour would normally be a deep tan. People in the tan spectrum tended to be practical and hard-nosed. You didn't push people with tan auras too much because they pushed back tenfold. I had to head this off at the pass before Stuart lost him on pure stubbornness.

'I'm going to be personally managing Slim Sledge while he's here,' I said confidently. 'I promise there'll be no issues with his behaviour. And we've just heard his new single is debuting at number two on the Aria charts.'

Stuart choked.

'Charts aren't due in until next week,' grunted Paolo.

I winked at him. 'Sure they're not. But I know

someone…'

Slim's gig at Paolo's was supposed to be this coming weekend. By the time the charts were out next week, I figured it wouldn't matter that I'd made it up.

Paolo opened his desk drawer and pulled out a large handkerchief. I glimpsed more packets of bullets—unopened—before he closed it. He mopped his brow with the hanky and looked at me with renewed interest. 'Not your average lesbo then, eh, Stuart? She's got connections.'

'Let's just say the music industry is my family,' I said with cryptic grace. Inside, though, I was getting annoyed. Did lesbians have to put up with this crap all the time?

'What do you say, Paolo?' Stuart asked. 'Sledge will pack this place out. You know that.'

Paolo shrugged. 'Okay, we'll go ahead. But you gotta assure me there'll be no hassles. I'm taking a risk on you, Stu. Certain parties won't be happy.'

'What parties? It's Aprile, isn't it? He wants my tour to go arse up.'

I studied Paolo's aura and his micro expressions. Nothing changed at the mention of Aprile's name. Speaking of changing auras, though, Stuart's was making like a greyhound around the racetrack.

'Or is it Giannoukakis?' he said.

'Who?'

Again, there was nothing to give me a clue. Either the man was an accomplished liar or Stuart was way off base.

Stuart unclenched his fists and took a deep breath.

'Thanks, Paolo. You're a good man.'

'Yeah, well, don't let me down.'

Stuart talked press call, sound checks and set times with Paolo's stage manager for a bit before we left. Leaving him to it, I plonked my bum on a bar stool and ordered a belt of rum. When in Queensland, home of Bundy rum, after a long flight sitting next to a biker, hiding from a criminal gang lord, what else do you do?

From my perch, I got to study the venue in more detail. It looked like the walls folded back to make one huge dance floor that'd fit, I estimated, around six hundred bodies. It was small by proper entertainment-venue standards, but I guess when you're on the comeback trail you had to take what you could get. Anyway, careers were often made on good word-of-mouth from small gigs.

The DJ had switched from the latest Rihanna to a Jason Derulo track and the dance floor was still full. This was a forgiving crowd who just liked music, not a cliquey audience. I hoped it would be the same for the Slim Sledge gig.

Truth was, I was excited about meeting him. I knew a few local musos in the Perth scene but I'd never met anyone on this scale of famous. Slim Sledge. Holy fuck!

He wouldn't be too hard to handle, I told myself. Everyone knew that the press demonised music stars.

Look at what happened to Eminem.

The rum was good and Derulo was bopping but it was around midnight and I knew it was time to either have a second shot to stay awake, or head to bed. Fortunately, Stuart turned up and crooked his finger at me. We left the venue and found the car.

'What do you think of Paolo?' he asked.

I shrugged. 'Seems okay. He didn't react to you mentioning Joel Aprile or the Andreas guy, but I'll do some digging around all the same. Can you email me their phone numbers and addresses? Include your girl Sofia's as well.'

'Sure, sure.' He seemed composed again and back in normal Cooper mode.

Before I could ask him where I was bedding down he pulled into a darkened driveway off Brunswick Street.

'I'd put you up at my place,' he said, 'but there's only one bedroom.'

'Oh?' I stared out of the window as he switched off the ignition and peered at the little old cottage. 'So who lives here?'

'You for the moment,' he said, rubbing his chin nervously. 'With a friend of mine.'

'What friend?' I couldn't keep the suspicion out of my voice.

'Inigo,' he said.

'Who?'

'Inigo Love. She … ah … works from home.'

'Doing what?' I heard my voice rise as I mentally ran through my own list of ideas.

'Oh, you know. New Age-y stuff.'

'Like tarot cards?'

'She's a medium. I'll get your bag from the boot.' With that he jumped out of the car and grabbed my luggage. Before I could think of a sound objection to the arrangement, he was at the front door, knocking.

I dragged myself over to join him and was met by a slim lady of about fifty with Kate Bush hair, skin as pale as ice cream and some tiny tattoos along the sides of her face. Incense wafted out the door and straight up my nose.

'Inigo, this is Tara Sharp. I'll be back to pick her up around eleven tomorrow morning.'

The small woman ignored Stuart but took my hand in a fierce, cool grip. She pulled me in close and sniffed me. 'Interesting,' she said.

'Stuar—' Before I could finish my protest, she tugged me inside, indicated that Stuart should put my bag down at our feet then shut the door in his face.

'Bye, Tara,' he said through the wood. 'Inigo will take good care of you.'

'Stuart, we'll talk in the morning,' I said meaningfully.

A moment later the car door slammed and the engine started. I thought about bolting back out the door after him, but Inigo was already pulling me down the hall into her living room.

'Stand here,' she ordered.

I didn't know whether to laugh or do as she said. Seeing as I couldn't afford a motel and it was late, I decided the latter was the most sensible option.

While she walked a slow circle around me, I looked around the room. It was furnished with odd and mismatched items which had either been either collected on eBay or in Op shops, or showed that Inigo Love had been to some interesting places: an elephant-foot side table, one shaggy-haired armchair, another shaped like a giant vulva, a Mexican sombrero lamp and a half dozen shrunken skulls hanging along the picture rail.

'Something wrong?' I asked when I finished my observations and found her staring at me, deep in thought.

'Where do you come from?' she asked.

'Perth—I'm a West Aussie,' I said.

'No, I mean where. On the psychic plane. There's a disturbance around you that I've never seen before. Should I be scared or thrilled?'

I stared back at her. I mean, what do you say to that?

'I'm really tired, Inigo. Could you please show me where I'm sleeping?' I asked in my most polite voice.

The woman smiled suddenly and a lot of the weirdness left her face. 'Follow.'

I grabbed my suitcase and she led me back into a short corridor and along to a small bedroom. When she swung the door open, I saw a single bed covered in a bright blue doona sprinkled with moon shapes, a white wicker table next to it, and a dream catcher hanging from the window latch. The room was cheerful and clean.

'The bathroom is next door and the kitchen is across the hall. Help yourself to anything except the Kombucha tea.'

No danger there, I thought. Bitter stuff.

She left me to it then, and I didn't bother to unpack anything except a nightie and my wet pack. A quick brush of my teeth in the bathroom next door, and despite the strange bed, I was asleep before I counted ten sheep.

Chapter 6

I was finishing off a slice of cashew and honey cheese log and sipping a cup of dandelion coffee when Stuart arrived the next day. Inigo didn't believe in caffeine or wheat, so cereal, normal toast and English Breakfast tea were off the table. I thought about asking her for eggs but reconsidered in case they came pickled or something.

Inigo and Stuart talked about mutual friends while I visited the bathroom to scrub my teeth. The mirror told me I looked a bit tired, so I dotted some foundation under my eyes and smoothed outward. I normally never bothered with such things, but this morning I was meeting Slim Sledge. Vanity dictated I look half decent.

To wit, I was wearing a sexy Free People fitted grape shift with a lacy black hemline. It was too hot for the boots I usually wore with it, so I'd opted for sandals. For once I left my hair out. I loved this outfit because it nailed sexy and comfort. Smitty liked me in this dress, but Bok said it made my shoulders look too big. I poked out my tongue at the mirror. Smitty wins!

Back in the bedroom, I tucked my toothbrush away and grabbed my handbag. Stuart and Inigo were talking about a new local band when I joined them.

I was about to thank Inigo when she placed a key in my hand.

'You look magnificent,' she said. 'I've decided to be thrilled. Mi casa es su casa.'

My house is your house. 'How kind of you,' I said, nonplussed.

'And tonight, I'll read your palm.'

'That's very … thoughtful.'

'Go well, Tara Sharp.'

'Sweet as a musk stick, isn't she?' said Stuart as soon as I'd climbed into the passenger seat.

'Sweeter even,' I said.

'You don't like her?'

'She's … um … a little freaky. Is there somewhere else I could stay? What about your place?'

'I live at work. Only one bedroom, sorry.'

'Oh.'

'Wal said you'd be cool with Inigo.'

'He knows her?'

'They go way back. She used to sing in a band he roadied for.'

'Oh. Well … I guess it's okay then…'

'Awesome!' Stuart beamed at me.

He looked different from last night and I suddenly realised how dressed up he was in his black chinos and blue shirt with a silver chain and cross tucked into it. His dressy clothes and freshly washed hair told me that he was just as psyched as me about meeting Slim Sledge.

'I've got Sledge booked under another name so there's no media circus at the airport. We'll meet Juanita, the publicist, there, collect Slim and head for the hotel. Juanita'll be his PA while he's here. I've also hired a bodyguard.'

'Wal could have done that,' I said, a little surprised.

'I asked him to,' said Stuart, 'but he said he had some things to sort out and wasn't available.'

'Oh?' I remembered how edgy Wal was when I'd last seen him.

'Gordy—the muscle—will do fine as long as we keep him away from the Sambuca.'

We? I hoped he wasn't including me in that.

'Did you get those addresses I sent through?' he asked.

I scanned my email on my phone and found them. 'Yes. Thanks. I'd like to check these out today.'

'Sure. After we get Slim to the hotel.'

I nodded, relieved. Although I was excited to meet Slim Sledge, I was used to working alone. I didn't want Cooper trailing around after me.

According to his email, Andreas Giannoukakis's business was in South Brisbane but Joel Aprile's was a

Sydney address.

'Joel is in Brisbane this week,' said Stuart, as if reading my mind. 'The third address I gave you is a men's club in the CBD he likes to go to when he's here.'

I saw a jpeg attachment on the email and clicked it open. It was a photo of a slim, average-looking guy.

'That's him,' said Stuart, glancing at it.

'Why would he be in Brisbane?'

'He's got family here—his mum and sister. It's only an hour's flight. He's up and down all the time.'

'And how do you know this?'

'Like I said, I worked for him.'

'I mean, how do you know he's here right now?'

Stuart licked his lips.

'Listen, if you want me to help you, you're going to have to share your sources, Stuart.'

'Yeah, yeah. I understand. It's just a bit embarrassing.'

'Try me,' I said.

'I … er… I see a girl who works at the club. She says he books a private room there when he visits.'

'And you keep track of this because…?'

'Good to know things about people who harbour a grudge against you, don't you think?'

I nodded. 'So your … girl tells you this? Which day has he booked for?'

'Tonight. Doors open at six but they take private appointments at five.'

'What's your friend's name?'

'I don't want her involved in this,' he said quickly.

'Well, she kind of is already,' I said.

'Please don't draw any attention to her, 's'all I'm saying. Her name is Jane but at the club they call her Strawberry Jade.'

He switched into the short term parking lane and grabbed a ticket while I added Jane—Strawberry Jade—to my notes.

'So how many in Slim's entourage?' I asked.

'Today it's just him.'

I glanced up.

'There was a problem with his manager's ticket at the last minute. He's arriving tomorrow.'

'Slim's travelling alone? What about airline security?'

'He's in first class and he'll exit the plane separately with an escort. I leaked his arrival date as tomorrow to his fan club, so there'll be no problem.'

'Who?'

'There's a hardcore Sledge fan group in Brisbane. I had a friend whisper to their president, Fran Dickle. His official itinerary on his Facebook site says he's coming in two days, so that's what the press think.'

'You don't want the press here?' I was a bit confused. Slim mightn't be as big as Taylor Swift or Katy Perry, but he was only one hit song away from being that hot. Australia was a buoyant market for some of these international artists. Hell, we'd almost turned Pink into a national treasure. If this tour went well, Slim Sledge could follow in her wake… Didn't they want the publicity?

'We have to handle the way he's exposed.'

I slipped my phone into my handbag. 'Say what?'

'He doesn't like too many people up close.'

'What does that mean exactly?'

Stuart's aura gave a little kink and jerk, and I knew he was hiding something.

'He's fine at concerts. You know, when he's on stage. And press conferences, as long as they don't crowd him. But anywhere that fans might swarm … well, let's just say we need to keep them back.'

As I digested this, we got out of the car and walked to the Qantas entrance. My phone rang as we rode the escalator. It was Wal.

'Hey,' I said.

'All okay there, boss?'

'Sure. I'm at the airport picking up the artist.'

'Where you staying?'

'With one of Stuart's friends, Inigo Love. I believe you know her.'

'Inigo's good people. But don't drink her tea.'

'What do you mean?'

'Gotta go, boss.'

'Wal? Wal?'

But he'd already hung up, and Stuart had taken off through the airport. I tucked my phone away and ran to catch up.

We arrived at a gate labelled Staff Only down at the

far end of the terminal. Through the windows, I saw a motorised cart zipping across from the next gate with two flight attendants and a passenger. Was that our man?

'Stuart!'

A stunning woman of around forty waved at us from over by the newsstand near the closed door. Her turquoise aura was so bright and clean that it almost hurt my eyes. Combined with her chunky bling and whitened teeth, she was a blaze of light as she tottered over to us on a pair of ridiculously high peep toe heels. The woman's shoes and tight-fitting red zipper-through tunic dress gave her a power executive meets rock-and-roll look. She sure had the figure to pull it off. Silky hair in a pull-up style completed the jaw-dropping appeal.

'Dah-ling…' She blew a kiss at the top of Stuart's head and then looked me in the eye. 'And who is this divine Amazon?'

I wanted to giggle. I'd been called many things before, but never 'divine'.

'Tara Sharp,' said Stuart. 'This is Juanita Venture from Venture Publicity. Tara is a … err … private investigator.'

'Oooh, how exciting. Do you have a gun? Investigate me any time you like.' She winked at me.

The giggle tickling my throat became desperate to escape. I managed to turn it into a splutter before it did.

Be mature, I told myself sternly.

But the scolding was wasted. Juanita already had Stuart by the arm, walking him closer to the gate while she ran through a string of publicity arrangements. I trailed behind them, not sure if she'd just made a pass at me or if this was her normal way of saying hello.

The gate opened and a female steward appeared. She scanned the group waiting there and fixed on Juanita.

'Ms Venture?'

'Yasss,' said Juanita.

'Your … arrival will be here soon.'

'Fabulous.' Juanita peered down the walkway.

On cue, Slim Sledge swaggered through: soft black leather jacket over a white singlet, baggy blue jeans and sneakers, oversized sunglasses, hair in cornrows and heavy silver chains around his neck. His smile was wide and riveting.

What the others couldn't see, though, was his swirling pink aura, which was dotted with grey clouds. According to Mr Hara's aura coding, swirling pink meant a hyped-up sex drive. The grey clouds were just like they sounded. Ominous.

He winked at the female attendant next to him. She sagged a little, as if her knees wouldn't lock in place properly.

'Sebastian?' said Juanita rather imperiously.

Slim looked up and spotted the gorgeous publicist. He left the flight attendant and sauntered over to us.

'Lay-dies,' he said, flashing us both a mega-wattage smile. 'My Oss-ie welcome mat.'

Stuart stepped forward. 'I'm Stuart Cooper, your … er

… promoter.'

Slim slapped Stuart's outstretched hand for a sideways five, ignoring the offer of a handshake. 'Good to be back here, man.'

'And we're thrilled to meet you, Slim.'

'You bring these shawties fo' me, Stu?'

'Charming of you to think so, Sebastian,' said Juanita smoothly. 'But I'm Juanita and I'll be far too busy being your publicist to be your… shorty. Tara will be keeping you safe.'

Slim looked me up and down properly and whistled. 'You look like a handful, girl. You my bodyguard?'

'One of them,' said Stuart before I could answer. 'The other one is currently waiting for us at the hotel. We should step this way quickly, if you don't mind. We don't want to risk word spreading that you're here.'

'Yes, we have a limo waiting for you downstairs,' added Juanita. 'Your luggage will be sent to the hotel by courier.'

'Slim!' called someone behind us. We all turned and the flight attendant waved. She'd been joined by two others. 'Could we have a photo?'

'No!' said Stuart and Juanita automatically.

But the attendants clustered around him, clutching their phone cameras and giggling. Sledge looked edgy but kept smiling. Stuart, on the other hand, was stressing.

Juanita extracted the rapper as quickly as she could, shooing the airline staff away. But the damage was done;

people were beginning to look our way.

As we headed down the escalator towards baggage claim and the exit, I could almost hear the whisper rippling ahead of us.

'Slim Sledge.'

'It's Slim Sledge.'

'Someone famous.'

'That singer.'

'The guy that sings "I Die For You".'

'Oh my God, it's Slim Sledge!'

'It's Usher.'

As we reached the foot of the escalator there was a shriek from above.

'He's here! I told you he was here!' A swarm of banner-carrying fans rushed down and surrounded us, demanding autographs.

'Shit!' said Stuart in my ear. 'I'm going to get airport security. Don't let anyone get their hands on him. He'll go psycho.' He bolted and left Juanita and me on either side of the rapper, waving the crowd back.

I could sense Slim's fear and his aura began to churn against mine. His cocky confidence was slipping away, leaving a healthy dose of panic in its wake.

'No autographs,' trumpeted Juanita. 'NO PHOTOS!'

But camera phones were recording like crazy.

'Slim, I love you!' shrieked a round-faced girl at the front of the growing congregation. Tears streaked mascara down her face.

Sledge began to hyperventilate.

'Where's the limo?' I asked Juanita.

'Through that door.' She pointed almost dead ahead.

'Close ranks and don't stop for anyone,' I hissed at the publicist.

We crowded in near Slim, acting as a shield. But halfway across the baggage-claim area, the speed was too much for Juanita's high heels. She wobbled and went down, leaving Slim unprotected on one side.

The crowd, which was moving with us, converged. The crying girl got to him first, clawing at his arm and blubbering her love.

'Get out o' m'grille!' Slim screamed. 'Get out, bitch!'

Before I could get between them, Slim let loose a two-handed shove that sent the girl sprawling back into the people behind her.

'Hey, he hit that girl!' someone shouted.

'He can't do that!' yelled someone else.

The crowd's aura switched from a golden, celebratory yellow into something the colour of stale urine. A tall guy fought his way to the front. I stepped around Slim and got in the guy's face.

'Don't even think about it unless you wanna spend the next year in jail, mate,' I said.

'But he hit Fran.'

'He defended himself because she was assaulting him,' I said. 'You can't grab a total stranger like that.'

'He's not a stranger. He's Slim Sledge.'

That about summed up how the mob felt. Sledge was public property.

'Airport security will be here in a moment,' I warned. 'Now back off or—'

'Or what? What're you gonna do about it? You might be big but you're still a chick.' He full-stopped his insult with a poke to my chest.

Before I even realised what I was doing I'd yanked him in close and kneed him so hard in the groin that I almost pulled a hamstring. The guy went down like a sack and then it was all whistles and shouting and security guards everywhere.

I grabbed hold of Slim and tunnelled through the crowd, shouting, 'Make way. Emergency! Make way.'

Juanita was just a few steps behind us, heels in her hands, hair torn loose. The limo driver beeped the car open and we tumbled in. Another beep locked it. Then Stuart's pale face pressed against the window from outside.

'In,' Juanita ordered, beeping the door open and shut again in quick time.

As Stuart fastened his seatbelt, a news van swung in behind us. And another.

We caught a lucky break in the traffic and the driver hit the pedal before the cameras started to roll.

'What the fuck, man? WHAT THE FUCK?' shouted Sledge as we left the media behind us. He was shivering like a junkie in withdrawal. 'You said the airport would be cool, man. That wasn't cool. That was WAY FUCKING

UNCOOL!'

'I'm sorry, Slim,' said Stuart. 'I don't understand what happened. I let it be known that you weren't arriving until tomorrow. Someone must have leaked the details to your fan club.'

'Storm in a teacup, Sebastian dahling,' soothed Juanita. 'But you can see how primed Australia is to see you again. They just LOVE you.'

'Call me Slim, woman,' said the rapper. He thumped the back of the seat. 'Only my mama calls me Seb.'

'Of course, dahling,' said Juanita, not fazed in the least. 'Now just sit back and relax, we'll have you at the hotel in a jiff.'

'What's a fucking jiff?'

'It means real soon,' I said. 'Take a breath. It's all good.' I deliberately made my own aura calm, hoping it would soothe his.

People's auras bang together all the time. When you think you have good chemistry with someone, it usually means your auras are doing something compatible. Right now mine was pouring calm onto the black storm around Sledge. It was the first time I'd tried something like this and it seemed to work. By the time we got to the Gateway Bridge, Sledge had settled enough for me to point out the sights. He even smiled again. He was rather gorgeous to look at, in a gangsta kind of way.

I glanced out the window and saw the Channel Nine helicopter taking a pass over us.

'Whas 'at?' hissed Slim, shielding his head dramatically with his hands.

'Rescue helicopter,' I said quickly. 'Must be a road accident on one of the majors.'

Juanita gave me an eye-roll in the rear-view mirror.

Stuart looked like he was one blood clot short of a stroke. His skin had a bright sheen of perspiration as he peered out the window.

The 'copter dogged us all the way into the city along the snaking brown Brisbane River. Despite the air-con, I was sweating up my nice dress. The humidity was something else.

By the time the limo turned into the entrance of the Stamford Plaza hotel, my dress was wringing wet and I was all out of platitudes.

Unfortunately, word had travelled and there was a cluster of media waiting for us. Stuart made a phone call and had a short, flustered exchange with someone at the other end.

'What do you mean? ... But you can't... Oh... He'd better be... His name is what?'

'Stuart?' said Juanita in a rather high-pitched voice.

'Um... Tara, can you escort Slim to his room? The concierge is waiting to show you through.'

I looked at the scrum of reporters surging towards the car. 'Where's your ... er ... other minder?'

Stuart cast me a desperate look. 'He was delayed. He'll be along in a while.'

'Where's m' bodyguard?' demanded Slim. 'Shawty here's got a nice ass but she's no brother. I want a man watching my back.'

No brother? I'd give him no freaking—'I'm trained in Japanese martial arts and I'm a former athlete. My ass and I are quite capable of looking after you,' I said tartly.

'An athlete? What's your juice, baby?'

It was then that I realised Slim Sledge could be easily distracted. That was handy.

'Basketball,' I said.

'A hooper. Lay five on me.' He held out his hand for me to slap. 'Lafayette junior college, starting guard— twenty-three points, five assists per game average. They got banners about me.'

I obliged then leaned close to him. 'Well, right now I'm gonna stay up on you, closer than a five-man setting a pick, until you're in your room, Slim. Got it?'

He took in the basketball analogy then stared out at the cameras. Fear flashed across his face. 'Don't let them touch me.'

'I won't,' I said.

We all got out of the car together and formed a triangle guard around the musician. It went well, with the concierge tutting around making sure the porters ran interference with the journos—until we reached the lift. As the concierge took out his key to open the staff lift, a reporter broke free from the rest and dived headfirst through the closing door. At any other time I might have given him a whoop and shouted 'Try!', but right now I was just plain gobsmacked. Then he rolled over and began snapping photos, his camera angled right up Slim Sledge's nostrils.

'Sir,' said the outraged concierge. 'Leave immediately or I shall call the police.'

The reporter ignored him. 'Are you over your drug addiction yet, Slim? Are you really clean now?'

'Get him outta here,' said Slim, shrinking into the corner of the lift.

The reporter's flash kept blinding us, until I reached down and ripped it from the guy's hand with my best basketball snatch.

'Gimme my camera,' he whined. 'You can't touch my camera. That's assault!' He scrambled to his feet.

'You wanna see assault?' I pressed the open-door button and threw the camera out into the gathered media huddle. It skimmed their fingertips like a planker in a mosh pit, finally coming to rest in the hands of a security guard who'd just arrived. He gave the journalist a nasty smile and beckoned him to come and get it.

The journalist puffed air. 'Don't mess with the press.'

I wanted to laugh in his face but I was too pissed.

The lift door closed and I turned to see Slim cowering in the corner with his face in his hands. The concierge, Stuart, Juanita and I all looked at each other as the lift shot towards the penthouse. No one spoke until we got

Sledge into the suite.

Juanita steered him into the room but he refused to take his hands from his face.

'Slim,' said Stuart.

No answer.

'Slim dahling, it's alright now,' Juanita assured him.

No answer.

They looked at me.

I sighed. 'Come on, hooper. Whistle's blown. Half time.'

Slim dropped his hands and looked around. His face brightened at the stylish Stamford decor and the huge-screen TV. 'You got ESPN, man?'

The concierge fell over himself explaining all the suite's extras. Slim didn't seem impressed by anything other than the size of the TV but he allowed himself to be toured into the bedroom and bathroom.

'Huddle,' said Juanita as soon as he was out of earshot. 'Stuart? What the fuck? Where's your bodyguard?'

'He's broken his arm. Said he's trying to find me a replacement but there's a freaking security convention in the city this weekend and they're all at that.'

'Haven't you got a friend who could do it?' I asked.

'No one who wouldn't be star-struck and make things worse.' He looked at me. 'You've got a connection going with him, Tara. Can you do it until I find someone?'

'Shit,' I said. 'I've got no experience as a bodyguard. I nearly punched that reporter.'

'He feels safe with you.'

I shook my head. 'He shouldn't.'

Juanita tapped Stuart on the chest. 'Okay Stuart, what's his deal? One minute he's "the man" and the next moment he's neurosis on toast.'

Stuart flinched at the bald assessment. 'Look, his rehab wasn't just drugs. He had a complete nervous collapse. Mostly he's fine, as long as fans don't crowd him or grab him.'

'Okay, no damage,' said Juanita. She had her phone out and was making notes furiously. 'As long as we can spin the airport thing, it will all help with ticket sales. I'll make some calls.'

'What about the reporter downstairs?'

'He'll be too busy arguing with the security guard for his camera.' Her eyes widened suddenly, like she'd thought of something. 'Tara, you keep Slim happy while Stuart and I smooth troubled waters.'

'But I have other things to do,' I protested.

'I'll come back before dinner,' promised Stuart.

'With a bodyguard?'

He nodded.

I sighed. 'Alright.'

Chapter 7

Slim Sledge took a bath and emerged with a towel tucked low around his waist, looking happier.

Too low! I tried not to goggle but he noticed.

'I'd give you the benefit of my lovin' right now, but you gotta do your job and keep this precious body of mine safe. You feel me?'

He was back in 'the man' mode, which made me much more comfortable. I nodded vigorously. 'Yes siree. Need to be alert. Why don't you catch some sleep? You must be jet-lagged.'

He yawned and stretched. 'And hungry. I'm tastin' waffles and syrup and eggs over easy. You do for me?'

'I'll call room service.'

He wandered off to the bedroom and I ordered two meals of pancakes with maple syrup and eggs. No point in me going hungry!

I settled behind the desk and fired up the complimentary desktop computer. As soon as it booted, I hit Google, looking for everything I could find out about Joel Aprile and Andreas Giannoukakis.

Aprile was easy to find information on. His family had been in the spotlight so long there were newspaper articles on Trove dating back to the fifties. Joel himself was even on Wikipedia. I scavenged the bare bones of the entry and typed it into my client file.

His parents had bought a theatre restaurant in Sydney in the late sixties and still owned and worked it today. Run on a Casablanca theme it was so successful they'd been able to buy other properties, including an old shoe factory which they'd converted into a club venue for live bands. When Joel was seventeen he'd pretty much taken over running the club, which was still one of Sydney's best live gigs. By the age of twenty-five, though, Joel had moved on to full-time promoting and installed a manager in the club. He named his new company OTB Productions, the initials standing for Only The Best.

OTB had its own Wikipedia entry, which was similar to the blurb on the company website. The only variation was that Stuart was listed on the site as a former assistant manager but his name was nowhere to be found on www. onlythebest.com.

Giannoukakis's company was called Easy A and showed he'd promoted a mixed bag of events and concerts, everything from Kitchen Superstar and Martin Delectable to old rockers like Deep Purple and Status Quo. In between were the Polka Dancers and a welter of stand-up comedians.

A knock at the door interrupted me and I opened it for room service.

'Slim,' I called. 'Food!'

'Bring it in here, babe,' he replied. 'I'm watchin' Sports Centre.'

Biting my lip in annoyance, I thanked the waiter—Aussies don't tip at home—then pushed the trolley through to Slim and opened the table leaf so he could sit at it.

'Right?' I asked.

He lifted the plate cover and gave a satisfied grunt.

'I'll be out here working,' I said and took my plate back out to the other room.

After two pancakes, I settled back at the computer. Giannoukakis's business had the feel of a variety show catering to all age groups. Only The Best, though, was definitely aimed at the sixteen to twenty-five demographic—and their parents, who, in many cases, would have forked out for the concert tickets. There were a few general articles, the most recent from the Brisbane News portraying Andreas as a family man with a big heart and deep pockets. Apparently Giannoukakis contributed generously to a number of charities every year. His online profile didn't fit with the kind of man who'd run a vendetta against his niece's lovesick suitor, but scratch any surface and it usually bleeds.

When I googled Sofia Zachariou, Stuart's ex-fiancée, I came up with pics of a beautiful Greek girl with dark curly hair and a nice smile. Altogether too sweet looking for Stuart—but that was an opinion I'd keep to myself. There were pics of her on social pages and she'd also modelled for one of her uncle's charities. She had Facebook and Tumblr pages and a Twitter account. I bookmarked her Tumblr but hesitated on sending a friend request to FB or following her on Twitter. I didn't want to leave a footprint behind. Her Tumblr looked like it was updated regularly, so I made a note to come back and read all the old posts. Softly, softly…

The only other item of interest I found was that Giannoukakis was a big fan of the Supanova Pop Expo, Australia's biggest pop culture convention. He was a regular at the event, dressed—according to the pics I found—as either Captain America or the Incredible Hulk.

I got up and stretched. My internet surfing had killed the best part of five hours. Where was Stuart?

I went to the toilet and peeked into the bedroom to check on my charge. Sebastian 'Slim' Sledge was asleep on top of his covers, on his back, stark naked. I thought about throwing a cover over him but he kicked out with one leg and started moaning. Then he rolled over, got on his knees, and began pawing at the sheets, giving me the full benefit of his naked butt. A few seconds later he was lying down again, curled into a ball.

I noticed a door on the other side of the bedroom. Some hotel suites had adjoining rooms, so they could accommodate families. With visions of snooping photographers copping an eyeful of a bare-arsed Slim, I checked it was securely locked then went back into the sitting room. It was after 4 PM and I was starving again.

Just as I started thinking about more room service, there was a knock at the door. Stuart was standing there with a Maccas bag in one hand and a briefcase in the other.

'Where's the bodyguard?' I whispered as he walked past me.

He shook his head. 'It's this freaking conference. No one's available.'

'Don't you know anyone?'

'Jade knows some of the Comancheros. Apparently, they hire out.'

'Bikers?'

He shrugged. 'I'm desperate.'

I nodded towards the bedroom. 'Slim ate breakfast and he's been out cold since you left, pretty much.'

'Let me know if you come up with something. We've got a press call tomorrow at nine.'

'Television?'

He nodded. 'And print press. Tara … er, thanks. I've kind of thrown you in the deep end here. Wal said you were a trooper.'

Did he just? I made myself smile. 'All part of the service. Did you smooth over the airport thing?'

His aura squirmed. 'Yeah, I think so.'

If I hadn't been in such a hurry to get out of the hotel

room, I would have pressed him on it but my feet were already heading out the door. I caught the lift and almost ran through the foyer onto the street for fear he'd call me back. I'd just learned something about myself: I don't like being trapped inside hotel rooms, babysitting rap stars. I'm pretty sure that'd apply to any other kind of star as well.

That revelation made my stomach rumble and I bagged a seat in a Gloria Jean's café. Googling a map of the CBD, I saw that the club where Joel Aprile was meeting with Strawberry Jade wasn't far away. I had time to eat, so I ordered a caramel milkshake and some raisin toast.

The toast came thick and buttery and I wolfed it down. The last slurp of the milkshake was best; caramel sticky and sweet with splinters of ice in it.

My phone rang as I sucked up the last bit. I checked the caller ID. 'Ed?'

'Tara, hi.'

We both started to speak at once then laughed.

'You first,' he said.

'No, you,' I insisted.

'Okay. Look, I'm sorry about the other night. I just … had some stuff to do.'

The night already felt like weeks ago. 'I nearly came over anyway then I remembered my manners.'

'You sounded drunk.'

I sighed. 'Smitty needed counselling. That doesn't happen very often. Bok broke out the bourbon.'

'Sounds like fun.' There was wistfulness in his tone.

I thought about Smitty's insistence that I spy on Henry, and how bad my hangover had been, and how Tozzi and I had parted on less than friendly terms again. 'Not really. Not the next day, at least. How are things with you, anyway?'

'Good. Great, really. I picked up a part in a music video.'

'You mean … for, like … a band?'

'I mean … for, like … the Hilltop Hoods!'

'The Hoods! For real?'

'Last time I checked.'

'What do you mean?'

'I mean I'm shooting it now. I'm in Brisbane.'

'You're in Brisbane.'

'Yeah. I'm sorry I didn't get a chance to tell you…' He trailed off as I burst out laughing. 'What's so funny?'

'So am I.'

'No way.'

'Way.'

'Where?'

'I'm in a café on…' I squinted at the street sign outside. 'Elizabeth Street. There's an empty Borders store across the road.'

'Surreal!' he said. 'Look at the next corner. Can you see the McDonald's sign?'

I scanned around and located it. 'Gotcha.'

'That's the Myer Centre. I'm in a boutique on the left

trying on clothes for the shoot.'

'Right now?'

'Yeah. Come over.'

I checked the time. Aprile would be at the club in about ten minutes. I'd do a fly-by on Ed and head over there.

'On my way.' I swished water around in my mouth to dilute the last of the caramel and paid the bill. A make-up stop would have been nice but I didn't have time now. Instead, I sprinted across at the lights and burst in the door of a boutique called Urban, Sex and Fancy. Two women who looked like staff turned, alarmed, but Ed pitched me a beautiful grin. There was no one else in the shop.

'Sorry,' I said. 'Didn't mean to scare you all. I'm in a bit of a hurry.'

'Tara's always in a hurry,' said Ed calmly. He was looking more divine than divine; dark hair long and curling around his shoulders, skin glowing. His shirt was unbuttoned, giving me a peek at his advertisement-ready abs. He didn't need a spray-on tan, either; his skin colour was naturally olive.

The sales assistants glanced back and forth between us. Both were quite glamorously dressed; one a tall redhead and the other blonde and perfectly petite. They both had the slightly flushed complexion and moist lips that women tended to get around Ed. I could have been possessive but it seemed pointless. A girl could drive herself nuts if she went that route. I still wasn't sure why he wanted to date me anyway, seeing as I was seven years older and a lot less beautiful than he was—it just didn't make sense. And if he was looking for some mothering, I was definitely the wrong bet.

He handed a coat to the redhead and walked past them both to give me a warm hug. When he drew back, my erogenous bits were sending smoke signals to each other. I hadn't had sex in a while now—months. Every time Ed and I had got close to doing the deed, something got in the way. And as for Tozzi … well, I wasn't planning to go there with Mr Mightily Married to the Material Girl.

'Shari, Lulu, this is Tara Sharp.'

The girls muttered unimpressed hellos.

'Nice to meet you,' I beamed in return.

'Shari, can I just have five minutes to talk to Tara?' Ed asked.

Shari looked me up and down. She was older than Lulu with a thin but strong dark red aura. In contrast, Lulu's aura was soft pink and mushy, like it might disintegrate at any moment. Shari was definitely the boss. Lulu looked like she might have trouble catching the bus in the mornings.

'Don't be long, darling,' said Shari. 'We have a lot to get through.'

Ed gave her a nod and steered me out onto the street. We stepped back into the alcove of the next shopfront and Ed pulled me against him. Without warning he kissed me, deeply and meaningfully. Taken by surprise I took a moment to respond, and then I did, very enthusiastically.

'Yum,' he said, when he finally drew away. 'You taste like caramel.'

'Sprung,' I said breathlessly. 'Milkshake.'

He ran his hands down my arms and slid them around my back to pull me closer. 'I'm so glad to see you.'

'I noticed.' I tried not to titter but didn't quite manage it. Ed wasn't usually quite so direct. 'Feeling's mutual but I'm late for something. But why so pleased? You can't have been missing me already!'

He shrugged. 'First trip away from home, I guess. I'm not good with new places.'

I recalled he'd had that slightly lost look when I'd first met him; fresh from the country and his mother's cooking. It reminded me that he was only nineteen going on twenty.

'Well, I'm here if you need me.'

He pressed his lower body against mine. 'It goes without saying that I need you.'

I wanted to giggle again but scolded myself serious. 'I've got to go. I'm in the middle of something.'

'I haven't even asked you why you're here,' he said.

'I'm on a job that came up quickly. Have you heard of Slim Sledge?'

His eyes widened. 'Slim Sledge? You're working with him?'

I settled for a nod and a grin.

'Tara, your life is so … random.'

'Well, what about you, boyfriend? A Hoods music clip. How cool is that?'

'I'm just a piece of meat. You get to use your brain.'

I pulled away and stared hard at him. I'd never heard Ed be cynical about his profession. He had his heart set on making a success of it.

He saw my surprise and gave a sheepish grin. 'Had a late night. Feeling sorry for myself. You want to catch up later?'

'Not where I'm staying,' I said automatically. 'We might get forced into a séance—or something.'

'I'm staying at the Sebel on George Street. It's just across town.' He pointed in a direction I thought might be north-ish. 'Come when you can. I have a night off.'

'I'll be finished about nine.' I hope. 'I'll call you when I'm done.'

'We'll have room service on my expense account.'

My day had taken a turn for the better. 'Deal.' I pecked him on the lips and ran off.

Chapter 8

The address that Stuart had given me was only a block away. At just after 5PM, with the commuters on their way home, Vixens was a dull black and red sign and a dirty closed door.

I knocked several times on the door before an untidy-looking guy came and cracked it open.

'We're not open until six.'

'Can I speak to Strawberry Jade, please?'

'Wait here,' he said sullenly and shut the door again.

Jade took so long that I was checking my email when she finally appeared.

'Who are you?' she asked, frowning.

She was pretty under her heavy make-up. Her red hair was pulled back into a tight plait and her slim figure just held up her red corset. Her skirt was long and black and slit up both sides, revealing clunky doorstopper high heels.

'Tara Sharp,' I replied quietly. 'Stuart Cooper said

you'd be able to help me out.'

Her slightly annoyed lip curl turned into something furtive. She stepped out into the street and pulled the door closed behind her. 'You can't come here now. It's appointment only. They'll wonder who you are.'

'Is he here? Aprile?'

She pursed her lips and nodded.

'I need to meet him. Can you say I'm a friend of yours or something?'

That set a bunch of crease lines crinkling along her forehead. After a moment, they fell away. 'We're interviewing for a new girl. You could pretend to be interested.'

'You mean … someone who does what you do?'

'No, we're looking for a hostess, not a dancer. You couldn't do what I do without a lot of training.'

'So what does a hostess do?'

No, Tara! my mother's voice told me.

'She books the girls for the rooms and makes sure the punters spend their money.'

'Does she take her clothes off?'

Jade shook her head. 'But sometimes she has to mind the rooms when the crowd controller is on a break—to make sure the clients are behaving.'

I could do that for one night.

No, Tara! Joanna again.

'What happens in the rooms?' I asked.

'Lap dances. Strictly no touching.'

'I'm in.' My mother would never find out.

She looked me up and down. 'I'll say someone gave you my name. But we don't know each other, okay?'

'Sure. Absolutely. Thanks for this.'

'Try not to ask stupid questions,' she added.

With that, she opened the door and led me down a set of narrow stairs. At the bottom was an unattended ticket booth. We entered the door next to it and walked into the club proper. Tables were scattered across the room, which had a bar on one side and a stage bordered by footstools and bearing half a dozen brass poles on the other.

Jade saw me ogling and nudged me. 'Stop staring like you've never been in a men's club before.'

I blinked and dragged my eyes from the gleaming poles. 'What are the footstools for?'

'Anyone who sits that close to the girls has to tip them with notes. Your job is to make sure they do. Come on.'

Jade took me over to the bar where a guy who could have been Johnny Viaspa's older brother was fitting bottles of spirits upside down into their holders. His long dark hair was pulled back in a tight ponytail and he wore an apron over a black t-shirt and dark jeans. His nose was aquiline and his lips thin and he was carrying a few extra kilos.

He narrowed his eyes and shot Strawberry Jade a look. 'What?'

'Sammy, this is Tara something-or-other. She heard

we needed a hostess.'

His eyes got even narrower. 'You know her?'

Jade shook her head. 'She says Meat-lover told her we were looking for someone. He gave her my name.' She drifted off as if bored with the whole thing already, and I noted that her acting skills were better than average. I wondered, briefly, what that meant for Stuart.

'Tar-ah, eh?'

I switched my attention to the sleazy guy giving me the eye.

'You worked clubs before, Tar-ah?'

'Nope.' Didn't seem much point in pretending otherwise. 'But I learn quick. And I'm good with men.'

He gave me another slow appraisal. 'So why you thinking you want to work here?'

'I need the money.' I tried to keep my tone as flat and practical-sounding as possible.

'Turn around,' he said.

I did as he asked.

'Bend over,' he said.

'Pardon?'

'Bend over and show me your arse. We don't employ bitches with big arses. Except for one of the dancers. Some guys like that, y'know.'

All I knew was that I was likely to break this scumbag's nose if he said another stinking sexist thing. My fists clenched and my muscles bunched, ready to swing. Every move Hoshi Hara had taught me so far flashed through my mind. After I hit him, I was going to roll this guy and stomp on his head. I couldn't think when I'd last been this mad.

Just then a door opened to my right and a thin, hawkish-looking girl in a clinging dress staggered out clutching her belly.

'Sammy, I got the shits real bad. Musta been that leftover sushi Meat-lover brought in. You better take over, the younger one's getting randy.' She ran off to the toilet.

'Fuck,' said Sammy behind me. 'Jeee-sus. Hey, Tar-ah?'

I relaxed my muscles enough so that they'd let me turn around without unleashing a roundhouse. 'Yeah?'

'Here's your chance. Go mind the booth until Shaz gets back.'

'And do what?'

'Keep quiet unless one of them tries to touch a girl. Then you find a way to stop him that doesn't piss him off. The guy with the white shirt is a regular who pays good. The young one in the other room is a newbie—first lap dance. Sounds like he's getting a bit overexcited. You do alright with them, you get the job.'

'What are their names?'

'Joel is the older one. Young one is Kosta. That's all you need to know.'

I forced my legs to carry me over to the entrance of booth the girl had vacated. About then my courage briefly deserted me and I hesitated.

'What you doing?' bleated Sammy.

'Getting my thoughts in order,' I said. Gritting my teeth, I stepped inside and shut the door.

It was just a cubicle with a rotating stool placed between a couple of two-way mirrors. The stool had a drink caddy and a microphone on one arm. Each mirror looked into a different room. Both rooms were furnished with lounge chairs configured around a central small, circular platform with a single pole connecting to the roof. Even through the two-way, the walls looked slightly grubby and the lounge chairs were patterned with cigarette burns.

The older of the two guys—Joel Aprile—was leaning back in his lounge chair with a glass in one hand and a cigarette in the other, while Strawberry Jade did her thing. He looked content and half asleep, like he was just there for a drink and a nap.

In the other room, a freckled blonde girl slow-danced. Her client—Kosta—was sitting forward on his seat, hands tapping the edge of the platform. Their auras were indistinct through the glass and the dim lighting, but there was no mistaking Kosta's jiggling knee and the way he kept licking his lips and brushing the sweat from his upper lip. The boy was excited. The redhead, on the other hand, seemed more interested in the brass pole than the young man ogling her.

I swallowed and tried to get a grip.

As the blonde got low, she reached behind her waist and pulled off her press-studded skirt. With a clichéd flourish, she swirled it once and dropped it over Kosta's head. He scrambled to untangle himself and then scrunched it into a ball and began sniffing it.

The blonde didn't seem to notice and continued about her business, grinding her panties against the brass. As she swung around and gave him her back view, Kosta could no longer contain himself. He launched forward and smacked her semi-naked butt cheeks, sending her sprawling off the podium onto the chairs opposite.

I flicked the microphone on and summoned my deepest voice. 'Now, now, Kosta, you know the rules. No touching or the pretty girl has to leave.'

But Kosta had his pants unzipped and halfway down his legs.

Sammy chose that moment to enter the booth. 'Jee-sus, stop the little bastard,' he hissed.

'Kosta!' I barked. 'I'd hate to have to come in there and tell you off.'

That seemed to excite him more and his hands found their way into his pants.

'Sammy!' screeched the blonde.

'Shit!' Sammy went to run into the room but I grabbed his shirt, holding him back, and spoke into the microphone again.

'Kosta, unless you zip your pants up and sit down,

it'll cost you a thousand dollars extra. We'll charge it straight to your credit card.'

The hands that had been working furiously stilled. Nothing like plain money talk to dampen a young boy's ardour.

'Good fellow. Now zip it up, sit down and we'll bring you a complimentary drink while our girl takes a short break.'

The blonde left the room and Kosta relaxed. So did Sammy, who nodded at me approvingly. 'How did you know that would work?'

'You said it was his first time. He's probably been saving for it.'

'Well, you got yourself the job. Get the girls to find you a dress. Staffroom's next to the cig machine. Time I cut this wanker off.'

I left the booth and made a direct line for the door with no markings at one end of the bar.

The blonde was in there knocking back a shot of something evil and black. When she'd swallowed it, she took another shot glass from her handbag, ripped the plastic lid off and downed it too. Her aura was giving off little explosions of light, like she might just combust. I'd never seen fear do that before and I tried not to stare.

'That you in there?' she said.

I nodded. 'Shaz got sick. She's in the loo.'

'Bitch is strung out.'

'Oh?'

'Didn't get her junk today. Anyway, thanks.'

I shrugged it off. 'Sure. You get that often?'

'Not if Meat-lover's here.' She saw my raised eyebrow and explained. 'He's our bouncer but he's off at some security love-in bullshit this week.'

'I heard about that.'

'Sammy tried to talk him out of it but he wanted to go real bad. All kinds of new tech and some ex-SAS guys talking.' She shuddered. 'I can't stand it when they touch me.'

'Sammy said I should put a hostess dress on. Said to ask you.'

She took a joint out of her bag and lit it. After a few deep drags she offered it to me.

I shook my head. 'Not on my first night.'

She shrugged, went over to the sideboard that held a small TV screen and a pile of women's mags and pulled open the top drawer. After a rifle through, she selected a dress. 'Change in here if you like. We don't worry much about that kind of thing.'

Considering she was standing in front of me in only high heels and a G-string, I got the drift. Still, I was Joanna Sharp's daughter and I turned away to do the change.

'You know the guy in the other room?' I asked, trying to deflect attention from my embarrassment.

'Listen, you helped me out in there but I'm not your

friend.' She tottered over to the sink and ran water on the end of the joint to put it out. Then she dropped it back in her bag and left the room.

I smoothed the dress down over my underwear. From the way it pulled tight in all the wrong places, I was glad I didn't have a mirror to look in. A deep breath, a quick promise to myself I was out of there as soon as I'd spoken to Joel Aprile, and I headed back out to the bar.

Aprile had left the private room and was sitting in the lounge area nursing a drink. He looked preoccupied and I noticed his orange aura showed some dull, metallic spots. People with orange in their aura tended to be powerful personalities but the flat spots indicated a change might be happening.

Sammy and Strawberry Jade were talking, so I grabbed a tray with complimentary peanuts on it from the bar and strolled over to Aprile.

'Can I get you something?'

He took a moment to look up and focus. It gave me time to get a first impression. Joel Aprile was a handsome man in his early forties, lean with shoulder-length hair and high cheekbones. He was dressed in jeans and a punk-style t-shirt and had four piercings in his right ear. He looked like he'd just stepped out of a recording studio and was ready to knock off a bottle of bourbon. Rumpled but attractive was how I assessed him, and (according to his aura) about to undergo some kind of life change.

'You're new,' he said.

'Like about half-an-hour-ago new.'

'Was there trouble in one of the rooms? I heard some shouting.'

'Not trouble,' I said carefully. 'Just a bit of excitement.'

He grinned and his attractive face got quite sexy. I bet he got his way a lot.

'You dancing?' he asked.

'No. Just getting your drinks and taking your money.'

'Pity. I'd like to see those long legs wrapped around a pole.'

I ignored the blunt line and decided to move quickly. 'You don't seem like the type of guy to come to a boys' club, but Sammy says you're a regular.'

He took a sip and rolled the alcohol around in his mouth. After he swallowed it, he patted the seat next to him. 'Things are quiet.'

I pretended to glance over at Sammy then I sat next to him.

'What brings you to work in Vixens?' he asked.

I waggled a finger and settled the little bowl of peanuts on the table next to him. 'I asked first.'

He chuckled. 'Can I tell you a secret?'

I pretended to zip my lip with my fingers.

'I have a lot of family here. When I visit Brisbane, they drive me nuts. This is the only place I can go where they won't come looking for me.'

I stared at him for a moment then laughed. Genuinely. 'You're just here to hide out?'

'Yeah,' he said. 'In a good way. If I get to look at a beautiful naked woman while I'm doing it, then it's a bonus.'

'Some men would just plug in their earphones at home and turn the music up.'

'I get enough of that at work.'

'Oh,' I said vaguely. 'You sell music?'

'Something like that.'

'I'd die without music,' I said a little melodramatically.

'You ever get to Sydney?' he asked.

'Not much. I'm saving to finish my voice tuition course. Want to go on Sing Factor.'

'So you like to sing?'

'Does a man like a woman in a G-string?'

He smiled. 'Say, I'm going to a party later on tonight. You want to come?'

I frowned. 'What sort of party?'

'Just some friends in the music industry. You might meet a producer or two.'

I gave another pretend worried glance at Sammy. 'We're not meant to see clients outside...'

'I'll square it with Sammy. How about I pick you up here about eleven?'

'No, don't tell Sammy—I'll just meet you there later,' I said quickly.

He shrugged. 'Okay. Come to Bizarre Bar in the Valley.

The party is in a private room upstairs.' He wrote the address on a coaster. 'Tell the guy on the door you're with Joel Aprile.'

I gave him a delighted, slightly awed smile. 'Thanks. I'd better get back to work.'

'Yes, you'd better … so I can watch you.'

He stayed for another hour or so while I wiped down tables and listened to Sammy's list of instructions about how the evening would unfold.

When Joel left he gave me a covert, one-finger wave.

I waited ten minutes in case he came back, and when I was sure he'd gone, I bundled my real clothes into my bag, ducked out the door leading to the cashier's booth, and set off the fire alarm.

Sammy, Strawberry Jade, Shaz, the blonde and two punters grumbled up the stairs and out onto the street to wait for the fire brigade to turn up and check it out. While they were milling around, complaining to each other, I tagged on to a passing group and stayed with them as far as the next street corner. Then I peeled off and headed straight for Ed's hotel.

When I was still a block away I got a phone call. Smitty.

'T, where are you? What have you found out? I need to know or I'll die.'

Her trembling voice worried me. She wasn't the sort to get hysterical. 'Calm down, Smitts. What's happened?'

'I followed him to work today. He stopped at a house in Claremont. He was in there for forty-five minutes.'

'Do you know the house?'

'It's hers.'

'Belle's house? You saw her?'

'There was a red Alfa Romeo in the driveway.'

Belle had a thing for red Alfas. Her daddy had bought her one as her first car.

'Could be a coincidence. I mean … maybe it's just a patient.'

'It's her. I know it! The kids and I are leaving him. How could he?'

'Smitts!' I yelled. 'Stop it! Let me investigate a bit further.'

Heads were turning on the street to look at me.

'Then where are you?'

'Brisbane,' I said.

'Tara, I need you.'

'Look, hon, I'll get Hoshi to look into it for me. He's better than I am at this sort of thing. Just be patient and give Henny the benefit of the doubt. Please.'

She began to howl. I was standing outside Ed's hotel by the time she finally cried herself into a snuffle.

'You're right,' she said finally. 'I'm being ridiculous. Of course he loves me.'

'I know he does! How are things between you? Are you fighting?'

'Yes,' she whispered. 'About everything. He says I'm acting weirdly.'

'Are you?'

'Yes.' She said it so faintly I wasn't sure I'd heard it.

My stomach churned a little. I hated hearing her so upset. She was my best friend. 'I'll ring you in the morning.'

'Okay.' Still faint. 'Come home soon.'

Ugh. Between Smitty's crisis and the clammy residue of Vixens I wanted to go and take a long shower and spend some time with Ed. Luckily both were on tonight's menu.

I rang Hoshi but he didn't answer, so I stood on the pavement outside the hotel and sent him a long text explaining that I needed him to check up on Henny. After pressing send I strode up to the desk and asked for Eduardo Pote, ignoring the fact the hotel staff were staring at my Vixens outfit.

'Mr Pote has been delayed and asked if we could escort you to his room. He said he'll be with you shortly. The concierge will take you up.'

'Thanks.' After a moment of disappointment, I realised it would give me time to unwind and have that shower.

As soon as the concierge let me in the door, though, the only thing I could see was Ed's bigger-than-king-size bed decked out in crisp white sheets and down-stuffed pillows.

Just for a moment, I thought…

Tozzi's lips were on my thigh, warm and soft. His tongue came next, leaving little trails of moisture that made my flesh pimple. I really should take my clothes off to make it easier for him but if I moved he might stop what he was doing and that would be terrible…

'Tara?' said Nick.

'Mmmm? You want me to take my clothes off?'

A chuckle. 'Sure do.'

I sat bolt upright and opened my eyes. Ed was kneeling on the bed beside me, his shirt off and his pants undone. He'd been kissing my thighs and I was overcome by guilt and confusion. 'Ed!'

'Expecting someone else?'

'No. I mean, I didn't… I was dreaming … and thought I was awake.'

He crawled forward and stretched so that our mouths were level. 'What is this?' he asked, tugging at the clingy hostess dress.

'I… Long story,' I said, and pulled him on top of me.

But as things started to get hot and heavy, so my brain began to wake up. Unwanted thoughts filed into my mind: Brisbane, Stuart Cooper, Smitty, Joel Aprile.

I freed my mouth from Ed's and he fell straight to kissing my neck. His hands slid up under my dress, teasing all my tender bits. My skin got so hot I wanted to tear off the dress.

'What time is it?' I panted.

He stopped what he was doing and raised his head from my neck. 'Uh?'

'How long was I asleep?'

He shifted slightly so he could see the bedside digital. 'It's quarter past eleven. I'm sorry but the shoot dragged on.'

'Crap!' I groaned. 'I have to go.'

'Go where?' His mouth, which was all soft and kissable, thinned.

'I'm sorry, Ed. It's work.'

'And you can't tell me…'

I trailed a fingertip gently down the side of his face. 'Well, apart from the client privilege thing, it's better for you if you don't know anything.'

He gave me a very serious look. 'Does that mean it's dangerous?'

''Course not,' I said lightly. 'Just … messy sometimes.'

'Like the Johnny Viaspa thing a few months ago.'

'Shhhh! Don't mention the devil's name or he'll appear.'

He frowned. 'You shouldn't make light of people like him. Everything I've read … and heard … says he's bad news.'

I blinked. 'Have you been researching criminals on my behalf? Ed, you're so sweet.'

He sat up, the last of his ardour deflating. 'Stop treating me like a child, Tara. You do it all the time.'

Do I? 'I don't mean to. I'm just trying to protect you from some of these seedy types I work with.'

'Do you think everyone from the country is stupid and needs protecting, or just me?'

'Just you!' I joked.

This wasn't going well and I was late for my date with Joel Aprile. 'Look, I really have to go but can we catch up tomorrow? Please? I promise I won't be frivolous.'

He suddenly relaxed his shoulders. With it came a look of exhaustion. I could tell he'd been 'on' all day and needed some time out.

'Ed, you're a great guy. I can't help my instinct to protect you,' I added softly. 'It's nothing to do with being from the country or anything else.'

'I don't want a mother, Tara. I have one.'

'Okay.' I leaned forward and kissed him on each cheek then on the lips. The last kiss grew firmer and deeper and pulling away from it felt like the hardest thing I'd ever had to do.

Chapter 9

Fortunately, Bizarre Bar wasn't far from Inigo's house, so I got the taxi to wait outside while I threw on some fresh clothes.

The lady of the house had retired to her room; trance music and the smell of something exotic emanated from under the door. That saved awkward conversation and I tiptoed around without disturbing her.

The taxi driver dropped me outside the bar at quarter to twelve and then rolled down the road to the nearest cab rank. Even though it was a Wednesday night Fortitude Valley was buzzing.

I gave Aprile's name at the door and a bald-headed bouncer pointed me up a flight of stairs.

The venue was an old house that had been redone in a modern cabaret style with lots of red down-lights. The stairs were narrow and creaky despite the little grey carpet runners and took me up to a closed door. It was just another club but right now I didn't feel like being there. I stood for a moment and made a deal with myself: find out whether Joel Aprile was targeting Stuart, then go home.

When I pushed the door open, the party was in full swing, the room crowded with the fuzzy auras you normally got when booze and other substances were involved. The music was loud but not loud enough to drown out the beat from the bar below, and the two streams of sound collided to make a weird hybrid. A couple of people were huddled over a coffee table sniffing coke and the sweet smell of hashish filled the air. It was likely I'd get stoned just being in here.

It took me a few minutes to locate Joel, who was over by a large double window, puffing cigar smoke up towards a vent and talking on his phone. I supposed they were keeping the windows closed so that the scent of hash didn't drift out onto the street. I studied his aura; it seemed settled and healthy enough. Nothing out of place.

He hung up when he saw me. 'Tara. I'd given up on you.'

'Busy at work,' I said. 'Had trouble getting away.'

'Drink?'

'Die for one.' I nodded.

'Full bar. What's your poison?'

'A beer, please. Something fancy.'

He threaded through the crowd to the small bar and gave me more time to take in the scene. I recognised a couple of people but couldn't put names to them. They were much-photographed faces, I thought.

'Trying to place people?' Joel asked, as he placed a beer into my hand.

'Thanks—yeah,' I said cautiously. The girl I was pretending to be would probably know who these people were. 'I'm kinda awed.'

'You don't look like the sort.'

'Maybe,' I murmured, shooting him a sideways look. Was he kidding? Or fishing? 'So, what about you? Are you rich or famous or both?'

He shrugged. 'I own a club in Sydney. We only do live bands, so I know a lot of people in the industry.'

'Cool,' I said. 'Had any big names in your place?'

'Sure. Ed Sheeran dropped in recently but not to perform. He was out clubbing.' He grinned.

'Wow!' I didn't have to pretend to be impressed. 'What about Slim Sledge? I hear he's in town on a comeback. He's pretty big.'

He shook his head. 'Let that one slide through to one of my competitors. Slim's too much trouble. I like my artists to be in control of their addictions.'

'I heard he got straight.'

'Rule number one when working with entertainers— never believe anything that you haven't seen for yourself.'

'So why did the other promoter pick him up if he's so much trouble?'

'Guess he figured he was worth the risk. Good luck to him. He used to work for me, actually. Not a bad guy. Say, you want another beer?'

His aura hadn't altered its regular movement the whole time we'd been talking. Perhaps he wasn't our man. 'You trying to get a girl drunk?' I said, attempting a weak flirtation.

'Will it work?'

I laughed. To tell the truth he wasn't bad company.

His phone beeped and he turned away to read a message. Straight away I spotted the change. Not only did his aura get choppy but it lightened into a more fluorescent colour. Something had got him excited. I wondered what.

We talked a bit more, had a couple of drinks and he introduced me to one or two producer types. One of them treated me like fungus while I forced myself to do the aspiring-singer thing, and the other tried to hit on me. Jonno Vebson, the hitter-onner, wore dark glasses, and had gelled hair.

When he squeezed my bum, told me to bring my demo to his office and said that he sensed we could go places together, I decided it was time to split. He hadn't pissed me off quite as much as Sammy at Vixens but he was batting in the same ball park.

I sought out Joel to say goodbye.

'Any luck?'

'Maybe. Thanks for inviting me.'

'Sure. No problem.'

'Can I ask for one more favour? My phone battery's died. Could I borrow your phone to call my ride?'

He grinned at me. 'Boyfriend?'

'You got me,' I said.

He hesitated for a split second then handed it over. 'Don't call China,' he joked.

I dialled a nonsense number and turned away, pretending to have a private conversation with my guy. From the corner of my eye, I saw a woman approach Aprile and start chatting. Capitalising on his distraction, I quickly killed the call and opened his text messages. The last text read: 2pm at the club. I've got some more info. Jx

I flicked back to the home screen and swung around, handing the phone back. The woman seemed annoyed at the interruption and moved on.

'Thanks again,' I said to Joel.

'Good luck.'

'Back atcha.'

I left and caught a cab to Inigo's, musing on the message. Could J be Jade?

Inigo's bedroom door was still closed with light leaking out from underneath, but the music was off. Maybe she'd fallen asleep with the light on?

As my hand touched the doorknob of my room, my stomach made a noise that was a cross between a buzz saw and deep drain gurgle. If I didn't feed it, I'd never sleep.

With a sigh, I tiptoed to the kitchen and opened the fridge. A slab of tofu sat sullenly on a plate alongside a dish of mixed butter beans. Ugh. I checked the freezer next and spied brown ice blocks and a frozen fish. Nope.

That left me with bread.

I read the label that told me which hundred and one gluten-free grains were in it and slathered it with what looked like peanut paste. Biting into it, I realised I'd made a mistake on the paste. A squint at the jar revealed it was sesame seeds. Not awful though, I thought, so I slathered up a second piece and took it to my room, trying not to think about Ed alone in his hotel bed.

Life sucked.

Morning came way too soon, in the form of a phone call from Stuart.

'Where are you?' he demanded.

'Asleep. Got caught up with Aprile late. How's the babysitting?'

'Some fans hijacked a room service trolley and tried to break in. It's all over the morning news. Tara, get over here.'

I sat upright. 'Slim okay?'

'Yes. Just.'

'Shit!'

'Fans are camped outside thanks to the media coverage and I can't find a bodyguard. You'll have to do a shift so I can get some sleep.'

Shit! 'But I've got to see Giannoukakis today. I'm still not sure about Aprile. He said he passed on Slim because he's trouble but he didn't seem bitter about you.'

There was a pause before Stuart answered. 'Really?'

'I spent the evening with him, drinking.'

'That means it is Andreas, the autocratic old bastard.'

'Nothing's certain yet,' I said. 'I have more leads to follow up on. And I can't do my job if I have to hold Slim's hand.'

'For chrissakes, don't do that!'

'What?' I said, confused.

'Don't hold his hand. He's OCD. Washed his hands eight times before breakfast and used that antiseptic stuff between his cereal and his toast.'

'What time does his manager arrive?'

'Lunchtime.'

'I'll watch him till then,' I offered.

'Fine. Come up to the room before eight. Juanita's scheduled a press conference for nine. I want you to scout the area beforehand and make sure there won't be any problems.'

It seemed pointless to tell him again that I knew nothing about being a bodyguard; he was in too much of a spin. Instead, I put in a call to Wal. Even though it was 5 AM in Perth, he answered quickly and sounded alert.

'It's me,' I said.

'Yeah, boss?'

'I think you should come over. Stuart needs a bodyguard for his muso and seems to think that I'll do.'

There was a long pause. 'Can't.'

'Pardon?'

'Got some things to sort out here.'

'Wal?' My voice rose a little, despite it being early morning—my normal croak time. What the hell is he up to?

'Unsecured line, boss. Sorry, you'll have to do this one without me. Call the Comancheros. They hire out.'

'The Comancheros?'

'Gotta go. If I'm out of reach for a few days, don't worry. Tell Stuart hey.'

'But Wal—'

Click.

Argh! I got out of bed and prowled over to the window, pushing the sarong-style curtains aside. It was a beautiful day outside already, cloudless and bright. Only the stickiness in the air and the high-set house next door offered a clue to the fact that I was in Brisbane not Perth.

Right now, perfect weather didn't soothe my frustration at the mess this job was turning into. Wal telling me to contact the local biker gang was kind of the last straw. I felt like ringing Stuart and telling him I was pulling out. I wasn't cut out for personal protection of neurotic musos.

Then I had an idea.

I searched the bottom of my handbag until I found a slightly crumpled card and dialled the mobile number on it.

'Who?' said a gruff and wholly scary voice.

'Tara Sharp. We met on the plane.'

'So?'

'I … er…' My tongue threatened to fail me by sticking to the roof of my mouth but I swallowed to create some saliva and forced myself to continue. 'Er… I need a bodyguard for this job I'm working on and there's no one around—some big security convention in town or something. I thought if you were here for a few days, you might be interested.'

'Bodyguard for who?'

'A US rapper on tour with Reverb Promotions. The fans have found his hotel and are causing chaos.'

'How much?'

'I'll have to talk to Stuart Cooper—my client.'

'Where are you?'

'On my way to meet him at the Stamford Plaza. You want to come down and check it out? That is … if you're not busy with … um … funeral stuff.'

'Funeral?'

'Your friend?'

'Oh, sure. Yeah, I'll come down.'

'Cool! I'll be there at eight.'

'So will I.' He hung up.

I sank back onto my bed and took a couple of slower breaths. I hadn't really expected Big Nuts—Bon Jovi Ames—to say yes. Had I just invited a tiger into the deer park?

'Tara?' said a voice at the door.

Oh no! 'Yes?'

123

'I wish to do a reading for you.'

'Um, I'm in a bit of a hurry, Inigo. Stuart just called.'

The door flung open in dramatic style and she stood there with a teacup in one hand.

'Well, come on in,' I said lightly.

Inigo was looking a bit wild, hair sticking out and eyes bloodshot. Her clothes were a mix of op shop and sex shop: cheesecloth dress, Madame Lash boots. If that was kombucha tea she was drinking, then she must have slipped in some cactus juice as well. Didn't look like she'd slept at all and her aura was the fluorescent orange of a toadstool.

She came over to the bed, placed the tea on the bedside table and sat next to me. 'Give me your hands,' she rasped.

As I obliged, she grabbed one of my thumbs and pressed it into her palm. Her eyes rolled back in her head and her lids gradually closed.

We stayed in complete silence for far longer than was comfortable before she began to sniff.

Sniff. Sniff. SNIFF.

And on it went; thumb pressing, sniffing, eyes shut, until eventually her eyelids snapped open and she glared at me with unnerving intensity.

'I smell salt and orange blossoms. Then I smell petrol and rubber. Petrol and rubber. Petrol and rubber.'

'Um...' I felt like I was trapped in a Twitter hashtag.

Suddenly, she let go of my thumb and sagged,

exhausted.

'Inigo, are you alright?'

'I have done what I can for you. Now I must sleep.' She got up and left the room.

Phew. I scurried to the bathroom and locked the door. A shower and some fresh clothes and I was out of the house and down the street looking for a cab.

The nearest street corner harboured a bakery, so I bought two custard tarts, a croissant and a fresh orange juice.

The carbs-and-sugar hit was spectacular and settling, and soon I was on my way to the Stamford in a taxi, feeling fortified and ready to handle the Slim Sledge show.

I checked my phone and saw there were messages from Cass, Joanna and Aunt Liv. Joanna would be asleep and I didn't fancy a dose of my mother right after the Inigo event. Cass would still be crashed out as well, so that left Liv, whose message had sounded quite urgent.

She answered after one ring. 'Tara! Thank goodness!'

'Liv, everything okay?'

'I fear not, my dear. Wal is in trouble—he's disappeared!'

'Disappeared? How do you mean?'

'I've been down to the flat and he's not there. He's not answering his phone. He always answers his phone to me. Always.' Her voice trembled.

'Did he say anything to you recently about a problem?'

'No, but he has been acting a little … paranoid.'

'How so?'

'Oh, you know, only opening the door a crack, keeping the curtains closed and the windows locked. He made me go and pick up our takeaway Thai dinner alone. And the ... you know ... things he keeps in that bag. He had them out, cleaning them. Honestly, Tara, I didn't know where to look. I told him to put them away but he said he couldn't.'

'Oh.' Crap. If Wal was cleaning his weapons in front of Liv, something was definitely up.

'Have you spoken to him, darling? Is this one of your psychic jobs? I hope not because I don't like the idea of the ... you know ... things in the bag.'

'Last time I spoke to him he sounded fine.' I didn't tell her it was only an hour ago because I knew she'd just ply me with questions.

'Where are you, darling? I want to see you.'

'Sorry, Aunt Liv, I'm in Queensland working for a music promoter. Wal did say he had some things to deal with and that he'd be out of circulation for a while.'

'For a while? How long is that? Deal with what things? Darling, this is far too Secret Squirrel for me. You must come back here immediately and find him.'

Double crap.

I owed Liv a lot. She'd been a shoulder to cry on about my difficult relationship with my mother, she'd always championed me on the family stage and never blinked an eye at some of the odd people I'd brought home to her place. She'd even set Wal up in a flat so I didn't have to have him sleeping on my couch. Sure, the latter was because she had some weird and inexplicable crush on him—Bogan Russian Mafioso meets Flamboyant Society Girl—but she hadn't had to go the extra mile and fit him out with curtains and a couch. In fact, I doubted Wal had ever owned curtains and a couch in his life. When we'd met he was living in a boarding house.

'I can't, Liv. I'm in the middle of a job. Wal is more than capable of looking after himself. Be patient, he'll sort it out.' I lowered my voice so the taxi driver couldn't hear. 'And whatever you do, don't go to the police.'

There was silence at the other end.

'Liv? You haven't, have you?'

'That rather superior female constable called around here yesterday.'

I racked my brains to think who she might mean. 'Fiona Bligh?'

'Yes, that's her. And that overweight ogler.'

'Bill Barnes?'

'M-huh.'

'What did they want?'

'They were after Wal's address. They had some questions to ask him about a missing truck.'

'Why did they come to you?'

'Well, apparently they'd been to your place but Joanna told them you were interstate.'

Triple crap. Now I definitely wasn't going to ring my

mother back.

'They remembered I knew him from that other time,' said Liv.

'Oh.'

'Is that all you have to say?'

'Look, I'm sorry the police came to you, Liv, but I don't know anything about a missing truck or why Wal has gone AWOL.'

'Tara Sharp, I'm telling you, you must come home and fix it.'

I'd never heard Liv so adamant about anything. 'I can't,' I said. 'But I'll get Hoshi Hara to look into it until I can get home.'

'He's the nice Japanese man, isn't he?' Her voice was quavering again. 'Very well. Tell him to come and see me right away.'

'I will.'

'Goodbye, dear.'

'Bye, Liv.'

Chapter 10

The crowd outside the Stamford were vocal and unruly. Even though it was breakfast time they were sharing burgers, fries and hotdogs around. Some had placards and most wore t-shirts that said Sledge Sisters.

I recognised Fran Dickle, the president of the fan club, from the airport. She was standing at the edge of the crowd with a paparazzi-type camera slung over her shoulder and was talking animatedly with the concierge. Not keen to be seen by her, I slipped past on the other side and almost ran in through the double doors.

Bon Ames was standing in the foyer near the reception desk looking like a cheezel in a packet of potato chips. His size alone drew attention, but when teamed with torn denims, a studded leather jacket, biker boots and a pissed expression, he must have been terrifying to the hotel staff.

I waved and his expression lightened a fraction. When I got close he hit me with a man-sized handshake that nearly dislocated my arm.

'How they hanging, Tara Sharp?'

'Better for having you here, Bon. It's mad outside.' We walked towards the lift.

'Just a bunch of kids,' he said dismissively.

'Yeah, but the guy we're minding's just out of rehab and psych counselling. He flips out every time a fan gets close enough to touch him. It's kinda weird actually. He enjoys the attention and he loves the ladies, but when fans grab at him he goes mental.'

'So that's all you want me to do—keep the fans from touching him?'

'Yep. Pretty much.'

'How much and for how long? I got to get home soon.'

'You'll meet Stuart in a minute; he'll talk to you about that. Slim is in Brisbane for a few days.'

Ames grunted.

'Don't want to hold you up—go home when you have to,' I said. 'But thanks for stepping in today.'

Another grunt. By this time we were in the lift heading up.

'How was the funeral?' For some reason, it was the only thing my brain would let my tongue say.

He shrugged.

There was a short awkward silence before the doors pinged open, in which time I smelled the rum leaking from his pores. His aura wasn't at all messed up with emotion as I would've expected. In fact, he seemed quite calm.

I led him out of the lift and along to Slim Sledge's suite.

There was a young guy in hotel uniform standing outside looking bothered.

'Hi, I'm with Mr Sledge's tour,' I said. 'This is Mr Ames, Mr Sledge's new bodyguard.'

'Please wait here.' He turned his head to speak discreetly into his phone. Before he'd hung up, the door to the suite opened.

Stuart stepped back when he saw Bon.

'Meet Bon Ames, your new bodyguard,' I said.

With his mouth open, Stuart stepped aside so we could enter. I glanced around the suite. Food plates littered the table but there was no sign of Slim.

'He's in the bedroom,' said Stuart. He looked like a man who hadn't slept in a week, all stubble and red eyes.

'Bon Ames, this is Stuart Cooper. He's Slim Sledge's promoter and tour manager. He'll talk to you about money and times.'

Stuart slapped me on the back nervously then pumped Bon's hand. 'Man, thanks. I mean … thanks.'

'I'll leave you two to talk business,' I said and headed to the bathroom. I rang Mr Hara from in there, waking him up.

'*Hai?*'

'Hoshi, sorry to call so early, but Wal is missing. I think it's by choice, but can you ask around about any trouble? My aunt Liv is about to bring in the SWAT team.'

Hoshi knew both Liv and Wal. After I won the Perth triathlon a few months back, we'd all played Monopoly together to celebrate. Immense fun after a couple of bottles of champagne.

'Surely, Tara. How's your job going?'

'Uh, interesting, I guess. Any news on Henry? Smitts is on my back as well.'

'Your friend is right 'bout one thing. The house is owned by Miss Bussey.'

'Crap.'

'Cass is watching the house today. Tell you more tonight, maybe. Depends on if he comes back.'

I heard Mrs Hara shouting to him in the background.

'Gotta go.' He hung up.

I felt sick. That wasn't what I'd expected. How could Henry be seeing Belle the Black Widow Spider? Didn't he know she ate her mates? Didn't he know Smitts would carve him into little pieces over this? I wanted to call and bawl him out for it, but Smitts would be in bed next to him right now. No, it was better to wait until Cass had done her surveillance and I had more proof. I didn't want Henny slipping out of this when I nailed him.

A quick face sponge and I went back into the main room of the suite feeling bolshie.

Slim Sledge appeared from his bedroom, dressed in a white tank top and black jeans. A baseball cap and shades completed the look. I was momentarily reminded that I was in the presence of a superstar.

'Shawty, where you been?' he said. 'I missed you.'

'Missed you too, Slim,' I replied. 'But I brought you

Mr Ames. He'll keep those germy little fans away.'

Slim walked a slow circle around Bon and we all held our breath—all except Bon. He looked like he wanted to grab Slim and tip him upside down, just because he could. But maybe he looked at all people that way.

'Will you do good for a brother, man?' Slim asked.

'Fucking A,' Bon replied.

Slim's mouth split into a wide, dazzling grin. 'Mothafucker.'

When the singer smiled like that I could see why millions of fans adored him.

Behind him, Stuart just looked relieved. 'Okay. Okay. It's about fifteen minutes until the press meeting in the Pandanus Room. Tara, you and Bon go down and make sure everything is cool then come back and get us. Juanita is already down there.'

Bon and I did as we were instructed, making very tiny small talk in the lift.

'Thanks for doing this, Bon,' I ventured.

'Fucking weirdo.'

'He's recovering from stuff, y'know.'

'I'll give him fucking *stuff*.'

OMG, what have I done? I know nothing about this guy at all. I swallowed the huge lump that had grown in my throat and was glad when the lift chimed open.

Juanita was flitting around the Pandanus Room, seating

journalists as they arrived and arguing with them about where their recording equipment should go. Hotel staff were also bustling about, handing out complimentary orange juice and sparkling water and setting up an urn and tea and coffee cups on a long, linen-covered table.

'Dahling,' Juanita said as she swayed over to us looking dead sexy in spiked heels and a Kardashian-style fitted dress. Her long hair was out and falling silkily on her shoulders today and her make-up was photo-ready-heavy. 'Everything alright at Ground Zero?'

'Um, yes. So far. Juanita, this is Bon Ames. He's agreed to be Slim's temporary bodyguard.'

Juanita gave him her sweeping once-over with a flicker of her eyelash extensions. 'Excellent. Someone who knows what they're doing. No offence, Tara dahling, but we really do need to keep those nasty little fans away from our sensitive artiste.'

For the first time since he'd arrived Bon's expression changed and his aura expanded. His eyes took on a predatory gleam that suggested he'd like to scoff Juanita for morning tea. But Juanita's aura was all focused and business-like and she flashed over to the coffee table to head off rumblings over the lack of sugar sachets.

'So, it's all good then?' I said.

Bon dragged his eyes from Juanita's bum and glanced around the room. 'One door, first floor. Windows are sealed. I'll stay out in the corridor and watch the lift and stairs and make sure no strays get past the hotel security.'

'What should I do?'

'You stay near him, keep the news scum at a distance.'

It was obvious Bon didn't have time for a lot of people.

'Roger that,' I said.

Bon stared at me. 'Who?'

'I meant … nothing,' I said lamely.

He shook his head. 'We'd better go get the weirdo.'

Instinctively, I wanted to defend Slim. His neurotic fits were annoying, but other than that, he was okay. I didn't know how sane I'd be if strangers wanted to touch me all the time. But Bon Ames wasn't the kind of man you'd take to task over his opinion, especially when he was helping you out. I suddenly felt grateful for one Wal Grominsky—for all his quirks and narcolepsy problems, Wal was a lot more user-friendly.

Stuart and Slim were waiting for us. Slim was looking smooth and ready to roll, so we trooped back into the lift and went down again. Once we hit the convention floor, Bon stationed himself between the lift and fire exit, and I trailed the others into the limelight.

Slim took to the podium and I kneeled in front of it like a concert bouncer ready to leap up and rescue fainting fans. I felt silly, but Slim relaxed a bit when I did it and began to flash his thousand-carat smile.

Juanita took the helm and made sure the media all got their moment. I was bored by the tenth question and marvelled at how many times a different journalist could ask the same question. Slim took it in good humour and even cracked some jokes that got them all grinning.

All in all, it was going smoothly enough that my thoughts wandered to visiting Andreas Giannoukakis. He was next on my list to investigate and I wanted to get on to that today.

'Last question,' declared Juanita. 'That young woman next to the pillar. Stand up, please, so we can see you.'

'I'll come a bit closer,' said the girl.

The nervous, breathy tone of voice should have alerted me; I am a body-language expert after all. But the truth is I'm sharper with visuals. It wasn't until the figure came into line with the front row of chairs that alarm bells clanged.

Fran Dickle was wearing a press pass and a cap for disguise but there was no hiding her erratic aura and round face. Her aura surged like the tide in a storm as she brought the microphone to her mouth.

'Slim...' she began.

I sprang up to act as a deterrent to whatever she was planning, but when she saw me she panicked.

She flung the microphone at me as I lunged to head her off. For an out-of-shape-looking girl, she stepped sideways like a footy pro. My lunge and grab fell on thin air and I went down with a crash, taking a table and water jug with me.

Slim squealed as Dickle secured him in a clinch.

'Unhand him!' shouted Juanita.

By the time I'd rolled over and scrambled to my feet,

Stuart had Dickle in a headlock and Slim was sobbing in Juanita's arms. Cameras were rolling and flashing and clicking.

I could see the headlines already: REHABBED R&B STAR STILL ROCKY. SLIM SLEDGE FIGHTING DEMONS. SLIM BREAKS DOWN—AGAIN. FAN ASSAULTED BY SLEDGE'S PROMOTER.

Just when I thought things couldn't get worse, Bon burst into the room brandishing a knife.

A knife? Shit! What is he thinking?

'Hey!' I bellowed at full volume.

All the camera attention swung to me and gave Bon the split second he needed to assess the situation and put the knife away.

'Hey!' I repeated, aware now that they were all watching me. 'You need to leave. This is over. Go suck someone else's blood.' I hadn't meant to say the latter; it just came out in the heat of the moment. But it set off a bunch of angry reactions and some eye-popping name-calling.

Bon took over at that point, half lifting the collapsed Slim Sledge into his arms. There was something desperately sad about the musician curled up and bawling like a little kid. But Bon's expression didn't show any sympathy. Lip curled, he kicked the door open and headed for the lift. We fell in behind him, Juanita bringing up the rear, madly trying to mend bridges with the offended journos.

By the time we got up to the room and Stuart had bombed Slim out with a couple of Xanax, the fallout

137

hit. Stuart, Juanita and I sat around the hotel computer watching #SlimSledge trend on Twitter.

'Who the fuck gave her a press pass?' said Stuart.

'I don't understand, I screened them all,' said Juanita. 'There was no Fran Dickle. She must have bought it from someone.'

'Bought it?' I said incredulously.

Juanita and Stuart both rolled their eyes at me.

'This is the music industry,' said Stuart. 'Fans will do anything!'

I knew that in theory but I'd never seen it in action. 'I'll follow it up. See what I can find out.'

Stuart's phone rang.

His side of the conversation went from disbelief to cajoling to terse in the space of a few sentences. When he hung up we waited.

'Sydney venue just cancelled,' he said.

'They can't do that,' I said. 'Isn't the gig only a week away? Won't it cost them a fortune?'

'Not if they can establish he's medically unfit to perform. That way they claim insurance instead and they'll probably come out ahead in the long run.'

'How do they prove he's medically unfit?' I asked.

'Won't be too hard,' said Bon Ames. He'd been out on the balcony smoking but was now standing behind us, staring at the muted TV screen. 'Crazy fucker like that.'

'Turn it up,' said Juanita.

Stuart reached for the remote.

'Comeback R&B star Slim Sledge showed he still had demons to slay at a press conference in Brisbane just a short time ago. When confronted by an overly enthusiastic fan, Slim appeared to become overcome, retreating to the arms of his publicist. It has prompted the concert-going community to question whether he is fit to be touring…'

'Overly enthusiastic!' said Juanita. 'The girl is a piranha. I swear she was scraping his skin to get DNA samples.' Her phone rang and she turned away to listen.

'Fuck,' said Stuart.

'Keep calm, everyone,' said Juanita. 'I can resurrect this. I've just had a call from some producers I know. They're shooting a music clip in Spring Hill tomorrow with a local band. They've invited Slim to do a cameo and then the Sunday paper is going to do an article on it.'

Stuart gave her a grateful, if wan, smile and turned to me. 'Tara, any more cancellations and I'm bankrupt.'

'Gotcha.' I stood up. 'You guys have got babysitting duty until tonight. I'll go track down who gave Dickle the press pass, then I have to go and see a man... When does Slim's manager get here anyway? I thought it was today.'

Juanita and Stuart exchanged looks.

'What?'

There was a long silence that got even Bon Ames's eyebrows kinking with curiosity.

'This mustn't go outside this room,' said Stuart, lowering his voice.

I nodded but Bon Ames just kept staring.

Stuart must have taken that as agreement because he continued. 'He doesn't have a manager. His last one quit and he hasn't been able to attract another.' He rubbed his fingers together indicating money.

'You mean he's broke?'

Juanita nodded. 'Stone cold. The previous manager ripped him off and then his last trip to rehab cleaned him out of his cash flow.'

I suddenly felt the weight of two careers on my back. 'You mean if this tour fails, he's ... like ... on the dole?'

Stuart nodded gravely. 'Or whatever the American equivalent is.'

'There isn't one,' said Juanita.

Another silence fell.

'When did he tell you?' I asked.

'This morning when I was making arrangements to go to the airport.'

Bon Ames gave a grunt that was a bit hard to decipher. It might have been in sympathy but I suspected it was more likely to mean I'm not surprised.

'Well, I'd better get to work,' I said.

And quickly. Even in previous jobs, when my life had been under threat, I hadn't felt this sense of responsibility.

'Juanita, can you email me the press list from this morning so I can go through it?' I added.

'Right away,' she said.

Then her phone rang again and I took that as my cue to get the hell out of there.

Chapter 11

The first thing I did was find the concierge, but he couldn't shed any light on Fran Dickle or who she might have bribed to get the press pass.

'Though I regret the incident,' he said primly, 'this was handled by Mr Sledge's publicist. We don't run security details for our guests, though of course we know how to be discreet.'

'Nothing discreet about that,' I said, pointing to the fans chanting outside on the footpath.

'The pitfalls of fame,' he said and went back to his computer.

I took the side exit and headed up the street until I found a café, where I ordered a hot chocolate and some more raisin toast.

Fortified, I searched Google Maps on my phone for Giannoukakis's address. It was a short walk across a bridge to South Brisbane. I memorised the route then had a thought. Checking the notes Stuart had emailed me, I saw that Andreas's niece, Sofia Zachariou, worked at a beauty salon in the city. Maybe talking to her as well would give me a better picture of the family's feelings about Stuart and whether they were likely to actively sabotage Slim's tour. The salon was called Finesse, and I found a phone number for it easily.

I sat for a moment before I rang. Would contacting Sofia upset Stuart? Even if it did, I reasoned, he needed results and this might help. I dialled the number and asked the receptionist for an appointment for a pedicure with Sofia.

'Sofia is booked out,' she said.

'Could you explain that I'm a friend of Stuart Cooper's, just in town for a short while, and that he recommended I contact her?'

'I'll pass the message on but right now she's with a client,' said the receptionist firmly.

I took a breath and counted to three then played the fame card. 'Look, hon, I'm a manager on the Slim Sledge tour and I'm on a tight schedule. Do you think you could just check with her quickly?'

'Slim Sledge! You mean, like, the singer?'

'That's right.'

'You're his manager?'

'Yes,' I said baldly.

'Please hold and I'll be back in a minute.'

The line switched to AM music and I had a bit of a grin while I waited.

She returned quickly and out of breath. 'Sofia can see you at three o'clock.'

I checked the clock on the wall. 'Fine. Thank you. My name is Tara.'

'Just Tara?'

'That'll do.'

'Lovely,' she gushed. 'We'll see you then.'

I hung up and rechecked my mail. Juanita had sent through the press list. None of the names meant a thing and I didn't have time now to google them. It would have to wait until I had a spare moment.

I drained my hot chocolate, paid my bill and headed out into the sunshine. It was good to get away from the hotel room. Though it was beautiful and spacious, the tension in there seemed to eat up the oxygen.

The walk across the bridge was picturesque—sunshine and brilliant blue sky—and I would have liked to stop and watch the river traffic for a while. Ferries scudded to and fro and there were rowing eights out, even though it was the middle of the day. Despite the water being puddle-brown, the Brisbane River definitely had its own charm. It spoke of cruise parties and drunken late-night ferry rides home. Something about it gave me a little buzz of excitement.

I got to the other side and found Giannoukakis's office in the basement of a decrepit but character-filled old building across from the expansive concrete Convention Centre.

There was a young man sitting at the desk in front of a computer. His dark hair and aquiline nose suggested Mediterranean heritage but his gum-chewing and iPod was all-Aussie consumer.

'Yeah?' he asked loudly, not bothering to take out his earphones.

'I've got an appointment to see Mr Giannoukakis.'

'Wassyourname?' Loudly again.

'Tara Tozzi.' Holy crap! Where had that come from? Right out of my mouth before I could even think about it.

Music Boy flipped through computer screens with one hand while drumming on the desk with the other. When he couldn't find the appointment, a scowl settled onto his face and he jerked one earphone from his ear.

'Got nothing in here about an appointment. You sure you got the right day?'

I decided to go plummy. 'Absolutely sure. I don't get dates wrong. I'm a journalist.'

He frowned. 'For who?'

I raised my voice so you could hear it out on the street. 'Last Rave magazine in Sydney. I'm here to do Mr Giannoukakis's profile piece for our next issue. It has been arranged.'

An inner office door opened and an older man peered around. 'Fubulo? Is there a problem?'

'This … woman says she has an appointment with you but I don't see a record of it.'

'What magazine did you say you were from, Miss?'

asked the older man.

'Last Rave,' I said, holding out my hand in greeting. 'Tara Tozzi?'

'No relation to Nick Tozzi?' he said.

The blood drained from my head and pooled in my feet. 'Who?'

He smiled and stepped into the room to shake my hand. He was an impressive-sized man with a girth to match his thickset shoulders and a booming dark blue aura that was twice as wide as most. He would be a hard man to take a stand against and I felt a pang of sympathy for Stuart, who hadn't met with his approval as a suitor for his niece. Though he was thinning on top, his face held character and humour. Smart, I thought. And tough.

'A businessman who you'd be better off not knowing,' he said.

'Oh, I'm intrigued,' I said.

'Please step this way and I'll aim to intrigue you a little more.'

Fubolo gave me a frown as I followed Andreas into his office.

The boss closed the door and gestured to one of a pair of slightly worn and heavily patterned armchairs squatting in front of a large tinted window. Outside the wind was picking up, bending some spindly new trees on the footpath in half.

'Please sit,' he said. Lifting the phone on his desk, he told Fubolo to bring in some iced water, then he folded his body into the armchair opposite me. 'My apologies for the mix-up, Ms Tozzi. How did you want to do this?'

'Just a little Q and A would be fine. I'll arrange for the photographer to come in next week.'

'Fine then. I'm at your mercy.'

He was quite a charming man and answered my standard questions with practised ease; how he got started, best moments in his career—that kind of thing.

Fubolo marched in with the water and marched out again without a backward glance at us.

Andreas smiled apologetically. 'My nephew.'

While he poured me a glass of water, I looked around the room. On the other side of the desk was a large table. It harboured an object that was hidden by a heavy cloth. I immediately had an itch to see what was underneath the cloth but that meant manufacturing a reason to get him out of there. I couldn't think of a reason on the spot, so I proceeded with the interview. Who were his influences, the best and worst artists he'd seen tour, his opinion of the state of the Australian music industry...

When his aura became expansive and soft around the edges from speaking on his favourite topic, I dropped the grenade.

'According to my research, you almost had another promoter in the family. I believe Stuart Cooper was engaged to your niece?'

His aura immediately shrank. 'That is correct.'

'Had you considered merging businesses?'

His eyes flicked to the covered table in the corner for little more than a micro-second, but I registered the movement.

'There is no point in discussing what might have been, Ms Tozzi. Stuart and my niece went their own ways. Suffice to say, family is everything to me. You have to watch out for your own.'

I wasn't exactly sure what he meant by that but flashes of red had begun to shoot through his aura. The colour red generally meant a person was strongly materialistic. I didn't know what this had to do with Stuart but it gave me a strong urge to search the man's office and computer. That, of course, would be highly illegal and I wasn't exactly experienced at B&E. It brought me back to my earlier thought: I had to get a look under that tablecloth.

'Well, thank you so much, Andreas. Perhaps we could arrange a good time for my photographer to come around?' I reached for my glass of water and 'accidentally' knocked it over. It rolled right into his lap and he flinched as the icy water soaked through his pants.

'Oh, I'm so sorry,' I cried.

He leaped up. 'It's fine, Ms Tozzi. Really. But if you'll excuse me, I'll just dry off.'

The moment he was out of the office, I ran to the table and tried to lift the cover. It was secured to the base of the table by hooks. I loosened a couple and peeled it back.

Beneath was a model of an office development. Andreas's name was printed on a label glued to one side. I grabbed my phone and took a picture of it. Then I dropped the cover back, hooked it to the eyelets, and catapulted into my seat.

The door opened again just as I was crossing my legs.

'Andreas, that was so clumsy of me. I'm so sorry.'

He looked a little annoyed and embarrassed by the wet patch across his crotch. 'Look, Ms Tozzi, I have to go to a meeting elsewhere. Perhaps you could talk to Fubulo about an appointment with your photographer. Or I could send you one of my press shots.'

'Lovely,' I said, standing up. 'I'll do that now. And thank you. What a pleasure to meet you.'

'And you,' he managed through gritted teeth.

I left his office and organised with Fubulo to email me a press photo. He wrote my (fake) address on a Post-it note, after which we exchanged a cool farewell and I split.

Outside it was still beautiful. I took my time going back across the bridge and drank in the rhythm of the riverscape. The sun was high now and every surface seemed to bounce light at me. The foot traffic had lessened with the increasing heat and those out and about wore the Brisbane sheen of perspiration.

My plan was to wait outside Vixens at 2 PM and see what transpired, then head on to the beauty salon. I couldn't imagine why Jade would be telling Joel Aprile to meet her at the club out of hours, but instinct told me it wouldn't involve a lap dance.

At 1.50 PM I strolled past the dirty black door of the men's club. It was locked and the place looked deserted, so I kept on walking until I reached a nearby juice bar, where I ordered an orange and beetroot blend and watched the juice guy throw fruit and vegies around like a juggler. The colour in the blender was rich and bloody and made my mouth water. As he banged a straw in the plastic cup and took my money, I glanced back down the street.

'Shit!'

'Pardon?' said Juice Guy.

'Um, look, could you stick that in the fridge for a sec? I'll be back.'

He shrugged. 'Sure.'

'Thanks.'

I bolted across the road as soon as there was a break in the traffic and hustled back down the street the way I'd come. The shop directly opposite Vixens sold Chinese foodstuffs. I went inside and found a spot to spy, standing in the window between hanging sets of glazed barbecued ducks.

'You want something, Miss?' asked the guy behind the counter.

'Just looking,' I said.

And I was: looking straight across the street at Joel Aprile knocking on Vixens' door.

The door opened and Joel stepped into Strawberry Jade's passionate embrace.

What the hell?

There was nothing businesslike about the way they twined around each other's bodies or the ferocity with which their mouths were exchanging fluids.

Shit! No doubt in my mind. They were a couple!

Finally, Strawberry Jade detached herself and peered out onto the street before closing the door. I shrank back to avoid being spotted and banged into one of the ducks. It hit me in the head and on instinct I ducked (ahem), hitting another one as I jerked my head back.

Suddenly, the whole row of ducks was swinging wildly on their hooks. The store owner raced out from behind his counter to settle them. I tried to help but grabbed too hard and one came clean off its hook. Momentum carried my arm forward and I smacked him square across the forehead.

'Whaaa—' he shouted, followed by something in Chinese that, thankfully, I didn't understand.

'I'm s-so s-sorry,' I spluttered, whipping the duck back.

His forehead bore a duck-beak imprint. I wanted to tell him but my tongue wouldn't form the right words.

'You try, you buy.' He finished steadying the other poultry and I followed him back to the cash register. 'Fifty dollars.'

'Fifty dollars! You're kidding me?'

'Best duck in town.' He held out his hand. 'Plus damages.'

'Damages!' I squeaked.

A customer entered the shop and stared at the owner's

forehead, bemused. I gulped and handed over my credit card before he could speak.

When the transaction was complete, the owner wrapped my duck in brown paper and I shoved it, as well as I could, into my handbag. Its head poked out near my elbow, beak open from the impact with the man's head. Refusing to be daunted, I adopted a nonchalant air as I crossed the street to collect my juice.

'Happy duck,' said the guy.

'Funny,' I said and headed off through the city to my appointment with Sofia.

The beauty salon was on the first floor of an arcade full of sushi bars and cute accessory stores. I took the stairs, not the lift, and was sweating heavily by the time I got to the door. What was it like here in the middle of summer?

The receptionist's eyebrows shot skyward when I entered but she didn't mention the duck. I gave her my name and she led me through to a cool, clean room furnished with an armchair, a bed, a cabinet, a basin and some cheesy repros of the sea hanging on the wall. Wind and chime music filtered through the O-shaped speakers hanging from the ceiling as I slung my shoes off and sat on the edge of the bed.

I should have been planning my strategy for dealing with Sofia, but all I could think about was the fact that Jade and Joel Aprile were doing the nasty behind Stuart's back—and not in a 'work' way, which suggested that Joel Aprile had been lying through his teeth to me. It certainly meant that he stayed on my suspect list. And how would Stuart take the news that his current girlfriend had a boyfriend? He was unluckier in love than me.

Andreas wasn't looking so squeaky clean either. There was no doubt he was carrying some baggage about Stuart but was that enough motivation to be trying to ensure that Slim Sledge's tour failed?

While I remembered it, I sent the picture I'd snapped in his office to Nick Tozzi with a message. Nick, can you tell me what this looks like? Important. Tara.

Tozzi mightn't have been an architect or an engineer but he knew plenty. And he loved to be able to tell me about things I didn't know. I was sure he'd get back to me with something but I didn't want it to be while I was talking to Sofia, so I turned my phone off.

Sofia walked in as I was sliding it back in my bag alongside the duck. She stopped, stared at the open beak and then at me.

'Hi, nice to meet you,' I said, holding out my hand. 'Tara Sharp.'

She hiccoughed in a way that could well have been concealing a laugh and stepped forward. 'Sofia Zachariou.'

'Excuse my duck,' I said. 'Long story.'

She nodded and her lips twitched upward. I saw immediately why Stuart had fallen in love: soft dark curls, flawless skin and a wide, generous smile. For me, though, the best thing about Sofia was her aura. It was the palest green and textured like shallow sea on a warm, still day. I could imagine people wanting to be near her merely for its calming effect. There was one medium-sized purple blemish situated over her left shoulder. I wondered if that psychic bruise was anything to do with my current employer.

'I have you booked for a pedicure. Would you sit in the chair?'

I did, and she scrubbed my feet in a basin of hot water and did all the toenail jazz while we exchanged pleasantries.

When she moved on to the leg massage, I fought a desire to just lean back and forget the world. Instead I got a bit more personal.

'That's heavenly,' I said. 'Stuart said you were the best.'

'Stuart?'

'Cooper. He said you were close friends.'

Through my half-closed lids, I saw her aura contract a little but maintain its serenity.

'Yes… Stuart and I … knew each other well.'

'The dude sounds like he's besotted with you,' I said baldly.

A red flush stole up her neck to her cheeks. 'Oh? What did he say?'

I yawned. 'Can't remember exactly. Something about your family not liking him. No … that's right … your uncle.'

153

As soon as I said the word uncle, her aura turned luminous. I pressed on while I had a reaction.

'Actually, Stu's asked me to come and work with him in his business,' I said.

'Oh?' She kept her head bowed.

'My job's so boring it would be good to have a change. It will cost me my life savings though.'

The bruise above her shoulder darkened and her aura began to swirl gently.

I let her reaction guide me. 'It sounds like it'll be worth the risk though.'

She nodded calmly but by now her aura was speeding up to whirlpool proportions. Just the mention that I might be investing in Stuart's company got her agitated. She knew something and I had a feeling it was connected with the model hidden in her uncle's office. I wanted to get out of here and ring Nick Tozzi about the picture I'd sent him.

I lifted my feet out of the tub. 'Look, that was wonderful and you've listened to me rambling on but I've just looked at the time—I have to fly.'

'But I haven't done your nail polish yet.'

'No need,' I said.

'But—'

I was already up and slipping my feet into my shoes. 'Pleasure to meet you, Sofia.'

She got up, soaped her hands in the basin and followed me out.

A few more pleasantries, a quick jab of the credit card in the chip reader, and she and the receptionist watched the duck and I depart.

Chapter 12

I caught a taxi straight out to Fortitude Valley, where Slim was having his publicity event. The driver talked so much I didn't get a chance to listen to my phone messages. Instead, I watched the city workers soldiering along the pavements looking hot and bothered and felt grateful for the blast of his air-conditioner.

The trip only took about ten minutes but the change in atmosphere was profound. While Brisbane CBD was all office bustle and sweat, Fortitude Valley was an invitation to a beer and a Vietnamese nosh-up. As soon as I got out of the car, I headed down the mall looking for a place to sit and make some calls. I still had half an hour before I had to meet Bon Ames and perform the security check.

Little Paolo's was about halfway along the mall so I went to Ric's Bar opposite so I could scope the entrance and order a coffee. There was a table right in the corner, outside, screened by some potted palms. Sinking into the chair, I got my phone out and checked my messages.

Smitty and Hoshi Hara. Nothing from Nick.

I called him first and he answered after the second ring. 'Tara?'

His voice sent a hot shot through me. I didn't realise I'd been missing him and yet it'd only been a few days since he'd picked me up on Queenslea Drive.

Tucking that thought away, I got straight to the point. 'Did you see the picture I sent you?'

'Nice of you to say hello,' he said.

'Sorry, but I'm in the middle of something.'

'You're always in the middle of something.'

And you're not? I nearly added. How's your coked-up wife doing? But then he'd get pissed and hang up.

'It's a model of a property development, isn't it?'

'Hang on while I have another look.'

I peered through the palm fronds while I waited. Paolo's was locked up in the way Vixens had been; dusty, dark double doors firmly shut, illuminated sign switched off. I wondered if Little Paolo had to shut the bar for the afternoon to accommodate Slim's media event.

'Tara! Tara, are you still there?' Nick's voice came back on the line.

'Sorry,' I said. 'Daydreaming.'

'You're right. It's a scale model of new offices. Why are you sending me a picture of it?'

'Is there any way of finding out where the development is going to be?'

'Where are you, for a start?'

158

'In Brisbane,' I said impatiently. 'I'm working on that job I mentioned.'

'How would I possibly be able to tell you anything about a business development in Brisbane? I live in Perth and sell sports gear.' He was sounding decidedly grumpy.

'Yeah, but you know lots of people.'

'So?'

He was being deliberately obtuse. 'Well, can't you ask someone who might know?'

'So you want me to drop everything to do you a favour?'

'Jeez, I'm not asking for your kidney, Nick,' I said. 'I thought we had a sort of ... deal about helping each other.'

I was playing the you-still-owe-me-for-saving-your-business card. He could have countered with the I-saved-your-life trump—but he didn't.

'Sorry, things are a bit rough here today,' he said.

'Anything you want to talk about?'

'No,' he said. 'Look, leave it with me and I'll ask around. I do know a guy who works in the government over there. He might be able to help. Or know someone who can. But before I do ... you did obtain this photo legally, didn't you?'

I thought about it for a second. 'Yes. Quite.'

'Quite? What the hell does that mean?'

'I mean that the enquiry should be kept confidential ... to protect my client.' I was being deliberately vague and he knew why.

'I'll call you,' he said, and hung up.

I sat for a moment, finishing my coffee. A shot of rum in it would have been nice, but I was working and rum breath was not a way to build client confidence or keep Sharp sharp.

Another peek through the foliage told me Bon Ames was looming up the mall towards me, managing to look at home and out of place at the same time. People in the street literally changed direction or speed so as not to get too close to him. He really did possess the scary factor. And now I had to go to work with him.

I sprang up from behind the palms, stepped out onto the mall and tapped him on the shoulder as he passed. His hand shot backwards and clamped on my wrist with an arm-breaking grip, yanking me around in front of him.

'It's me,' I croaked, my mouth suddenly dry.

For a second I glimpsed a terrible ugliness in his face, then his expression relaxed. 'Don't sneak up on me.'

'Got it,' I squeaked.

He let go of my wrist, walked over to Little Paolo's door and pounded heavily. It took a few minutes but a bleary-eyed young guy opened the door.

'We're here to do the security check for Slim Sledge,' I said.

He took one look at Bon and let us in. He probably should have asked for ID but this was Australia—we are way too trusting like that. Especially when a monster-dude with a West Coast Cheaters patch stitched onto his leather jacket comes calling on you.

We followed the young guy upstairs and into the club. I realised then that Little Paolo's took up the top level of over half the businesses along the mall—must have cost him a fortune in sound-proofing.

The young guy pointed to the stairs that led to Paolo's offices. 'I'll buzz him. He'll be down in a mo' to let you in.'

'Thanks,' I said.

Bon Ames just grunted and scoped out the room.

I followed in his wake, trying to imagine ways someone as crazy and obsessed as Fran Dickle could get in here. It was hard to concentrate, though, with a storm of thoughts rushing about in my head: Andreas, Joel Aprile and Jade, Wal and Smitty. My energy was being slowly siphoned away.

'No windows,' Bon pronounced. 'Looks fine, as long as the fire exit stays locked.'

More precisely, no windows you could climb through. They were set high in the walls and painted in and looked like they hadn't been opened in forty years.

'What about the back offices?' I asked.

Bon Ames got a weird, almost predatory look on his face. 'Let's go check them out.'

Little Paolo came through a door and down the stairs just as we reached them.

'Slow down, lesbo. Where would you be going?' Paolo boomed, dropping a heavy hand on my shoulder. His aura buffeted me like an airbag in a car crash.

'This is Stuart's security guy, Bon Ames. Well, we both are actually.'

Paolo looked over my shoulder at the biker and something strange happened. His aura shrank so fast that I thought I felt the swish of the vacuum it left. What was warm and forceful suddenly chilled. I wanted to turn and see the effect their meeting was having on Bon but it would've looked too weird. I did know, though, that I had to stop Paolo's panic so he didn't throw us out before we could finish our sweep.

'Slim won't come into the premises until we've done the full recon. You don't mind, do you, Paolo? Just a quick scope around.' I gave him my most congenial smile.

'Well, I don't let people I don't know back here, so you can go but he can't.'

Bon growled under his breath behind me.

'Sure,' I said loudly. 'That's cool. Bon will wait out at the bar.'

An awkward moment followed as Paolo and I squashed past each other. His body was so large and soft that it folded around me, and I was overcome with a panic that I might suffocate. It spurred me to push forward harder and I champagne-cork-popped out the other side.

Paolo's back receded down the stairs, which meant that Bon had retraced his steps. I waited until they were both out on the dance floor and I gave Paolo a little wave. The light was dull out there but I could have sworn Bon's aura was jagged like broken glass. What the hell was that about? They didn't seem to know each other but their reactions to the encounter were pretty damn strong for complete strangers. It rattled me enough that I made my recce as quick as possible, not wanting to leave them alone together. The back offices were all as dirty and untidy as each other. The windows to the outside were long-time-locked and I couldn't see any way even Determined Dickle could get inside.

The last room I checked was Paolo's. Nothing had changed from our visit the night before last other than that the water cooler was less full and the bin brimmed with lolly wrappers. There was a pizza box on the floor behind his chair. I shut the door and headed out to find my offsider.

Bon was leaning against the bar, scanning the room to bite someone's head off. Paolo was nowhere to be seen.

'Looks fine,' I said. 'Shall we step outside?'

His eyes were so narrow I could barely see them, but he nodded. Once we were back on the street, his face settled into thundercloud status, which was better than head-biting status.

'I think we can give Stuart the all-clear.' I initiated all the conversation with Bon. Like I was on a date and nervous.

'Maybe,' he said.

'Care to elaborate?'

He stuck his thumb to his lips and bared his teeth. Passers-by gave us a wide berth.

'Do you know Little Paolo?' I ventured.

'No. Why?'

I had no reason to doubt him, but something nagged at me. 'Oh, it just seemed like you did. Or he knew you.'

He nodded slowly. 'Some weird psychic shit telling you that?'

I straightened my back and stood tall. 'Not weird psychic shit, Bon. Intuition.'

The fallout I expected from my rebuff never came. He wasn't bothered by me correcting him. In fact, he now seemed to be deep in thought.

'Shall I call Stuart?'

He nodded absently, and while I got out my phone and waited for Stuart to answer he made his own call, walking a few paces away so I couldn't hear.

'It's Tara,' I said when Stuart picked up. 'Bring Slim down. We've checked the place out.'

'Okay. We'll be there in fifteen minutes.'

I hung up and glanced over at Bon. He was pacing back and forth in front of the Irish pub. I would have given anything to know what he was saying.

He suddenly shoved his phone back in his pocket and stalked over. 'Right?'

'He'll be here in fifteen minutes.'

'I'll wait outside near the taxi rank,' said Bon. 'You go and watch the vultures as they come in. If that crazy bitch got a press pass at the hotel she could have got one here too.'

'Check.'

I went and found a perch at the bar. From the high bar stool, I could see the door and all of the room at a glance.

The bartender slung a free beer my way.

'Thanks,' I said.

He winked and smoothed his long hair through an elastic band. 'Boss said to keep the visitors happy.'

'Them too?' I gestured to the journos and photographers now entering. They lined up around the edge of the stage, each trying to take up as much space as they could to make less for the others. No sight of a Dickle-like shape.

'Crisps and peanuts and cheese and pickles for them.' He nodded towards the little bowls on a trestle table near the bar. 'They have to buy their own drinks. They're supposed to be working.'

I sighed. So was I, but the sun was well and truly over the yard arm and I'd had enough of today. The beer was cold and sweet and slick on the back of my throat and I drank it in a few gulps.

'Needed that, huh?' he asked.

'Pretty much,' I said. 'You worked here long?'

'Few months.'

I nodded towards Paolo, who was up on the stage rolling out posters and laying them across the back of the chair. He'd set up a seat and microphone and a little side table with water on it. 'Good boss?'

'Bad as most; good as most,' the bartender said cryptically.

I shot him a look. 'You sound ... unconvinced.'

He shrugged and began loading dirty glasses into the dishwasher under the bench. 'Club owners have always got it going on, you know.'

'What?'

'Y'know. Shit?'

'Oh? Educate me.'

'Whatever.'

I sensed him withdrawing so I changed the subject. 'You a fan of Slim Sledge?'

'Massive. For years. Back when he was just a support act.'

'Me too.'

'How did you score a gig working with him?' he asked.

'I'm working for his tour manager.' I remembered the story that Stuart had told Paolo. 'Stuart's a... err... friend of a friend.'

'Lucky you.'

'I gather you're not planning on making a career in

bartending then?'

He turned the dishwasher on and tore open a packet of beer nuts, dumping them on a little plate near me. 'Actually, I'm planning on being one of them.'

'What? A journalist?'

'Nah. Not great with words but I love the camera work. Studying it at uni.'

'Cool,' I said. 'I'm Tara, by the way.'

'Brendan.'

I looked at him properly for the first time. With his hair pulled back in a ponytail and the soft bar light on his skin he looked about seventeen but his voice and the confident way he moved told me he was older. He wasn't nearly as beautiful as Ed but he wasn't too shoddy either.

Ed. The thought jolted me guiltily.

I pulled out my phone and called him. He answered quickly, as though he was expecting my call.

'Tara?'

I turned away from Brendan and kept my voice low. 'Hi.'

'Is everything okay?' he asked.

'Fine. But I've been working flat out all day. What are you doing in a couple of hours?'

'I'm heading out to dinner with the producers. Expecting it to go late.'

'Oh.' I couldn't keep the disappointment out of my voice.

'Sorry.'

'That's cool. I'm sorry about last night too.'

'We could try again tomorrow?'

'Actually, about that… Are you shooting that music clip in Spring Hill?'

'How did you know that? It's supposed to be top secret.'

'My client's doing a cameo on your video. I'll be bringing him down there, so let's make some plans for after.'

'Slim Sledge?'

'Uh-huh.'

'It's a date.' His voice went all deep and melted-chocolate-like. 'Tomorrow then, hon.'

Hon. I gulped. He'd never used an endearment like that before and it sucked my breath away.

Fortunately, Bon, Slim, Stuart and Juanita walked in. 'Gotta go, Ed. Bye.'

Slim saw me first and came straight over. 'Bitch, where you been?' A different kind of endearment to Ed's and one that made me wince. Jacinta must have seen my expression because she shot me a warning frown.

I took a breath and smiled at Slim. 'You feeling better?'

He wiggled his hips. 'Bring—it—on.'

I became aware of Brendan hovering behind me and turned towards him. 'Slim, this is Brendan, a friend of mine. He'll get you whatever you want to drink.'

Slim banged his knuckles in Brendan's direction in an air five. 'You a friend of my girl here?'

'Ah … yes, sir…'

'Then you can make me something high-ball and sweet.'

'No alcohol,' I added.

Slim nodded. 'My girl knows what's good for me. You listen to her.'

Brendan flushed with fan-boy fervour and I noticed his hands shaking as he whipped up a pineapple mocktail in a high-ball glass. He handed it to Slim with a little umbrella, a curly straw and a strawberry wedged onto the lip.

'Brisbane special, Mr Sledge. It's called Paradise Punch.'

Slim took the glass, careful not to touch Brendan's fingers, and had a sip. 'I'm gonna remember you as the Paradise guy.'

Brendan's face flamed so red I thought I'd have to find a fire extinguisher.

'Slim, Slim, welcome to my humble bar,' said a booming voice.

We all turned around and absorbed the impact of Little Paolo's size and personality. He'd slipped an enormous black jacket over his t-shirt and turned the collar up so that he looked like a giant balloon gangster.

Bon stepped forward and placed himself right between Paolo and Slim. It seemed more a power play than necessity but I was happy to be safe rather than sorry. A touch by one of Paolo's big clammy hands might send Slim into hysteria.

'First, man, you can call me Sledge,' said the rapper.

'Second, don't sell yourself down. Place here reminds me of the clubs that my boy Nelly and me used to do back in the day.'

Paolo looked sweatily pleased. 'Let me show you to your chair, Sledge. The press are pissing themselves to talk to you.'

Nice.

'Tara!' Bon gestured me across to one side of the informal aisle made by the journalists and photographers. He went to the other.

Juanita took the lead while we covered the sides. Stuart and Little Paolo brought up the rear behind Slim. No fan was going to get past us this time.

Protected by our guard, Slim made it to the stage without incident and the interview began. It was the same round of questions as earlier, with the added, 'What happened with the fan?' and 'Tell your side of this morning's incident, Slim'. Juanita had drilled him well and he just stuck to the 'no big deal' and 'jetlag' line.

A journalist from a community radio station kept pinging personal questions. When he asked about the details of Slim's rehab, Juanita flicked Bon a look.

The biker sidled closer to the journo and stood a few feet behind him. I held my breath, not sure what the pair had planned. But Bon stood there quite casually, arms crossed, legs apart, and I relaxed. It was going to be cool.

'Is there any truth in the rumour that you developed obsessive compulsive disorder as a result of your past drug abuse and can't bear to be close to people?' asked the community radio dimwit.

There was an awkward silence in the room and even some of the hardened music reporters glanced at each other.

Bon suddenly shifted position and in the process kicked the cord that ran between the reporter and his sound gear.

This was NOT going to be cool.

The reporter stumbled backwards as he lost his headphones and yelped, 'Fuck man, you did that on purpose.'

'Say what?' Bon's scowl made me want to shrivel up and die.

I began to pray. Don't pull your knife. Don't pull your knife.

The reporter blanched at the ferocity of Bon's manner. Everyone else saw the biker's expression, and muscles. Only I saw his aura expand and totally smother the journalist.

'Um, er, nothin' … nothing, man,' the community radio guy stammered.

Juanita jumped up on stage and took the microphone, explaining that Slim would now be signing posters which would be auctioned for charity and that they were all free to photograph him while he was doing it.

Everyone immediately lost interest in Bon and Mr Community Radio and began fiddling with their cameras. As a mini furore of equipment-rustling ensued, Juanita beckoned me over. I walked the long way around, staying clear of Bon and the radio guy. She met me at the edge of the stage and kneeled down.

'Nicely handled,' I said.

'Practice makes perfect, dahling,' she whispered. 'Slim wants you on stage with him while he's signing. He says you make him feel safe.'

'Me!' It came out as a squeak.

'You have a fan.' She pulled a face.

I hid my urge to laugh hysterically and climbed on stage, finding a spot behind Slim where I'd be out of camera shot.

From my possie alongside some speaker brackets, I looked out into the room. There must have been sixty or seventy cameras pointed at Slim while he signed his name with a giant sharpie. I scanned the crowd. No sign of Fran Dickle, thank goodness, and the event was nearly over. We'd survived this one.

Then I saw something that made me start. Bent over a bunch of camera cases, face averted from the stage, was someone I knew.

Harvey T? It couldn't be!

I'd run some home 'social skills' classes when I was getting started in my business; they kept me in petrol money while Hoshi taught me how to use my gift. I didn't have many students but Harvey T. was one of them. Last time I'd seen him, Enid Bell, one of the other class members, had been riding his butt cheeks hard into the lino floor of my flat as if she was trying to win the Perth Cup. Even now the memory made me blush.

I squinted at the figure by the camera cases. Maybe I was wrong. The lights were dim and his Coke-bottle glasses were missing... No. Harvey T. was... Come to think of it, Harvey T. had never told me what he did other than to say he worked for the government. I'd always assumed it was IT. Before I could decide whether to call out and wave, Juanita was back at the microphone again, telling the media it was time to wind up and that they should all take home a complimentary gift bag which would be given to them at the door. 'Strictly one per person.'

Slim stood up and I hurried to his side to escort him from the stage to the cordoned-off area near the bar, where Brendan was waiting with another Paradise Punch.

Our trajectory took us past Harvey and as we got closer I waited for him to make eye contact. When he didn't, I called softly, 'Harvey?'

He stiffened but didn't look up. Now I was close, I was sure it was him—dressed differently, hair bleached—but he didn't seem at all keen on renewing my acquaintance.

'Harvey, it's Tara.'

He dropped his head lower and I was forced to keep moving. Once I had Slim ensconced safely on a bar stool with an umbrella and a strawberry on his glass, I had another look around for my former student.

Most of the reporters had either left or were milling

near the freebie box by the door. Harvey had vanished and I didn't know whether to be hurt or amused by his failure to acknowledge me; I'd certainly failed to impart any social skills.

'Tara?' said Stuart in my ear. He pulled me aside a little from Slim and the others. 'That went well, I think. Other than the jerk from community radio.'

I grinned. 'Bon sorted him.'

'He's terrifying,' said Stuart. 'I'm scared of him.'

'Me too,' I said.

'Where did you meet him?'

'On the plane.'

'True? Well, lucky for me I guess.'

'Hope so.'

'Listen, how did you go with Andreas? Is it him?'

I took a breath. 'Look, we need to talk about some things, but not here.'

'Well, I'm taking Slim to dinner at Cha Cha Cha. He's hankering for a steak. You want to come?'

'Er, I've got a few things to do. Can we take a raincheck?'

Stuart looked relieved that I'd declined. 'Sure. Sure. Stretching the budget anyway. The place is not cheap. I'll be in the office at eight tomorrow morning. It's walking distance from Inigo's place. Come by and we'll go over it all.'

'Sounds good.'

'The gig's in two days. It has to go ahead.'

'I got you. It will.'

'Ta-ra!' carolled Slim. He was giggling at something Brendan had said and was looking pretty relaxed now. I wish I could say the same for Bon. He looked so watchful that I felt guilty I wasn't acting the same.

'Yeah, Slim?'

'You coming to eat meat with us, girlfriend?'

I shook my head. 'No can do. Have to work.'

He pouted and tugged dejectedly on the lapel of his coat. 'What you doing for dinner, homey?' he asked Brendan suddenly. 'You gonna come eat with us?'

I thought that Stuart might have a heart attack. The bartender, on the other hand, looked like he might faint.

'Love to,' he managed to gasp out. 'B-but I'm working for another half hour.'

'Your boss'd be happy for you to come with me.' Slim turned to Paolo. 'Ain't that right, big man?'

Paolo hesitated and I saw his aura undulate like a snake around his huge frame for a second or two. Then he nodded. 'You can go early, Brendan. I'll lock up.'

Slim's good humour returned almost instantly. 'Let's shake it then. A brother is hung-*ry*.'

The last of the reporters had gone, so Bon Ames and Paolo escorted us out.

We said goodbye out on the mall. Paolo re-entered his club and locked the door on us. Slim, Juanita, Stuart, Brendan and Bon disappeared off down the mall to the limo that was waiting for them in the taxi bay.

Marianne Delacourt

Chapter 13

I hung around until they were out of sight, then I rang Lloyd Honey. Lloyd was my first-ever client. I'd kinda sorted his love life for him and he seemed to think he owed me some type of debt. He owned an IT business that handled enormous amounts of information: I wasn't sure exactly how, or who for, but he'd never failed me yet when I needed to know something.

'Hello, Ms Sharp,' he answered.

'Tara!' We did this dance every time we spoke. He tried to be polite and formal and I countered with something a little more friendly. 'How are you, Lloyd?'

'Extremely well. We just got back from an overseas holiday.'

He really did sound good; vibrant, in fact. This, for Lloyd, was outstanding. He was a nice man but he was never … vibrant.

'You sound great!'

'I've got some good news.'

'Oh?'

'I'm going to be a father.'

Well knock me down and pick me right on up again! 'Oh, Lloyd, how wonderful!' And it was. I just hoped his sexually wayward wife was feeling the same. 'We should have a celebratory drink when I'm back in town.'

'Indeed. That would be nice. Now, what can I do for you?'

'I need to trace an identity. I have a first name and a photo. Is that enough?'

'Are they Australian?'

'Um … yeah.'

'I'll see what I can do. Can you give me some context Ms … Tara?'

'He called himself Harvey T. and he'd be in his late twenties. He attended one of my home-run courses on Improving Your Communication Skills. I haven't seen him in months and he's turned up in a place I didn't expect to see him. Not only that but he pretended not to know me.'

'And you think it might be relevant to the job you're working on?'

'Probably not, but I thought it was worth checking. Curiosity at worst.'

'Hmmm. Did he tell you what he did?'

'He said he was a public servant. I have a photo from when he did the class. I'll send it straight through to you.'

'It might take a few days but I'll let you know what I unearth.'

'Thank you, Lloyd. I really appreciate your help. And I'm truly thrilled for you—about the baby.'

'As am I. Goodbye, Ms—goodbye, Tara.'

'Bye.'

I hung up and searched through my photos until I found the one I was looking for: a group shot with Wal, Harvey, Enid and me. It was a tad blurry but I'd kept it as a reminder of my first-ever paying gig in my new business. I texted it to Lloyd, then I stood for a moment and contemplated the idea of dear Lloyd and his narcissistic and promiscuous wife becoming parents. I guess the baby had half a chance at least. Better than many.

A group of teens dressed up for clubbing bumped past me and jogged me into real time. The mall was rocking out now, people everywhere, in the outdoor cafés, music blaring from Ric's. It gave me the same holiday feeling as Cottesloe Beach in summer, except here the air was full of sweet, musky city air not sea salt and pine cones; pavement and potted palms instead of sand and salt scrub.

I consulted Google Maps. It was no more than four blocks to Inigo's place, so I crossed at the Brunswick Street lights and left the mall behind. Restaurants and a gelato stand replaced the clubs and by the time I'd reached the last block before Inigo's house, the pedestrian traffic had all but dropped off. The bakery was well and truly closed for the day and the little trattoria next to it had no patrons sitting at its outdoor tables.

I stepped into a pool of darkness between a row of

new offices and a grand old converted home which had a sign advertising performing arts space. An alley ran down between them as if keeping the old building safe from the new. Two steps into the shadow, a hand fell on my shoulder.

I reacted immediately, twisting, ducking and punching. A slight ooph told me I'd hit my mark, but a second set of hands grabbed me around the waist from the other direction and a hand went over my mouth.

I scrabbled in my bag, searching for a weapon, and latched onto something slippery. With all my strength, I began whacking the guy in front of me with the barbecue duck.

He put up his hands to ward off the unexpected assault but the guy behind shoved me forward. The three of us went down in a sandwich, with me flailing the duck every which way.

'What the fu—' yelped the guy behind me. 'Get hold of her!' He had an American accent. Not a been-in-this-country-for-ten-years kind either. His was fresh-off-the-plane-my-luggage-got-lost-in-transit.

At the back of my mind, I was already wondering what an American (West Coast-sounding, from my vast knowledge of Los Angeles-based crime shows) visitor was doing assaulting me on a Brisbane street.

'Bitch has a weapon,' said the guy underneath me. He was Australian. Queenslander for sure. They had a broader accent than the rest of the country.

'Say what?' said the other.

'A fucking weapon. She's hitting me with a fucking weapon.' The guy underneath me wrapped his legs around both of us as he spoke, so I couldn't wriggle away.

The one on top's—the American—breath was sour on the side of my face and his spit wet my cheek. Oily hair draped over my face. 'Listen up. Pack your bags and go home. And take that fucking biker bastard with you.'

I opened my mouth to shout for help but he punched me in the jaw. My head exploded with pain, and with the agony came a wild surge of righteous fury.

Arsehole!

I bucked and writhed and began to fight in deadly earnest, clawing and slapping, and shoving duck where duck shouldn't be shoved. Somehow, I managed to get enough space to knee the underneath guy in the groin.

He made a gargling noise. 'Gaaaagh. You—fucking—crazy—bitch.'

'Eyes up!' hissed the American, and with that his weight lifted off me. The underneath guy rolled sideways, slamming me hard onto the pavement and I ate concrete.

With that they were gone, running down into the strip of darkness between buildings.

'Hey, are you alright?' The voice came from across the road.

I rolled onto my butt and sat up. Two girls, dressed for clubbing, stood under a streetlight, staring across at me.

'Fine.' I wasn't actually. Mad and shaken didn't even

begin to describe it.

'You want us to call the cops? We saw those guys knock you down. Did they rob you?'

I swallowed to make some spit so I could talk more. 'No, it's fine. They didn't get anything and I live in the next block.'

'You sure? You look like you're bleeding. I can call someone.' The girl held up her phone.

They weren't coming across the road to help me up and I didn't blame them. I was still clutching a skinned duck.

Blood was trickling from my mouth and my palms stung from pavement burn, but I made the effort to get to my feet. With a reassuring wave, I limped towards Inigo's house. The next time I looked back, they were walking in the other direction, talking excitedly.

Though Inigo's was only in the next block, by the time I crossed the road and had her garden fence in sight, reaction set in. I was still mad as hell, but my body was starting to shiver and jerk.

I saw Inigo standing on the veranda, silhouetted by her front light. She looked taut and alert.

'Inigo?'

She ran down the front path to the gate and hugged me. 'Thank the heavens you're alright.'

I stood unsteadily in her embrace.

She drew back. 'They hurt you. Look at your face. Come inside and I'll get antiseptic.'

I followed meekly and let her push me into a kitchen chair. She prised the duck from my fingers and laid it gently, almost reverently, on the sink. Then she found a basin and poured in hot water and some foul-smelling black liquid.

'Clean the worst of it here before you have a shower.'

As I soaked my hands in the liquid, she boiled the kettle and made me some tea with honey. I was relieved to see the plain old chamomile tea bag dangling out of it—no sign of white fungus.

'H-how did you know?' I asked. 'You couldn't see from here.'

'The disturbance you've caused across my psychic sphere is great. I sense peaks of danger. One has just passed.'

'What do you mean by disturbance?'

She flicked a dark batwing of hair from her eyes with her bony fingers and gave me a sardonic look. 'Have I not explained this to you already?'

'Kinda… You told me you smelled things. Orange blossoms and salt and rubber and petrol.'

'I'm a clairescent.'

I sipped the tea and felt the welcome rush of sweetness soaking up my shock. 'I don't know what that means.'

With a dramatic sigh, she perched on the seat opposite me. It was only a little kitchen table—three rickety chairs around its odd triangular shape.

'My clairvoyant skills are attuned to scent,' she

explained.

'You mean you're a smelling psychic?' It was impossible to keep the scepticism out of my voice.

'You're so naïve about your gift, Tara, that it hurts me here.' Another dramatic gesture as she cupped her hands over her heart. 'Clairvoyants read in different ways; some through touch, others through taste. Others simply know. They are the ones who create doubt. And, I'm sad to say, there are far too many charlatans around. True clair-cognisance is rare. My mother had the gift of clair-audience. It was impossible to lie to her. She heard everything in the way people spoke.'

I thought of Joanna and wondered if she, perhaps, had the same hidden talent. 'So you smell the future?'

'Goodness, no. You watch too much television. The things a clairvoyant sees might be meaningful to a person's future or their past. But the reading itself comes from the present.'

I nodded, trying hard to open my mind to the possibility. I mean, hell, I saw auras around people! Who was to say Inigo couldn't smell things? It seemed ridiculous but, under Inigo's earnest scrutiny, I had to give her the benefit of the doubt, if only because it was rude not to.

'What do those scents you talked about mean, though?' I asked. 'I don't think that I've even smelled orange blossom before.'

'The orange blossom is a sign of something or someone who is affecting your life. So is the rubber.'

I felt inside my handbag and got out my phone. Then I put the words orange blossom, salt, petrol and rubber into Google. All it came up with was some tyre sales and perfume sites. I tried again with the question 'What smells like...' and got the same answers.

I sipped some more tea and tried again. Wikipedia told me that orange blossoms were grown all over the world and that there was even an orange blossom festival right here in Australia.

I added salt to the search but it didn't narrow it down at all. In frustration, I threw the phone down on the table and slumped in the chair. Inigo didn't say a word but kept drinking her tea.

We sat in an uncomfortable silence until I had a thought. I picked up my phone again and rang Bok.

He sounded tired but pleased to hear from me. 'T? Where the hell are you? Smitts said something about Brisbane.'

Had I forgotten to tell my other best friend I was going out of town? My bad!

'I'm on a job. It came up quickly and I've been flat out ever since I got here.'

'Is that some kind of weak apology, Tara Sharp?'

'I guess so.' My jaw was starting to throb from the punch I took.

'You realise you've left me here with a hysterical Smitts.'

'It's under control, Bok. I've got Mr Hara and Cass

looking into it.'

'Cass? You've got Cass lurking around Claremont in torn black stockings and purple lipstick? She'll get arrested!'

'She'll be fine,' I soothed. 'Listen, I have a question for you. What's the first thing that comes to mind when you think of orange blossoms, salt, petrol and rubber?'

'I don't know about petrol and rubber,' he said. 'But orange blossoms and salt mean California for me. Maybe that's because I've been to the Orange Blossom Festival in Riverside.'

A little shiver ran through me. One of the thugs had been from the West Coast—I was sure of that.

'Why?' asked Bok.

'Just the case I'm working on…'

'Which you can't tell me about,' he finished.

'Not much to tell at this stage.'

He sighed. 'Well, get your arse home soon. One of your best friends needs you. Has Hoshi come up with anything?'

Bok knew Hoshi and Mrs Hara nearly as well as I did. In fact, he knew Mrs Hara better—she'd adopted him as her pet and regularly fed him delicious meals. I was lucky to be offered a glass of water.

'Nothing confirmed,' I hedged.

'T?'

'I can't talk now,' I said, glancing at Inigo. She hadn't wavered in her stare.

'Then call me when you can.' Bok hung up still huffy with me.

I placed my phone gently on the kitchen table. 'One of the men who threatened me earlier had an American accent. West Coast, I'm pretty sure. My friend says orange blossoms and salt remind him of California.'

'The scents do not lie,' Inigo said quietly.

It seemed such a ridiculous statement—'The scents do not lie'—but I was too rattled to challenge her. I felt a deep strumming inside me that I was beginning to recognise as connections being made. Where they were leading, though, I had no idea. I had two potential suspects and an improbable link to California.

Right now, though, I needed a shower and some sleep. Now that the shock was wearing off, fatigue was after its spot. I hated jittery tiredness.

Inigo got up and went to the fridge. She returned with an ice pack and some soapy-looking cheese and dry biscuits which she took from a pottery container on the bench. While I rested the ice pack against my jaw, she made a second trip to the pantry then placed the cheese, rice crackers, a jar of jalapeños and another of sweet gherkins in front of me. 'You should eat before you sleep.'

I didn't argue. Soapy cheese and chillies had never tasted so good. 'Thank you,' I said between mouthfuls. 'Please let me know what I owe you for food.'

She nodded distractedly. 'Later.'

While I ate, she sat down opposite me again, closed

her eyes and rocked. It was strange but soothing and by the time I'd finished eating I could feel myself relaxing a little. My knees and palms were still stinging, though, and I wanted to take some painkillers and sleep.

'Inigo?'

'Goodnight, Tara,' she said without opening her eyes.

'Oh… Goodnight.' I got up and stumbled across the passage to my bed.

Chapter 14

I slept like the dead. In fact, waking up was so hard that when I finally peeled my eyes open and got vertical, I contemplated the possibility Inigo had slipped something in the tea.

Then I remembered everything that had happened yesterday and my heart pounded me into wide awake. I tried taking some slow, steadying breaths and lay back down to try to sort through what I knew and what it might mean.

Andreas and Sofia were very sensitive about Stuart but that could mean just about anything. Joel and Jade had more than a professional hook-up, so I assumed Joel had invited me to that party knowing I was working for Stuart—which suggested that his answers to my casual questions were staged. He was definitely trying to make out that he was cool with Stuart, so chances were, he wasn't. I wondered which of the two men had sent the two thugs after me. Or was there a third party in the mix?

After chewing it all over for a bit, I decided to wait and see what the day brought. If I was lucky, Tozzi might get back to me on the picture I'd sent him.

On my to-do list was meeting Stuart at his office and then some more snooping and a security check before the video shoot tonight. I'd be seeing Ed there and the thought perked me up a bit. Maybe we really would get to spend the evening together afterwards. My jaw was sore where the guy had punched me but not as swollen as I expected. I ran my fingers along it and winced. As long as I didn't open my mouth too wide, I was okay.

First off, though, I had to leave my room and face Inigo and the unsettling fact that she could read my life through her sense of smell.

I picked my phone up from the bedside table and surfed until I found a Wikipedia entry on clairvoyance. Sure enough, one of the subheadings was for *clairescence*. The description was pretty much the same as the one Inigo had given me. I wondered if Hoshi knew anything about it and decided to ring him in an hour or so. It was still early in Perth.

While I was staring at my display, the phone beeped and a text popped up. The number was unknown. I opened it.

Wotch yr and Coops backs 4 JV. WG.

I sat up quickly. It was from Wal.

Where r u? R u OK? I texted back immediately.

After ten minutes of staring at the screen willing it to

beep again, I sat up and got dressed. Wal either wasn't going to or couldn't reply.

The sun shining in through my window was no longer so cheery, and my date with Ed later tonight seemed tainted.

JV had to mean Johnny Viaspa.

I felt shivery, like I was coming down with a cold. Not so long ago Viaspa had hired a hit man to get rid of me. I'd survived thanks to good luck and good friends. But here in Brisbane, I didn't have the luxury of knowing my way around, or knowing anyone who'd help me. Wal's warning suggested that maybe Viaspa had sent the thugs after me. But why would the thugs warn off Bon Ames too? Had Viaspa had seen us together at the airport.

Suddenly, I was scared. REALLY scared. But for me, scared always kept company with stubborn. I wouldn't run home, because that's what they wanted me to do. No, I was going to finish this job.

A quick glance at the time told me I had fifteen minutes to get to Stuart's office, which according to the Google map was two streets down from the Valley mall. Looked like breakfast would be from the bakery on the way. Anything to avoid Inigo's 35-different-kinds-of-wheat-free bread and extract-of-hummingbird juice. Not that I had much of an appetite right now. When Johnny Viaspa got in my face, it was like having a metal rake across my nerves.

I pulled on jeans and a ruffled singlet top, dabbed

foundation over the bruise on my jaw and put a slash of mascara on my lashes. That would have to do; I was in no mood for clothes angst.

I called a soft goodbye to Inigo, whose bedroom door was still closed, and scooted out onto the street.

It really was a beautiful day, a little windy with air like warm sticky fingers, sky a blinding blue, traffic bright and noisy. Brisbane managed to be sultry and shiny at once. It was no mean feat. But my attention was drawn away from its beauty to the early morning shadows that might be hiding someone.

I forced myself to stop at the bakery and buy an orange juice and a custard tart and walk at a normal pace down Brunswick Street. When I reached the mall, I turned right and headed past a bunch of boutiques that were still closed, and a café that had been open a while by the look of the weary counter guy.

A sharp right turn brought me into Winne Street, a tiny little affair with some narrow old brick peak-roofed houses as well as a deserted Victorian building that must have once been a church.

The first house I passed had a sign that said Q-Music alongside posters for the Valley Fiesta. Its equally rundown next-door twin's sign was in an upstairs window and read Reverb Promotions. Relieved that I could finally get off the street, I hopped through the door and almost ran up the steps.

Music was blaring from the upstairs office and I had to

knock three times before Stuart opened the door.

'Hi,' he bellowed. 'You're early.'

He hit the mute button on the stereo and waved me across to one of the couches in the tiny sitting room.

'Coffee?'

I shook my head and showed him my OJ.

He nodded, disappeared downstairs for a bit and returned with a large paper cup. After plopping down opposite me he had a couple of sips. He looked tired and his skin had a sallow tinge.

'Nice place,' I said.

'Yeah. My uncle left it to me. I live downstairs but spend most of my time up here in the office where the view is better.'

I glanced out the window. There wasn't much of a view, just the narrow house fronts and glimpses of the empty Victorian-style church next door. The windows let in a lot of light, though, and the street had a last-century feel about it; old and decayed but refusing to die.

'Infinitely better than living in your parents' garage,' I noted.

'Yeah, I get asked to sell it every other day but there's not a snowflake's chance I'll do that.'

'Sentimental reasons?' I asked.

'Pretty much. Been in the family forever. Closest thing I have to a family history. My grandparents used to go to church next door before they closed it.'

'I didn't think they closed churches.'

'Something about the bell tower being unsafe. I never believed that story though.'

'Fair enough. How did it go last night?'

'Fran Dickle's lot camped outside the hotel for the night but they were pretty quiet.'

'Slim?'

'Watched college basketball on TV, took his Xanax and went to bed.'

'Sounds like he was a little lamb.'

Stuart pulled a face. 'Yeah. After dinner.'

'Why? What happened?'

'Bon didn't fit the dress code so they wouldn't let him in the restaurant. I offered to lend him some clothes but he refused to change. It's not like I was gonna argue with him.'

I could so picture it: Juanita flapping, Stuart stressing and Bon standing there with his arms crossed being scarily obstinate. 'What happened?'

'They let him into the restaurant bar, so he watched us from there. Trouble is, Slim wanted to go to the men's room halfway through dinner.'

'You went with him, right?'

Stuart looked a bit sheepish. 'I was outside trying to persuade some reporters to leave us alone. Juanita told him to wait until I got back but he said he had to go.' He rolled his eyes.

I nodded. That sounded like Slim.

'Anyway, a fan followed him in there and tried to take

a picture of him on his mobile phone … you know…'

'What … peeing?'

'Yeah. Good internet stuff.'

'People are weird.'

'Work in this industry a few years if you want to see weird. Some fans know no limits. Anyway, when he tried to kick the phone from the guy's hand, the guy grabbed his arm. Slim started screaming bloody murder. I heard him from outside. Bon did too. He came thundering through the restaurant like a bloody bull, knocked over a waiter and the dessert cart.'

'He saved the day?'

'Uh-uh. Juanita beat us both in there.'

'Juanita went into the gents?' She really was a girl after my own heart.

He nodded. 'Straight in. Pushed the guy off Slim and told him to zip up and leave.'

'What happened to the phone?'

'Dropped in the urinal. Bon made the guy pick it out and delete the photo in front of him before he let him clean it off. By then half the management was in the john with us. They made lots of apologies—said the fan guy was "new staff" and that he wouldn't be returning.'

'Blah, blah,' I said.

'Yeah. We left then but the journos outside were sniffing around waiting until the place closed so they could get to talk to the rest of the staff. Haven't been game to look at the paper this morning.'

Wow! All the fun I'd missed while I was being roughed up on the pavement.

Stuart took another few sips of his coffee and stared at the rug on the floor between us. 'Jeez, Tara, I'm not sure how much more of this I can take.'

'I feel your pain,' I said, and touched my jaw.

'Is that a bruise?' he asked.

'Fell over in the shower,' I said.

He narrowed his eyes at me, but I kept my expression serene. He didn't need more stress.

'So how did you go yesterday?' he asked eventually.

'I'm following a lead on Andreas. He didn't say anything that suggests he's running some type of vendetta against you but you're still a hot spot for him.'

He raised an eyebrow.

'When we talked about you his body language got all messed up. I also paid Sofia a visit.'

'No!' He started up off the couch.

'It's cool,' I said, waving him down. 'But she got pretty wound up when I told her I was thinking of going into business with you.'

'Why did you say that? What do you mean, "wound up"?'

'I was just casting a hook. See if she was nervous about your business in any way.'

'Sofia wouldn't do anything to hurt me.'

'Fine. But she might have heard something. Or have her suspicions. See, this is how I work—I read people's body language, see what jacks them up. That tells me where I need to investigate. Right now, Sofia is really nervous about your job.'

He frowned. I didn't blame him. It sounded kinda flaky.

'What about Aprile?' he asked.

Here was the tough bit. 'Yeah, well, at first I thought it was all sweet. He invited me to a party. Even with some liquor in him he was nothing but cool about you. Just before I left, he received a text that I managed to get a look at. It was a date to meet someone called J at a club.'

Stuart waited for me to finish.

'So yesterday I went by Vixens on the way to Sofia's. He was there again.'

'So?'

'I saw him in the doorway with Jade. Stuart, I'm sorry but they … they're together.'

He blinked a few times while it sank in. 'She works there. He probably pays her to—'

'This was out of hours. The club was locked but she came up to let him in. They stopped in the doorway and … believe me, it's more than professional.'

'Together?' He seemed confused, not able to compute.

'So, I think Jade told him who I was and he was ready for me. Everything he said about you, everything he said in general, was probably a lie. He was hiding stuff. How much have you told Jade about the tour schedule?'

Stuart hunched forward, hugging his knees and rocking

slightly. 'I don't talk about work much but…'

'But?'

'She's been here. I guess it's possible she snooped around.'

'Does she know your computer password?'

'It's the same as the one on my phone and she knows that.'

I sighed. 'The fact that they've gone to that much trouble to deceive me means he could be the one behind your problems, but I don't want to discount Andreas until I've investigated a little further.'

'Aprile,' said Stuart in a menacing voice. 'Aprile, you bastard!' He began to rock harder and his aura was pulsing like an artery bleeding out. Time for damage control.

'Don't get ahead of things. It might not be him. But listen to me, Stuart,' I said urgently. 'There's something else.'

The serious tone of my voice got his attention. 'What?'

'Wal is missing.'

'Grominsky?' He gave a short, harsh laugh. 'He can look after himself.'

'Maybe,' I said. 'But I got a random text from him this morning from an unknown number, warning you and me to watch our backs for Johnny Viaspa.'

That got him alert and focused. 'Johnny Viaspa? What for?'

'That's where you come in. You know Grom's past better than I do. What's he been involved in that could have blown up in his face? And how would that involve the two of us? How do you know Viaspa?'

He rubbed his eyes. 'I'm going to get another coffee first. You want something?'

'Tea, white, one sugar,' I said. 'And a sausage roll and sauce, please.'

'Café's around the corner. Won't be long. Let the phone go to voicemail if it rings.' He got up and left.

I tried to sit still, I really did, but my agitation drew me to the window to make sure I hadn't been followed.

Stuart walked dejectedly down the road and turned the corner while I watched. There was no one else on the street, just the normal flow of vehicle traffic and an empty KFC box cartwheeling in the wind. I wondered what this area had been like a hundred years ago. This close to the river it was probably mud and scrub. Strange to think it was now defined by old bricks and used takeaway cartons. Stuart had said his place was the closest thing he had to a family history. Perhaps that was more significant than he realised.

Before I knew what I was doing, I was in Stuart's office, riffling through his desk drawer, looking for something, anything, that might be useful. My search yielded nothing more than some dried out mandarin skins, a bunch of flyers for Slim Sledge's tour and assorted paperclips and staples. His computer was in front of me but without his password I couldn't get in.

The phone started ringing and I let it go as instructed.

It cut out just as the downstairs door banged open and shut. I tiptoed back to the couch and dropped back in the same spot as before.

Stuart entered and passed me a white paper bag with a sausage roll in it and a white styro cup filled with brown liquid that had a greasy film across the top. I ripped the bag open, squeezed tomato sauce on the roll and bit into it. The pastry was flaky and the mince soft, and for a moment I forgot everything except my carbo-gasm.

Then Stuart started talking. 'There're a couple of things that I always thought would come back to bite him. One time we were touring a big Irish folk band.'

I stopped chewing and swallowed. 'Folk? Wal?'

'Yeah, we didn't always do rock. I mean, in Western Australia you gotta take whatever work comes along. A lot of big acts never make it over there.'

'Don't I know it,' I said ruefully, thinking how I'd still never seen U2.

'Anyway, he slept with one of the singers. Can't remember her name now but her husband was in the band as well. The husband found out the day they were leaving to go to South Africa. Always swore he'd pay someone to kill Grom.'

'I never figured Wal as a ladies' man,' I said.

Stuart blinked and almost smiled. 'You'd be surprised. The man's confident.'

Maybe that's what my Aunt Liv had fallen for? 'Ireland is a long way away. Do you think he meant it? And even if he had, then something would've happened before now.'

'I s'pose so. But if he has put out a contract on Wal then Viaspa would know about it. I mean… it's Perth.'

What Stuart meant was Viaspa was the whole deal on the west coast. You didn't run a hit without his knowing about it.

'There was one other thing…' He stopped and I could see the indecision on his face.

'Stuart, this is important—not just for Wal but for you and me as well.'

'This can't ever go past this room, Tara. Understand?'

I nodded.

'A year and a half ago, Wal and I drove a truck from Perth to Adelaide. It was a dump and run job. We'd been touring a Sydney band around W.A. and they wanted their gear taken on to South Oz. We just had to drive it over and hand it to the roadies working the gigs over there. We caught the bus back.'

'And?'

'Turned out this particular band's tour was being paid for by a guy they call Ash Machete.'

I snorted a bit of my tea. 'Ash Machete? You actually know someone called that?'

Instead of smiling, his face darkened. 'Ash Machete is the guy who set Viaspa up in Perth.'

'Viaspa has a mentor?'

'He's a Sydney "businessman". A powerful one, if you move in those circles.'

I hadn't heard of the guy, but that didn't mean much. I was a west coast private school girl. I grew up going to the beach and to boozy Claremont parties. The Sydney underbelly was a universe away. 'So what does that mean about the truck that you and Wal were driving?'

'Ash Machete isn't one to sponsor local bands for the love of music. He and Viaspa were shifting…' He stopped again and turned the music back on, soft enough so we could hear each other but loud enough that it filled all the background space. 'We drove a shitload of heroin across the border without knowing. Thirty-five kilos plus some methamphetamine.'

I felt my eyes open wider.

'We made it there safely. No dramas.'

'And?'

'Trouble is, when we arrived the drugs had gone.'

'What?'

'Wal and I spent a week locked in the dealer's garage while Machete's guys worked us over. They figured we found the stash and offloaded it.'

'Jeez.'

'It didn't matter what they did to us, we had nothing to tell. Have to say, though, I thought about making something up, just to get them to stop. Wal convinced me to stay with the truth. He was right in the end. It's the only reason we're still alive. But I always wondered if it might come back on us one day.' His shoulders sagged and his aura had disintegrated into a grey cobweb. 'After that I decided to move here and try promoting.'

'And Wal got fixated on weapons.'

'He'd always been handy with that kind of thing, though it was more like knives and stuff. The guns came afterwards. The kind of experience we had makes you re-evaluate your life. It made me want to follow my dream. It made Wal paranoid. His narcolepsy started soon afterwards.' He paused for a moment. 'So what do you think?'

'Well,' I said slowly, 'the drug thing's a more likely option than the jealous Irish husband. But why chase you down again now? And it doesn't mean it has anything to do with the tour, except…'

'Except what?'

I hesitated. I hadn't planned to mention last night but in the light of what he'd just told me he had a right to know, in case he was next in line. 'Two guys roughed me up a bit last night.' I rolled up my jeans to reveal my skinned knees. 'My jaw as well. And my back. They got me on the way home to Inigo's. Warned me off the tour— told me to go home and take Bon with me. One of them was American.'

'American?' Stuart's face drained to the same colour grey as his web-like aura. 'Why didn't you call me? Are you alright?'

'I'm fine. Inigo gave me some witchy brew for my scratches. Like I said, it was a scare tactic.'

'You think Viaspa sent them?'

'Maybe. Maybe not.'

He put his coffee down on the table and buried his head in his arms. 'I don't get it. Why is this happening when I'm touring my first big act?'

'Could just be bad timing, things from your past colliding with your current life,' I said. 'As I see it, you've got three options. Go to the cops with no evidence about the saboteur and have them tell you to stop wasting their time. Let whoever's messing with your life win. Or try and take control.'

He raised his head. 'People like you and me can't beat people like Viaspa and Ash Machete.'

'Yes, we can,' I said with a confidence I didn't feel.

I did something then that surprised me. I told Stuart about some of my history with Johnny Viaspa. How he'd tried to have me killed and how I avoided it. I stopped short of mentioning Nick Tozzi and the reason it had all begun. Stuart's mouth dropped open as I talked.

'You're crazy.' He got up and paced around the couch and back.

I sipped the last of my tea and contemplated that pearl of wisdom. It wasn't a new concept to me.

'The gig's tomorrow,' he said.

'Yeah. I say you focus on keeping Slim Sledge right for tomorrow night. Viaspa hasn't been a direct threat yet. It's only Wal's warning that's got us worried.'

'True. I mean Viaspa is all the way over in Perth.'

'Uh, actually, he's not.' I told Stuart about Viaspa seeing the placard at the airport.

'I didn't see him. Why didn't you say something?'

'He was the reason I asked you to meet me in the other terminal. Besides, I had no idea you even knew him,' I said.

We took up carpet staring for a bit.

Then Stuart pushed his shirtsleeves up. It was an unconscious gesture and I knew what it meant before he spoke. 'Okay. Well, you do your thing and I'll do mine. And like Wal says, watch your back.'

'Same to you. Just one thing I need to know: did you steal Viaspa's drugs?' I watched hard for a reaction to my surprise question.

His aura stayed steady. 'No! I already told you that!'

I nodded. 'Just had to be sure.'

'You believe me?'

'Yes.'

'I'm glad. By the way, I've had an enquiry about booking Slim in Perth next week. Sydney's cancelled, so the time is open. There's a big gig at a winery and one of their headline acts had a fall and broke his foot. They've asked Slim to slot in. Will you go back there with us? On the payroll, I mean.'

'Uuh?'

He flushed. 'The way things are going, it'd be good to have you on the ground in Perth.'

'Sure. I guess so. When do you leave Brisbane?'

'If the booking confirms and Slim agrees, we'll go over a few days after this gig. But you could go before us and do some groundwork.'

I brightened up. 'Like find Wal?' And sort out Smitty.
'Yeah.'

'Same terms?'

Nod.

'Fine, book me a flight for the day after tomorrow
then,' I said. 'That'll give me time to get down and scout
the winery.'

The idea of going home sooner than I'd expected
boosted my spirits. My phone vibrated and I saw the
message was from Tozzi. 'Let me check this, it could be
important.'

Stuart got up and walked into his office and checked his
landline for messages while I listened to Nick's voicemail.

'Tara, go to the café next to the Pig and Whistle bar on
Eagle Street Pier in the city at eleven this morning. A guy
will find you there. I sent him a photo of you. He might
be able to help with your enquiry. But this is a once-off. I
had to pull a big favour. Understand? Yeah, and one other
thing … can you please come home soon?'

The last sentence was so unexpected, and said in such
a thick, emotional voice, that I nearly dropped my phone.
My heart banged against my ribs. What the heck did that
mean?

'Tara?' Stuart was standing in front of me wearing
an expression that I guessed almost mirrored my own:
bewilderment mixed with excitement. His aura had lost
almost all its grey web and was expanding as I watched.

'What?' I asked.

'That message was from Sofia. She said she had something to talk to me about.'

'Really? Maybe I rattled her conscience with my visit?'

'I'm going downtown now to see her and then to the hotel to take over from Juanita.'

'Fine. Let me know what she says—if it's … ah … useful.'

'What about you?'

'Going to check out something from yesterday. Should be through in an hour. Do you have Jade's home address?'

He nodded, took a notebook out of his pocket and scribbled something on a page. 'What're you going to do?'

'Just have a bit of a look around. If she contacts you, act normal—but don't let her anywhere near your computer.'

He blinked but he didn't say anything. Instead he ducked into his office and returned with two ID badges. He handed me the notepaper, which had two addresses on it. 'The first address is Jade's. The second is for the film shoot this afternoon. Can you and Bon Ames do a security check before we get there?'

'Sure.'

'We're bringing Slim over about four. You'll need these to get in.' He gave me the badges with Reverb Promotions and his logo on them.

'Cool.' I took them and gave him a quick salute. 'Can you let Bon know?'

'Sure. Nil bastardo carborundum,' he said solemnly.

Don't let the bastards get you down. 'Back atcha.'

Chapter 15

I decided to walk to my city rendezvous. The light wind was still cool enough to be pleasant and I had a stomach full of nerves that needed exercising. There was also something about the traffic and the people on the street that made me feel safer now it was proper business hours. Surely even Johnny Viaspa wouldn't risk a drive-by shooting or abduct me in broad daylight.

I tried to enjoy the sights—palms dotted on balconies of high-rise buildings and glimpses of the river—but every car with tinted windows flipped my stomach. By the time I'd walked the length of Ann Street and down towards Eagle Street Pier, I was panting from the quick pace I'd set.

My phone rang just as the Pig and Whistle came into sight.

'Tara—here,' I managed.

'I'm going to call the police.'

Only one person I knew would be that dramatic. 'Liv?'

'I can't wait a moment longer,' my aunt said with true

theatrical flair.

'There's no need. I've just heard from him.'

'You what?'

'I had a text from him this morning about … business. He didn't say much but he's clearly alright.'

'Where is he?'

'He didn't say, Liv. But he's lying low. You just need to be patient. Give him some time and space to sort out whatever it is.' *Give me time and space too!*

'How do you know he didn't send the message under duress?'

'I don't,' I admitted. 'But honestly, I think he's fine.'

'I'm sorry, Tara. That's not good enough for me.'

Damn! What now? 'Liv, have you considered that he might be cleaning up something from his past? Wal's not exactly a saint, you know. If the police start sniffing around looking for him, it might land him in serious trouble.'

I could hear her breathing into the phone while she thought that angle over. 'You know something, don't you?'

'No. But I know Wal. He's got more skeletons than Karrakatta Cemetery.'

'So you don't think he's off having an affair or something?' She tossed the comment out light-heartedly but I picked up the slightly hysterical undertone.

Jeez, not Liv too! 'Hell, no!'

She sighed heavily. 'Very well, I'll wait a little longer— but I'm telling you, Tara, I will not wait forever.'

'I'll be home in two days. We'll get together as soon as I'm back.'

'I'll expect you,' she said in a very Joanna-like tone. Who knew my aunt could channel my mother when she wanted to?

'Bye, Liv.' I slipped my phone into my bag, turned off the street past the tavern and walked into a café called The Feels.

The Feels took up nearly the entire ground level of a huge office block. The decor was all glass, chrome and white fixtures, and the waiters wore white tux jackets over dress shorts and white sandshoes. The effect was kooky but cute.

I chose a seat back from the front windows, next to a pot of fake lilies, and waited. My inclination was to fidget with my phone but I made myself pay attention to the street outside and those entering the café.

My guy came in a few minutes later. I picked him straight away from the nonchalance in his step and the turmoil in his aura. He scanned the café and saw me almost immediately. All I got was a brief head shake, as though he didn't want a direct acknowledgement. He went to the counter and ordered a drink.

I left my seat and did the same. By the time I was served he was seated next to my table so that our chairs were almost touching back to back. He briefly looked up from his newspaper as I settled at my table with a small bottle of orange juice. We sat in silence for a while and I began to think I had picked the wrong guy.

'I'm going to put the paper down in a minute,' he whispered. 'Ask me if I've finished with it. We can talk casually after that.' He dropped it on his table and proceeded to stretch.

'Are you finished with your newspaper?' I asked loudly.

He turned as if surprised that I was even there and handed it over. 'Sure. Not much in there today.' In a low voice he added, 'I slipped it inside.'

I opened up the newspaper and held it at an angle that only he and I could see. With the paper in front of my face, I was hidden from most of the café.

He sank back in his chair so that our heads were almost touching. 'Tara, right?'

'Yeah. Look, thanks. Do you want to go somewhere else to do this?'

'No. A public place is best.'

'It is?'

I heard him take a sip of his coffee but I didn't turn my head.

'Let's make it quick,' he said.

'Do you know what the photo is about?'

'It's a proposed development in Fortitude Valley. I've written the address on the back of the photo. Please destroy it when you've read it.'

'Umm, sure… But why?'

'It's a heritage-listed area. If there's a green light in the works for this project then someone must have paid off the environment minister, and I don't want to know about it.' I could almost feel him shudder.

'Does that mean it's been approved?' I asked.

'That's not my area. Listen, I gotta go. I don't want to know where you got it and I don't want to ever see you again. This is a favour for Nick, not you.'

He got up and left the café before I could fold the newspaper and put it in my bag. As soon as I had, though, I headed straight to the loo and locked myself in a cubicle. A quick leaf through and I found a printed copy of the photo stuck onto a page with sticky tape. I peeled it off and looked at the back.

Winne St, Fortitude Valley.

I got a stomach cramp. The development was on Stuart's street. No wonder Andreas got a bit agitated when I mentioned his name. Did Sofia know that her uncle was in on an office development that would see her ex-fiancé lose his house and place of business? And was that a reason for Andreas to sabotage the Slim Sledge tour? Perhaps he was hoping that the failure of Slim's tour would bankrupt Stuart and he'd be happy to take whatever price he was offered for his home? I needed to find out more about the rules of heritage listing. Sitting on the loo, I used my phone to search for the right government department. From what I could tell, it seemed to be situated in a building on George Street which was only a few blocks away.

Okay, I told myself. Go there, get more information and see what pieces fall into place.

I shot Tozzi off a quick text before I left the cubicle. Thanks. Yr guy was a big help. I'll b home Sunday.

A quick loo-flush for appearance's sake and I was out the door.

George Street was on the west side of the CBD. I chose the route that took me past the Stamford and the Botanic Gardens. Fran Dickle and her fan crew were still camped outside the hotel and a couple of police officers were standing talking to them.

I crossed the street to avoid getting caught in conversation and power-walked down towards the Riverside Expressway. The gardens, on my left, were filled with Moreton Bay fig trees and garden beds of orchids. I wished I had time to wander through and have a proper look but sightseeing was off the table right now. I could still enjoy the wafts of frangipani and the dappled light on the grass as I passed though. Brisbane CBD was actually a pretty cool place.

The gardens ended in a conglomeration of buildings that made up the Queensland University of Technology. I took a right into George Street and headed in the direction of the casino and the government executive offices. Heritage was on the tenth floor of one of them and I had to sign in and have my bag searched. As I went through the protocol and stepped into the lift, I had a feeling I was being watched. A few quick glances revealed nothing other than the usual suits and delivery guys you'd expect in government offices. Still, I was relieved when the doors shut and I was alone in the lift.

When they reopened, I walked straight into a foyer that contained several chairs occupied by bored looking punters and a man sitting in a little booth peering at me over the top of a desktop computer.

'Identification, please,' he said in a nasal voice.

I handed over my driver's licence and waited while he ran his checks. Either the bandwidth was crap or he was making me wait for the sheer hell of it. By the pinched expression on his face and his equally narrow, hard aura, I was going with the latter.

'Take a number and a seat,' he said eventually.

I snatched my ticket and grabbed a bunch of pamphlets from the plastic holder on the table next to the water cooler before I retreated to an empty corner chair. I don't wait well, so I got busy skimming through pamphlets.

My phone beeped and the man in the booth frowned. I quickly switched my setting to silent and read the message. Good. It was from Tozzi.

Still three people to go before me. I got up and approached the man in the booth.

He gave me a suspicious stare. 'Yes?'

'Do you have a piece of paper I could have? I need to write some notes.'

Begrudgingly he dipped into the drawer below his computer and pulled out a blank sheet of A4.

'Thanks.'

I took it back to my seat and got out a pen. Slanting the paper so no one could see, I began to make a list of everyone I'd come into contact with over this job, and anything relevant to the Slim Sledge tour.

Andreas G.—planning a development on Stuart's heritage-listed street. Prevented Stuart and Sofia's engagement.

Joel Aprile—bitter about Stuart leaving and setting up his own business. Having an affair with Strawberry Jade, Stuart's current date. Is she the leak?

Johnny Viaspa—in Brisbane. Why? Who met him at the airport?

Slim Sledge—neurotic recovering addict. OCD. Broke.

Bon Ames—scary biker.

Juanita Venture—talented media and people wrangler.

Little Paolo—club owner, lolly lover. Took instant dislike to Bon.

Harvey T.—why did he pretend he didn't know me?

I tried to see connections between the people on my list but it wasn't giving up its secrets yet. No amount of staring at the paper helped, yet I must have been lost in thought for a while because suddenly I heard my number being called in an impatient voice, as if it had been called a couple of times already.

I stuffed my piece of paper into my bag and hurried over to the woman standing in the open office doorway. She was everything a heritage officer should be: bespectacled, cardigan-wearing, thin. But to contradict that look, she had a flaming dyed-red fringe set against a crop of light brown hair.

'Come in,' she said in a weary but refined tone.

I plopped in a chair while she closed the door and resumed her place at an orderly desk.

'How can I help you, Miss Sharp?'

'It's about my dad's place,' I said glibly. 'He died just recently and left it to me.' I paused as if letting a wave of sadness well and ebb.

She nodded sympathetically. 'Take your time, dear.'

'I just want to know where I stand. My friends say I can't do anything to my house or even sell it because there's a heritage-listed house next door. Is that true?'

'I can assure you that you are perfectly entitled to sell your property.'

I feigned relief. 'Oh, that's good news. And can I knock it down and build a new place?'

She frowned. 'Redevelopment is another issue. Permission must be given to redevelop land adjoining a heritage-listed property in case it affects the preservation and aesthetics of the building.'

I wrinkled my nose. 'Aesthetics? What do you mean?'

She gave me a rather superior smile. 'How it looks. It wouldn't do to put up something … unsuitable next to a gracious old building, would it?' She peered at me in such a way that I wondered if she was thinking of herself as the gracious old building and me as the trashy nouveau apartment.

I set my expression to dumb and stared back at her. 'Who gives permission then?'

'The Heritage Council appraises every application and makes recommendations to the environment minister.'

'Oh. Can I talk to him about my dad's—my house, then?'

'No, my dear, you cannot. Should you wish to develop your property you can go through the application process like everyone else and you will be advised of the decision in due course.'

I got some gum out of my bag and made a show of unwrapping and chewing it. 'Wow,' I said eventually. 'So, like, some government man somewhere can say no to me renovating.'

She gave me a quizzical look. 'I suppose you could put it like that. The thing is, Miss Sharp, our job is very important. We never make an ill-considered decision.'

Unless someone pays you off, I thought sourly. Or your minister. 'Okay,' I said, intentionally chewing with my mouth slightly open. 'Got it. Well, thanks a lot then.'

She saw me out the door with a palpable sigh of relief. I waved breezily at the man in the booth as I headed for the lift.

Sandwiched among the other lift-goers heading for the lobby, I thought about what I'd learned. It looked like developing Stuart's property into apartments would firstly require getting Stuart to sell, and then the developers would need to bribe the minister to green light it. But how would they get him to sell?

As soon as I got out of the lift, I ran through the revolving door and along the street until I found a laneway. Ducking down it, I pulled out my phone and rang Stuart.

'Hi,' he answered.

'Pardon the personal question, but is your house insured?'

He hesitated for a moment. 'No. I can't afford the premium at the moment.'

My breath caught in my throat. 'Look, it's only a hunch but I think someone might be going to set fire to Winne Street.'

'What? Slow down.'

I could hear Juanita in the background asking him who was on the phone.

'Look, I'll explain in person. But can you ask Inigo to scope the street out for any disturbances?'

'What's a "disturbance"?'

'She'll know what it means.'

There was a pause. 'Tara?'

'Just trust me,' I said.

'I'm not liking where this is going,' he said.

I glanced up and down the street to check for a possible tail. 'Me neither.'

Chapter 16

There was only a day to go before Slim's Brisbane performance and every time I learned something that might be helpful, the jigsaw I was trying to assemble got messier. It was like all I had were the blue-sky pieces and none of the image.

One thing I knew for sure, though: if tomorrow night's gig at Little Paolo's went down in flames then Stuart might as well put Slim Sledge on the next plane home. Not even a successful gig in Perth next week could help him recoup his money.

Asking Inigo to scope out Winne Street was a bit of a shot in the dark but if she was as psychic as she claimed to be, it might be the only advance warning we would get that trouble was brewing. But I still had to find out what was going on with Joel Aprile and Jade before I pointed the finger squarely at Andreas Giannoukakis.

On impulse, I went for another walk past Vixens. It was mid-afternoon now, around the same time I'd been here yesterday. This time, I walked along the other side of the road and went into the shop next to the Chinese food store. One barbecue duck experience was more than enough.

It turned out to be a phone and accessories shop and the guy pounced on me in seconds. I only half paid attention while he prattled on about connectivity and good looks (the phones'—not mine). There was no action over the road and after a few minutes I decided to cut my losses and walk to Jade's apartment.

'Yeah, look, I'll think about it, mate,' I said, cutting through his flow of talk.

He handed me his card and I escaped before he could sign me up for twenty-five years' hard labour on a Siberian railroad or an expensive phone deal that would make me wish I had.

Outside, I planned a route using Google Maps. The Hoods' video shoot was in a house in Spring Hill at the top of the CBD; a twenty-minute walk or five minutes by taxi. Jade's flat was along the same route, which meant I wouldn't have to go too far out of my way. Also, if I walked I might be able to pick up if I had a tail.

I headed off, dawdling then suddenly speeding up, ducking at random into clothes shops and crossing roads. By the time I got close to the Central train station, I had spotted my tail: a short, stocky, dark-haired guy who periodically spoke into his phone. Who was he updating about my movements?

Just before the Central Station traffic lights I spied a little arcade. I waited for a break in the traffic then bolted across the street. The second door along opened into a tiny boutique bookstore called Fine Fiction. There was no one in the shop other than a young guy behind the counter. On impulse, I ran past him and ducked down behind the counter.

'Whoa!' he called. 'What do you think you're doing?'

I smiled appealingly. 'I'm a private investigator and I'm trying to lose a guy who's following me.'

Seemingly immune to my charms, he reached for the phone.

'Please,' I whispered. 'He'll be along in a moment—short, thickset, dark, wearing a tight black shirt and talking on his phone. I just need him to pass by and I'll leave.'

He looked sceptical. 'You sure you're not just crazy?'

'Oh, I'm definitely crazy,' I replied. 'But I'm also telling the truth.'

'Why is he following you?'

'Not sure. Could be one of many reasons.'

His fingers tightened. 'Tell me one of them.'

'Honestly, it's in your best interests not to know.'

He stared ahead for a moment. A bell tinkled, signalling the door to the bookshop had opened. I could see the book guy's expression freeze into polite. 'Can I help you, sir?' he said.

'Just lookin' for my cousin. Can't remember where I

said I'd meet her.'

'No one in here, mate,' Book Guy said.

'She's kinda tall with messy hair and big shoulders. You haven't seen her walk by or nothin', have you?'

Messy hair and big shoulders! I was sorely tempted to spring up from behind the counter and slap him for that description. The only thing that stopped me was the knowledge that Book Guy would most definitely call the cops.

Book Guy maintained his polite face. 'Sounds like someone you'd notice,' he said to the tail. 'Big shoulders, you say.'

'She could have been a weightlifter.' The tail sniggered.

'Well, I haven't seen her but I'll keep an eye out. Pretty quiet today so she should be easy to notice. You got a card? I could ring you if I see her.'

The tail hesitated before he answered. 'No card, man. But I'll write my number down for you.'

'Cool.'

Book Guy was smart.

There was some fidgeting and scraping as the tail handed over his number. 'Thanks, man,' he said.

'No worries,' said Book Guy. 'You want me to give her a message?'

'Nah, mate. Just call me.'

'Sure?'

'Yeah.'

'So where're you going to look? Down the arcade?

You know, in case I see her a minute after you go.'

'I'll head to the station across the road. What's it called?'

'Central?'

'Yeah, that one.'

'You not from here then?'

'Sydney. Listen, mate, I gotta go. Call me.'

'Sure thing.'

The bell tinkled and I felt a whoosh of the air-conditioning as it adjusted.

Book Guy fiddled with the cash register for a bit then said, 'It's safe.'

I uncurled and stood up. 'That was exceedingly cool and clever of you,' I said.

He shrugged and handed over the slip of paper with the number on it. 'Livened up a quiet day.'

I slipped the paper in my purse and looked around. 'You sell crime books?'

'Sure do. And science fiction.'

'How weird that I came in here!' I held out my hand in proper greeting. 'Tara Sharp.'

He smiled and shook it. 'Ben Bower, bad-assed bookseller.' He was a little shorter than me with brown curly hair. Cute as a teddy bear.

'Well, Ben Bower, if I was going to be in town a bit longer, I'd buy you a drink to say thanks.' I had a thought. 'Hey, do you like music?'

'Sure.'

'Slim Sledge?'

'The rapper? My girlfriend's a big fan.'

'I'll leave your name on the door of Slim's gig tomorrow night at Little Paolo's in the Valley.'

'Awesome. Thanks, Tara.'

I went to the door and peered out into the arcade. 'Maybe see you tomorrow, Ben.'

'Bye.'

I headed out onto Edward Street and kept up a fast clip past the train station.

Jade lived in an apartment block directly behind it. The building was about ten storeys high, an ugly 1970s coloured-glass construction that screamed noisy and dirty. The foyer reeked of dog pee and the lift was out of order.

I walked four flights to Jade's floor and cruised the corridor. It was as foul-smelling as the foyer and her door stayed firmly shut. Short of breaking in, or knocking and announcing that I was spying on her, there wasn't much more I could do.

The lift pinged open and a scruffy guy got out.

'I thought the lift wasn't working,' I said.

'That sign's been up for months. No one took it down when the lift got fixed.' He saw where I was standing. 'You looking for Jade?'

'Uh, yeah. You know where she is?'

'Just passed her at the laundromat. Next door.'

'Cheers,' I said and moved towards the lift he'd just vacated.

He waited for me to pass and brushed up against me, leering. 'You work at the club too?'

'Yeah,' I said. 'Security. I came to drop off a taser for her.'

The guy took an involuntary step back. 'Can't be too careful.'

'Can't,' I agreed, and stepped into the lift.

I got out of the building as quick as I could and walked next door to the laundromat, pausing to peek around the edge of the glass. Jade was there all right, and she wasn't alone. A tall, thin guy was talking to her and into his phone at the same time. He was really familiar, but I couldn't think who he was or how I knew him.

I set my phone to camera and took a quick shot of the two of them from my spot at the edge of the window.

Something poked me and I turned to look down into the face of an old woman holding a walking stick. 'That's illegal, taking photos of people without their permission.'

I slipped my phone away. 'Madam,' I said, 'I need you to keep your voice down. I work for the government. The tax department—in the area of serious non-compliance.'

She reacted like I'd told her I had leprosy, scuttling off as fast as her Kumfs would allow.

Time to get out of there. I took a deep breath and crossed the road.

By the time I reached the venue for the film shoot I was

panting and sweating heavily. Minivans lined the street outside a grand old house that looked like it had been rejigged into apartments. I knocked on the front door and was greeted by a security guy. I showed him my Reverb Promotions badge and he let me in.

'They're filming on the left,' he said.

I went through the open doors into a huge room with high ceilings and peeling plaster. It was buzzing with people setting up cameras and rummaging through carry bags.

Lulu and Shari from the boutique stood next to a rack of clothes. A stylist bent over one of two make-up chairs set up by the window. She was attempting to paint pancake on a face I knew and frequently wanted to kiss. I would have just stood and stared at how beautiful Ed was, but he spotted me and bounded out of the chair.

'Tara!' He threw his arms around me and lifted me off my feet, planting a noisy kiss on my lips. He smelled and felt so divine that the morning's traumas almost melted away.

'Hi,' I said, laughing.

'I've got to get ready, back soon.' He lowered me gently to the floor and returned to the chair. It was only then that I realised he had nothing on but a nude stage G-string. Everyone on set was staring at me.

'Er, hi,' I said awkwardly, waving my badge. 'Reverb Promotions. I'm here to check the premises ahead of Slim Sledge's arrival.'

'She means we're here,' said a voice behind me.

Bon walked in and I pulled the second badge from my pocket. 'Bon Ames and Tara Sharp,' I said to our audience.

Something akin to a group shrug happened and the silence broke. They all turned back to whatever they'd been doing when I walked in.

A harassed-looking man with bleached hair and a rampant red aura detached himself from the women he was talking to and approached us.

'I'm Levin, the director. Make it quick. We'll be shooting soon.'

'Do you have a seat for Slim?' I asked, surveying the chaos. 'He'll need a chair and some space around it. He doesn't like to be crowded.'

Levin sniffed. 'Crowded? He's from LA for fuck's sake.'

'Please. Things will go a lot better.'

Levin gave an impatient nod and barked an instruction at one of his assistants who scurried off, returning a minute later with a canvas chair that looked like it had seen one too many barbecues.

'Dust it off and cover it with a towel,' said Levin. 'We haven't got time to source anything else. This isn't Hollywood.'

I bit my lip. Levin had attitude.

There was a call for 'On set' and three rappers came through an adjoining door. I had a complete fan-girl freeze when I recognised Suffa, Pressure and DJ Debris from the Hilltop Hoods. Their hit single 'Nosebleed Section' had been my anthem for years—got me through my furniture-stealing ex-boyfriend doing my housemate. I owed these guys big time; nothing like a pub-anarchy evening and a lot of beer to empower a girl going through a break-up. More recently, their song 'I Love It' was all over the shop, in sports commercials, on TV ads. And their Walking Under the Stars album was sublime. We loved our Hoods.

'Sharp!'

Bon's gruff tone snapped me from my trance and I reluctantly followed him around the perimeter of the room while he checked that all the windows were locked. By the time we reached the internal door, the music was amped up and Suffa and Pressure were mucking around with cordless microphones. DJ Debris had set himself behind a vinyl turntable and was making scratching noises. I wanted to stand and watch but Bon grabbed my arm and hauled me through the door.

On the other side was a much smaller, darker room which must have once acted as a servery for the house's huge front reception room. It was still lined with dusty shelves and there were several sliding hatches in the walls. Clothes hung from a mobile chrome rail in the middle of the room and a heap more were spread over plastic chairs. A lamp set down on the floor was the only light. The makeshift dressing room smelled of rodent. The only other exit—which I assumed had originally led to the kitchen—was locked. Bon Ames rattled the door handle a few times to be sure.

'Looks tight,' he said. 'And those hatches go through into the front room.'

'Sweet. How was Slim doing before you came over?'

'See for yourself. He'll be here soon.'

Bon sounded grumpy and preoccupied. Despite that, I took a breath and asked him something that had been bugging me since the day we met. 'How do you know Johnny Viaspa?'

His gaze shifted from the ceiling and settled on me. 'And you'd be askin' me that because…?'

'I thought you might know why he was here—you know … in Brisbane.'

He waited to see if I had more to say and his silence somehow compelled me to keep talking.

'It's just that … Wal's in trouble and I think it's got something to do with Viaspa.'

'Grom?'

'I think he's in hiding. He sent me a weird message… I'm worried.'

Bon stroked his beard. If the light had been brighter I could have read his aura but in the gloom it was coming off dull and diffuse.

'You got history with Viaspa?' he asked.

'Yeah,' I admitted. 'A bit. A, er, colleague of his went to jail because of me.'

Bon frowned, and I immediately knew what he was thinking—that I was a narc.

'Nothing like that,' I assured him. 'He sent someone to

kill me. I got away and the guy didn't.'

His frown stayed right where it was for a bit. 'Finn Fiegal?'

I nodded wordlessly.

He grunted with surprise. 'You put The Finn away?'

'Well, not exactly. The cops did that. Hope he wasn't a friend of yours … but in my defence, he did try to kill me.'

'Pricks like that don't have any friends,' he said in an approving kind of way.

I let out the breath I didn't realise I'd been holding. 'Anyway, something's telling me that Stuart might be in danger.'

'Why?' A curt demand.

I took a deep breath. I didn't know if I was doing the right thing but I had to share this with someone. I didn't want to disappear forever without at least one person knowing the full story. That I was trusting Bon Ames to be that person was a sign of my desperation.

'Well, two guys roughed me up last night as I walked back to where I'm staying. They told me to go home and take you with me.'

One giant paw shot out and crushed my shoulder. 'Describe them!'

I did my best but it wasn't until I mentioned the guy's American accent that Bon reacted.

'You sure?'

'I watch NCIS: LA,' I said. 'He sounded just like LL Cool J.'

'Who?'

'Never mind.'

Bon fired a bunch of questions at me in rapid succession. How tall? What was he wearing? Was he armed? Did he mention any other names? I got a taste of what it might be like to be interrogated by him. I didn't like it much, but I'd opened this can of worms.

'What do you think?' I asked when he eventually fell silent.

'When are you going home?' he asked.

'Sunday morning, after the gig.'

He nodded. 'I'm bringing in some more help. You square it with Stuart.'

'You think they're serious then? You think Johnny Viaspa sent them?'

'Maybe.'

I tried my original question from another angle. 'At the airport you said you knew Viaspa. I heard you call him a snake.'

The grip on my shoulder eased. 'I'm sergeant-at-arms for the West Coast Cheaters. What do ya think?'

I nearly said 'Over drugs?' but caught myself in time. Really, I didn't want to know. And if he told me, no doubt he'd have to kill me. 'I think that I appreciate your concern, but I don't know that Stuart can afford more help.'

Then he said the words I'd been half expecting to hear for a while. 'No charge, but you'll owe me.'

'I guess … I will.' My moment of relief ebbed. What

would that mean down the track—owing the sergeant-at-arms of an outlaw motorcycle gang a favour? Best not dwell on it now. That worry could join the queue.

Bon's phone rang. It was Stuart; they were outside in the car.

'Let's go,' said Bon.

I followed him out of the dressing room. The Hoods were running through their act with Levin, and Ed was now dressed in faded jeans, a torn jacket and no shirt, and he had a cap on backwards. If he hadn't been so perfect in every way, his look would have said 'street'. As it was, it said 'way too good-looking to be out alone'. Levin had set him up in a corner by a picture window where he squatted down while they discussed camera angles.

Further along the wall a girl sat in a second make-up chair. She was drop-dead stunning: long brown hair, oval face, big eyes. If Bon and I hadn't been striding through the room on a mission, I would have stopped to stare. Instead, I kept pace with the biker out to the roadside.

Slim was in the back seat with Juanita. Stuart was in the front talking to the limo driver. They all got out together and Bon and I closed around them. I noticed Bon was glancing up and down the street with more than usual suspicion. He even glanced at the top of the surrounding buildings. That sent a shiver down my back. What the hell was he looking for? A sniper?

'Everything alright inside, Tara?' asked Stuart. He didn't look much better than when I'd seen him that morning; bags cradled the bags under his eyes.

Juanita, on the other hand, was fresh and ravishing in a blue dress and black spike heels. Her hair was pinned up with some soft curls escaping at the back.

'We've done a check,' I said.

'Excellent. You hear that, Slim?' beamed Juanita.

'Morning, Slim.' I held out my fist for him to knuckle-five me but he left me hanging.

'You been ignoring me, bitch?'

Bon rolled his eyes and Stuart's breathing got heavier. Only Juanita wasn't bothered. I swear it would take an apocalypse to faze that woman.

'Now, Slim, Tara's been busy making sure that nothing gets in the way of your success,' she said.

Slim lost his sulky expression. 'That true, ho'?'

'I'm not a ho', Slim. Or a bitch. And yes, that's true.'

He stared at me hard for a moment then pointed to my jaw. 'Say, baby, who gave you some trouble?'

'I fell over,' I said.

'We should get off the street,' growled Bon. 'Now.'

It was impossible not to obey Bon when he used that tone. Even Slim did what he was told without a quibble.

Inside, Juanita swung into action. She had Slim's dirty canvas chair swapped for a make-up recliner and was sorting out food and drinks before Levin could open and shut his mouth.

Stuart introduced the Hoods to Slim, and then Ed and the other model came over and it was all matey for about three minutes until Levin stood on a stool and shouted, 'Places.'

I found a crate behind the crew and settled in to watch my favourite band and my almost-boyfriend do their stuff.

The first hour flew past with me in fan-girl heaven. It was only in a break that I realised Bon wasn't in the room. I sidled around the wall to the main door and slipped out into the entry hall. The hired security guy was still there, sitting on a stool, reading from his iPad.

'You seen Bon Ames?' I asked.

'The big biker guy? He went down the street.' He pointed to a white building.

'What's that?'

He shrugged. 'Old bread mill. Closed up for renovations now.'

'Oh.' I hedged for a moment. I knew I shouldn't leave the shoot but I was curious about where Bon had gone. Besides, Slim was surrounded by professional musicians and there was a security guard on the door.

My justification gave my feet permission to jog half a block, past a public phone booth and a graffitied brick letterbox out front of a vacant cottage, to see what was going on. But after a full circuit of the base of the old mill I'd found nothing, certainly no giant biker.

The sign outside said Closed for Renovations.

I was about to head back to the shoot when I heard a

muffled noise inside. Perhaps the builders were in there? Yet I couldn't see any sign of that kind of activity.

My phone rang, interrupting my sticky-beaking, and I pulled it out of my pocket. I didn't recognise the number.

'Hello?' I said cautiously.

'It's Inigo,' she whispered.

'Hi! How did you get my… Nevermind. Is everything alright?'

'I'm at Stuart's. There's someone outside.'

'What do you mean?'

'I sensed a disturbance. Right now I'm standing on the toilet looking through the little window into the backyard. Someone is fiddling in the fuse box.'

'What does he look like?'

'He has dark hair and he smokes.'

'You can see him smoking?'

'I can see the cigarettes in his top pocket.'

'Is he wearing jeans and a tight black shirt?'

'Yes.'

'Dark joggers?'

'Yes. How did you know that? Are you channelling me?'

The question wasn't a joke. 'No. He was following me earlier.' I stepped back from the mill's door, heart pounding. 'Inigo, I'll call you back in a minute. Keep watching him.'

I hung up and ran back to the public phone box. From there I dialled the number on the slip of paper Ben the book guy had given me.

It was answered on the third ring with a whispered, 'Yes?'

'Get away from the fuse box or I'll call the cops,' I said in a deeper, rougher voice than my own.

There was a pause and I imagined him glancing over his shoulder.

'I know you're plannin' to start a fire,' I said. 'Get away from the fuse box and don't come back or I'll have the cops crawlin' all over you.'

He hung up.

I rang Inigo back straight away on my own phone. 'What's he doing?'

'He's taken off like someone's after him.'

'Good,' I breathed. 'I doubt he'll be back. Thanks for ringing me—I think you just saved Stuart's street from arson.'

She didn't reply.

'Inigo?'

'You need a cleansing.'

'A what?' I asked as I walked back down the road to the mill.

'Your spirit is stained. I will arrange it.'

'Um ... well, thanks, but I'm heading home on Sunday and tomorrow's going to be pretty busy.'

'It will be done,' she declared, and hung up.

I walked back to the mill and rested my head against the door in despair. What was a cleansing?

From inside came a sound like a strangled scream.

On impulse, I grabbed the iron door ring, twisted it and shoved hard. It gave a groan and swung inward. I followed it, stumbling over the threshold before regaining my balance.

Bon had a guy pinned up against the wall on my right side, his huge hands tight around the fellow's neck. He stared at me with cold eyes. 'Get out of here.'

I wanted to do what he said more than anything I've ever wanted in my life, but my traitorous feet would not move.

He raised his voice. 'Get out!'

'I can't, you'll kill him,' I squeaked.

Bon made a face that caused every hair on my body to stiffen at their roots. Then his hands tightened until the man in his grip passed out.

'Oh my God! He's dead!'

Bon lowered the body to the floor and stepped over it. He walked over to me, grabbed my arm and hauled me outside, pulling the door shut behind us.

He didn't speak until we reached the garden hedge near the brick letterbox. There he suddenly stopped and said, 'Get down.'

My feet were still having trouble with instructions, and when I didn't move, he yanked me down so hard that I fell on top of him. A Bon/Tara sandwich was not a pleasant experience.

'What—?'

'Shut up!'

I held my breath and listened. A car drove along the road and stopped close by. Bon parted the hedge just enough so that we could peer through without being seen.

The car had parked next to the phone booth. Two men got out and walked across to the mill. I only recognised one of them and it made me break out in a cold sweat. Johnny Viaspa. Even from here I could see his pus-filled aura.

'Who's the other guy?' I whispered in Bon's ear.

'Ash Machete.'

'He met Viaspa at the airport.'

Bon let go of the hedge and slapped his hand over my mouth, half suffocating me. 'Shut the fuck up!'

I could feel my eyes popping in fright as I nodded.

He let go then and went back to spying through the leaves.

Viaspa and Machete were at the mill door, trying to get it open, but Bon had slammed it so hard they were having trouble. Machete went back to his car and grabbed a tyre iron from the boot. With a bit of gouging around the lock, they got the door open and went inside.

A few minutes later they came back out with the guy Bon had half strangled hanging limply between them. They dumped him in the back seat and the car vanished up the street.

We lay there for a few moments, to be sure they

weren't coming back.

'Everything alright?' said a voice.

I looked up from my horizontal position and saw the security guard from the shoot leaning over the hedge. I was up and off Bon in a flash. The biker was much bulkier than me and took a few seconds to get his feet under him.

'Saw you fall behind here, and then that car pulled up near the mill. Thought youse might be in trouble.'

I opened my mouth to reassure him but Bon beat me to it. He reached across and seized the security guy by the shoulder. I winced, knowing just how that felt.

'Best you forget you saw any of that,' said the biker.

The guy knew enough not to argue or question.

'Who's watching the door?' I asked.

'Pretty quiet over there. Thought it'd be alright while I checked you were okay,' said the security guy.

No sooner had the words left his mouth than there was a shriek from up the end of the street. The three of us swivelled in that direction. Fran Dickle and a posse of ten or more fans were peering in the windows of the house where the shoot was taking place.

'Shit. How did they find out?' I was off and running before the other two reacted.

At a flat-out sprint, I wasn't going to make it to the door before them, so I fumbled in my pocket and rang Stuart.

He answered straight away. 'Where the hell are—'

'Dickle's on the doorstep,' I panted into the phone. 'Head her off. I'm coming.'

'But where's the guard? And Bon?'

'Not there. Long story.'

I was fifty metres away and Dickle's hand was on the door.

'Oi!' I shouted, forgetting that only a short time ago I'd been trying to stay invisible on this street. 'Fran Dickle, you're not allowed in there.'

She squinted at the madwoman running at her. Realising it was me, she gave me the finger and pulled the door open. The others piled in behind her.

Heavy breathing in my ear told me Bon or the security guard had caught up. I didn't even turn my head to see which one, but leaped up the small set of stairs after the fans.

They were crowded into the entry hall, facing off against Stuart and Juanita.

I pulled up sharp behind them, chest heaving. 'Please leave the premises,' I panted. 'This is a private event. We'll have to call the police.'

The tall skinny guy who'd been with Dickle at the airport spoke for them. 'We just want an autograph. Doesn't Slim appreciate his fans?'

Alarm bells screamed in my brain as I recognised him. He was the guy who'd poked me in the chest at the airport. The one I'd kneed in the tenderloins. And he was the one I'd seen in the laundromat with Jade earlier today. Which meant Aprile and Jade had to be the ones trying to sabotage the tour.

He turned and, seeing me, began to back away.

I squeezed between two girls so I could get closer to Dickle. I didn't trust her at all, and if it came to a scrap, she'd take Stuart down in a heartbeat.

She saw me coming for her and shoved one of the girls, trying to block me. I squeezed out from between them like toothpaste, but my momentum had a ripple effect. The posse started falling like tenpins, the tall guy collapsing onto Stuart like a toppling crane.

'What the fuck is going on?' roared Bon from the doorway, in a voice that could've parted the sea. Unfortunately, it was too late to stop the Tara Sharp domino effect.

Dickle sidestepped the melee and ducked into the room where the shoot was taking place. I shot after her but tripped on a power cord.

The whole room had frozen in disbelief; Hilltop Hoods lounging on their chairs, camera and crew about their business, Shari madly stitching one of her garments, Ed and the model having their make-up retouched. Slim Sledge stood in the middle of the room under lights like a true star. Or a rabbit in the headlights—he'd seen Dickle.

'Ed, stop her!' I shrieked.

My voice broke the paralysis and Ed lunged out of his chair towards Slim and the converging Dickle. But

Juanita beat him there. She stuck out a stiletto and tripped Dickle, who tumbled to the floor just in front of her idol.

Though stunned, Dickle was still close enough to touch him. Slim saw her hand reach out and lost his composure. His face contorted in terror and his aura went colour-ballistic. He began to scream in the way you do when you discover a large huntsman on the dashboard as you're driving along a freeway and can't stop.

Don't kick her! I pleaded silently. She'll charge you with assault.

His foot drew back and I seemed to be stuck in molasses. Even Juanita could only stare with wide, incredulous eyes.

Ed, on the other hand, kept moving. He stepped right in between them and kneeled to help Dickle up.

'You took a bit of a tumble,' he said sweetly and calmly. 'Are you alright?'

All the fervour and combativeness went out of her face when she saw who was talking to her. Both her expression and her aura liquefied into something resembling melted butter.

I didn't blame her really. In his set make-up, wearing street clothes, Ed looked like a Latin James Dean: hip, beautiful and totally irresistible.

I wanted to shunt Dickle out of the way and demand his attention. Instead I walked straight over to Slim and put out my hand. 'It's all under control. Come over here and I'll get you something to drink.'

Slim's eyes lost a little of their white-ringed fear when he saw me next to him.

I deliberately got in his face, blocking out his view of Dickle. 'It's under control,' I repeated.

The confident rapper persona slipped back into place and he knuckle-fived me. That, from a guy phobic about being touched by strangers, I took to be a sign of affection.

'You got some crazy-assed bitches out here,' he said.

'We do,' I agreed.

A buzz of conversation started up and suddenly the whole incident was over. I got Slim an OJ from the refreshments table, the Hoods joined the tea party and Ed led Dickle by the hand to Bon, who looked like the Big Bad Wolf about to huff and puff and blow the fans out onto the street.

They went surprisingly quietly once Ed had given Dickle his autograph. She flashed a triumphant look back at me as she left and I knew it wasn't over. Dickle was worse than a starving dog after a meaty ham hock. She wouldn't give in until she got her tasty treat.

Chapter 17

The shoot wrapped soon afterwards with Levin issuing high-pitched orders to make sure nothing was left behind.

While the crew ferried out equipment and props, I got in a huddle with Stuart outside and explained what had happened earlier and why Bon Ames and I had been missing in action.

'Viaspa was here?'

I nodded. 'The guy that met him at the airport was Ash Machete. They were together here today and Bon recognised him.'

Stuart groaned. 'Ash Machete as well? This can't be just about Wal and me. Something else has to be going down.'

'That's what I'm thinking. But what would it be?'

He shrugged. 'Please tell me that's all.'

'Nope. There was a guy following me through the city today but I lost him. Then Inigo called me a little while ago. The same guy had turned up at your place and was fiddling with the fuse box. Between us, we scared him off.'

'How? Is Inigo alright?'

'She's fine. I don't think he'll come back again. I have his number—literally.'

Stuart stared at me open-mouthed.

'Long story,' I said.

'That all?'

'No. I swung past Jade's place. She was in the laundromat next door with Dickle's boyfriend. She's definitely your leak to the fan club.'

'Then Aprile is trying to make the tour fail.'

'Looks like it,' I said. 'He'd know that Slim can't handle too much close fan attention. He and Jade have been making sure that's what he gets.'

'Shit,' said Stuart with heat. 'So Andreas...'

'You know, Stuart, I don't think the Andreas land development thing has anything to do with Aprile.'

'You mean both of them are interfering in my business?'

'Yeah, but for totally different reasons. My suggestion is that you just feed Jade the wrong information on Slim and the Joel problem will go away. Andreas, on the other hand...'

Stuart's phone rang and he turned away from me, a finger in his free ear, while he answered.

Bon stomped through the front door and over to me.

'Bon, the guy in the mill—what's the story?' I whispered. 'I mean, I was being followed earlier today but it wasn't him.'

'That's 'cos he was following me.'

'Oh?' Clear as mud. 'Why?'

He shrugged, clearly not prepared to say any more.

'Stuart!' called Juanita. She was standing at the door with Slim, ready to get into the waiting limo.

Stuart hung up from his call and waved to her. 'Juanita needs someone to go with her back to the Stamford.'

'Not me,' said Bon. 'Need to find some extra security for tomorrow.' With that he strode off down the street. We stared after him.

'STUART!' called Juanita, rather more insistently.

'Tara, can you do a babysitting shift?' pleaded Stuart.

'Why? Where will you be?'

'I'm going to check on Inigo and meet with … Sofia.'

'Oh. Okay.' I saw my romantic evening with Ed evaporating—unless… 'Can I bring a friend?'

'What friend?'

'Ed, the model on the shoot.'

'The guy who bewitched Dickle? Sure. Buy him dinner on me.'

'Thanks. Call me later if you learn anything.'

He nodded.

I left him standing on the pavement and told Juanita to hold the limo while I collected Ed.

He was inside still, talking to the beautiful girl he'd been acting with during the shoot. When he saw me he disengaged from his conversation and came over. Half a dozen set guys rushed in to fill his space.

'Sorry to interrupt. You want to come and have dinner with me and Slim?' I asked.

He gave me a melting-moment grin. 'Love to.'

I glanced at the men hovering around his model partner, while she was gazing wistfully at Ed. 'Are you sure?'

'Couldn't be more sure,' he said. 'I'll grab my gear.' He swung by the make-up chair and picked up a backpack. After a quick handshake with Levin and a wave to Lulu and Shari, he linked his arm through mine.

All the stress of the last few days faded for a moment. 'Listen, thanks for handling the crazy fan. I didn't know you had super smoothing powers.'

'I have all sorts of talents.' He shifted his hand to my butt and cupped it for a second.

I had an embarrassing notion that I might orgasm on the spot—put it down to the tension of the day—and I pulled away a little.

He gave me a puzzled look and I shook my head and grinned. 'Later.'

By the time we were safely tucked up at the Stamford and Juanita had taken herself off to do whatever Juanita did, Slim and Ed were mates.

They set themselves up with drinks and room service,

switching between NFL replays, basketball and cricket, discussing the merits of the different codes.

I kicked off my shoes, dipped into their platters of chips and mini-burgers, and used the desktop computer to catch up on my research.

Ash Machete made Joel Aprile's assets look like Lego pieces. He owned clubs in Kings Cross, property in Double Bay, Subway and Cold Rock franchises and a yum cha place in Chinatown. And that was just the stuff that was public. Mr Big was truly Big.

So what was he doing up here with Johnny Viaspa? And why the pressure on Wal and Stuart for something that happened a few years ago? I leaned back in the chair and stared at the ceiling, letting the noise from the television and the boys' sporadic conversation recede into white noise.

I had a border for my jigsaw but no inner picture yet. I wanted to chew the furniture with frustration. I was tempted to ring Hoshi Hara and pour the entire story out to him.

No! I told myself. This was my case. I had to stand on my own feet if I was going to do this kind of work.

I thought through the pieces. What was the common thread? Machete, Viaspa, Wal and Stuart were all connected over crime. Aprile and Stuart were connected over past employment and a woman—Jade. Andreas and Stuart were connected over Sofia and possibly Stuart's house. But which one of them had set the tail after me?

Andreas or Viaspa? And who had set the thugs on me? And why was one of them American? And why was Viaspa's guy following Bon Ames? Or was that completely random and nothing to do with Slim Sledge, Stuart and the tour? Argh!

My phone rang just in time to stop me banging my head on the desk.

'Tara,' I said curtly.

'Ms Sharp? Is this a bad time to call?'

'Lloyd? No, not at all. Bad day. Please tell me you found something.'

'Well, actually, I did. Are you somewhere private?'

'Hold on.' I put my hand over the receiver. 'Slim, can I take this in your bedroom?'

'Sure thing, baby girl. Turn my sheets down while you're there.'

I made a rude noise and closed the door on them.

'Right,' I said. 'What've you got?'

'My searches found no information but set off some curious return traffic.'

'What do you mean?'

'I'm not certain, but I think this Harvey T. fellow might work for "the government".'

'What?'

'Secret services.'

'You mean ASIO?'

'Well, national security in some form or other. Is that possible, do you think?'

I quickly went over in my mind what I knew about Harvey. There wasn't much. Socially incompetent, smart and overly horny completed my picture of him. He'd bonked Enid on the floor of my flat while I was outside taking a call. Wal was there at the time but sound asleep and snoring. I'd discontinued my classes after that and Harvey and Enid had gone their separate ways. Wal had come to work for me.

'I guess so. I barely knew him. Are you sure?'

'No. But I've seen this sort of ping-back before. I had to withdraw from the search. It wouldn't do for me to draw attention from … them.'

ASIO—the Australian Security Intelligence Organisation—was Australia's version of MI6 and the CIA. No doubt there were other similar covert groups the public didn't even know existed.

'Of course.' I wasn't sure what Lloyd was worried about, but then again, I wasn't exactly sure what he did either. Whatever it was, I didn't want to bring him any grief. 'Look, thanks, Lloyd.'

'I hope it helps.'

'It certainly makes things interesting.'

'Ah, well, it's what I'd expect from you, Ms Sharp.'

I sighed. 'Goodbye, Lloyd. See you soon.'

'I hope so,' he said. 'And Ms Sharp…'

'Yes?'

'Be careful. This pool you're swimming in may be deeper than usual.'

'Always careful.' I hung up and stood still, thinking. ASIO? What in the hell would Harvey the maybe-secret service agent be doing at a press call for Slim Sledge in Little Paolo's bar?

I could feel a headache of major proportions building in my head. My eyes hurt and my jaw still throbbed where I'd been punched.

I walked into Slim's ensuite to use the loo and splash my face with cold water. After several rinses, I stared at myself in the mirror.

Calm down, keep thinking.

I looked for the spare towel and dried off. Maybe there was something about Slim I was missing. On impulse, I opened his Louis Vuitton wet pack and started riffling through it. Nothing but the usual: toothpaste, aftershave, condoms.

I left the bathroom and glanced into the sitting area. They were still riveted to the screen, so I slid the door over quietly and did a quick recon of his suitcase. Most of his clothes were hanging up and his suitcase only held a few belts and caps and several pairs of sneakers.

His carry bag sat on the luggage rack next to the wardrobe and I tried that next. I felt bad touching his personal items, so after a cursory glance inside, I closed the main zipper.

The only other thing I could see was his iPod on the bedside table. I flicked through the menu and tapped on the photos. They were arranged in albums and I opened one with a recent date. From what I could tell they were happy snaps from rehab showing a bunch of complete strangers. I went back to the folder menu and opened one of the older albums.

These pictures were ancient: Slim with some tough-looking dudes in singlets. Each of them wore a bandana around his head or a cap, like it was some kind of uniform. All of them had tattoos.

'What you doing with my stuff?'

At the sound of Slim's voice from the doorway I froze. I quickly thumbed back to the song menu and took a breath before I answered.

'Just checking out your iPod. It's newer than mine.'

He stepped forward and snatched it out of my hand. 'Don't touch my stuff, bitch.'

'Everything alright in there?' called Ed.

'Client talk,' I called back. 'Out in a minute.'

Slim gave me an ugly look that suggested he was thinking about hurting me. He'd forked a previous assistant.

I made a split-second decision.

Lowering my voice, I said, 'I have something to tell you, Slim. I'm not just your bodyguard; I'm here doing an investigation for Stuart as well. We think he's … well, let's just say there's trouble brewing with his local competitors. I'm going to tell you something that I need you to be calm about. I also need you to help me.'

The ugly expression was replaced with a look of

curiosity. 'I'm listenin'.'

'I found out today we're being watched by government people.'

'Whach you mean, girl? Like Spooks. Like CIA?'

I nodded. 'The Australian equivalent, at least. Is there something about your past that might interest them?'

Suddenly, all his energy and aggression dissolved and he sank onto the bed.

'What? What is it?'

He shook his head and dropped his face into his hands. 'I'm clean, man. I don't do that stuff no more. I haven't done it for years. Couldn't be that.'

'Be what?'

'Kings and Aces. I used to run with them back in the day. A lot of us were bangers. Snoop Dogg, Ice-T, Tupac and Young Dre. Can't help where you grow up, 'n what you have to deal with. Some of the best music comes from street corners. But I'm done with that. That's history, man.'

'How did you get out?' I asked, curious.

'My baby cousin got shot in a drive-by. His mama gave me the money she'd be savin' to send him to college and told me to get out. I used it to record my first song. I owe that woman.'

I nodded as If I understood. But the truth was that Slim's childhood and mine couldn't have been further apart. I suddenly felt ashamed of what I'd had, the opportunities I'd squandered.

'Can I ask you… are you ever really done with a gang like that?'

He shrugged. 'I'll always be one of them that did good. In a weird-assed kind of way they're…'

'Proud of you?'

'Somethin' like that. All I really know is that I gotta get me through tomorrow night. 'Cos I need this. I need it bad. I got a third chance. Two more than most get. Ain't gonna fuck it up again.'

'I understand.' And this time I did. 'You don't happen to know a couple of guys called Johnny Viaspa and Ash Machete?'

'Nada.'

I took a deep breath. 'Let's join Ed.'

He held out his knuckles for me to tap. 'Don't you go touching my shit again.'

I nodded.

He suddenly smiled, the storm clouds gone. 'Say, your man is okay. Don't you go blowing it wid him by bein' a crazy-assed bitch.'

I rolled my eyes. 'You sound like my mother.'

'Yeah? Your mom must be cool.'

'My mother is not, nor will ever be, cool.'

We watched sport until past midnight, drinking beer, arguing with the referee's decisions and laughing at each other's jokes. It would've been the best night I'd had in a long while if my subconscious hadn't been worrying that we were being watched by feds.

My phone rang just before 1 AM. It was Stuart.

'Listen, can you stay tonight with Slim?' he asked. 'I can't make it.'

'Everything alright? Inigo?'

'Inigo's fine. She said to tell you that she'd do the cleansing tomorrow when you come back.'

'So why can't you come back here?'

'Um...'

He sounded slightly embarrassed and straight away I knew. 'You're with Sofia?'

'Yes.'

'In a good way?'

'I think so.'

I sighed. Stuart needed to catch a break and he was my current boss. My night with Ed was getting another raincheck. 'Sure.'

'Thanks. I'll be around by eight.'

I hung up, stood up and turned off the telly. The boys looked at me in open-mouthed protest.

'Bedtime,' I said, pointing a finger at Slim. 'Big day tomorrow.'

'That woman of yours is damn bossy,' Slim complained to Ed.

Ed grinned. 'She packs a punch too.' He was referring to the time I accidentally punched him in the nose, thinking he was some guy who had been spying on me.

'Where's my man Stu?' Slim asked.

'Stu's been caught up making some last-minute, er, arrangements. I'll be staying here with you.'

'Cool dat.' Slim got up and stretched. He was wearing track pants and a T and his eyes were heavy. He looked as tousled as a man with cornrows can look and it suited him. I forgot for a moment how demanding he could be and felt a surge of affection.

'Don't let the bedbugs bite,' I chimed.

He gave me a wide-eyed look then saw I was grinning. 'There ain't no bugs, right?'

'Just kidding—no bugs,' I promised solemnly.

He wagged his finger at me and swaggered from the room.

Ed was on his feet too, looking at me.

'I'm sorry about tonight,' I said. 'Things just keep getting messed up.'

He put his hands on my shoulders and pulled me close. 'It's you, Tara. I'm used to it.'

I gave a weary shrug. 'I guess you must be.'

'You okay? You seemed distracted tonight.'

I had the same urge as before, when I'd been thinking about ringing Hoshi—to unburden myself. But this was Ed; a lovely, handsome guy on his way somewhere. I couldn't drag him into my stuff. If it came back to bite him I'd never forgive myself.

'Just tired,' I said. 'Got a few things to figure out.'

259

'Well, I head home on Monday. We can always set a date for then.'

'Might have to, because I'm going Sunday. But you will come to the concert tomorrow night? Please?'

'Where is it?'

I grabbed the hotel notepad and jotted down the details. 'I'll make sure your name is on the door.'

'Cool.' He took the paper and stuffed it into his jeans pocket. Then he slid his hands down my arms and began to massage the small of my back.

I leaned as close as I could and we kissed slowly and deeply. My whole body heated and felt like it might ignite if this went on much longer.

Ed must have been feeling something similar because his breathing grew ragged and shuddery.

'Uh-uh,' carolled a voice.

We jumped apart as if someone had shouted 'Bomb!'

Slim stood in the doorway, hands on hips. 'I don't get no action, baby girl, you don't get no action either.' He went off back to his room, chuckling to himself.

Chapter 18

I slept on the couch with the spare pillows and doona I found in the cupboard. It should have been okay—I mean, the couch was a four-seater and wider than most single beds—but I woke up feeling like garden mulch.

My jaw was still tender and my neck and back seemed to have snuck out to a gymnastics competition without me during the night and fallen off the bar. I wanted to go home and sleep in my own bed and eat food from my mother's fridge.

Suck it up, princess, I told myself. This is far from over.

So I got up, peeked in on Slim softly snoring and went to the bathroom. After a quick shower, I donned yesterday's clothes and made a cup of tea.

The view from Slim's room took in an expanse of Brisbane River and two of its many bridges. Settling into an armchair in front of the window, I watched the ferries getting busy, a cruiser or two heading out to the harbour and some little dinghies packing up and puttering towards their moorings after a night of fishing. The sky was a silky grey and lightening by the second. Soon it would be brilliant Brisbane blue. I thought about slipping out for a swim in the hotel pool but, knowing my luck, Dickle would find a way through the air conditioning vent while I was gone. Plus, I would've had to swim in my underwear.,

I had an ominous feeling about the day. So much hinged on Slim giving a good concert tonight—Stuart's livelihood and Slim's career, not to mention me getting paid. But more than that, I couldn't rid myself of the notion that I knew too little to keep things right.

The river view faded as I put the big puzzle pieces in the front of my mind: ASIO, Viaspa, Machete, Slim Sledge, Stuart. How were they connected?

I turned on the hotel desktop again and gave myself a crash course on the LA gangs. There was no shortage of information. Jeez, they even had an educational website to enlighten local youth about the realities of being a banger.

The self-education did nothing to allay my nerves, which were stretched beyond tight by the time Stuart arrived. I dispensed with pleasantries and pulled another armchair over to the window.

'Sit. Talk.'

He sipped his takeaway cappuccino, refusing to be hurried, savouring something. His aura was calm and had a sheen that made me jealous.

'You spent the night with Sofia,' I said. 'What did she

tell you?'

His face reddened. 'Well, it's not like Jade would be broken-hearted.'

'Stuart, I don't care who you sleep with either. But I want to know if you found out anything about Andreas.'

The serenity faded and his aura started to pick up speed. 'You were right. Andreas's brother, Sofia's other uncle, talked him into putting up money for a big development in the Valley. It's caused a big rift in the family. Sofia's dad wants nothing to do with it; says it's wrong and likely to fail. But Sofia thinks some of the other investors have the environment minister in their pocket. They're planning to turn my street and three others into a huge office city.'

'So it could have been Andreas who tried to start a fire in your fuse box?'

'No… Andreas wouldn't do anything that radical.'

I frowned at him. 'You're the one who said he might be sabotaging your tour. Why wouldn't he do the same to your home?'

'He just wouldn't. He's not a criminal.'

'You're talking about the man who told his niece you weren't good enough,' I said with exasperation.

Stuart waved his free hand in the air. 'I know, I know. But that's family. I still don't think he'd try to torch my place.'

'Who then?'

'Sofia said he and his brother were the face of some

overseas investors. She said there were big guys putting up serious money.'

'Who?' I repeated.

'She didn't know—but she might be able to help us find out.'

'How?'

'There's an investor's meeting today. She heard Andreas and her papa talking about it.'

'Where? When?'

'She's going to text me when she finds out.'

'Do you trust her?'

A little of the sheen reappeared. 'After Jade, I don't know. I think so. She came to me to tell me about it. She got worried after you came and talked about becoming my partner.'

'Andreas wouldn't have put her up to it?'

'No. I don't think so. She respects him but she says she loves me.'

I sat back in the chair and let go of my breath. 'Okay. I'm sorry to push you on this, Stu, but things are getting weird. I recognised a guy at the Slim's press call at Paolo's. A guy I knew, from the west. He pretended not to know me. It was strange, so I asked a friend to make some enquiries about him.'

'And?'

'My mate thinks he works for the government.'

Stuart snorted some coffee and gave a choking laugh. 'Tax?'

'No. Secret service kind of thing.'

'Bullshit!'

'I wish,' I said quietly.

A long silence fell between us as he absorbed what that might mean.

'But even if these developers were pulling some dirty tricks, trying to mess me round, that's all local shit. ASIO's the watchdog for national security–why would they be interested?'

I nodded. 'That's the bit I don't understand either. Though I'm starting to get a feeling.'

'Care to explain?'

'You know much about gang crime in the US?'

'No more than the TV shows. Why?'

'I dunno. I'll get back to you on it.'

Stuart rubbed his forehead like he had a headache. 'Listen, whatever the case, this is getting way off the dial. If you want to pull the plug, I understand.'

I appreciated his consideration, but I wasn't quitting on him yet. 'Let's just get through tonight. We'll talk about it again after that.'

He sighed. 'Thanks, Tara. Have you heard from Wal?'

'Not a thing,' I said.

'Me neither.' He looked at me. 'He'll be alright. He's like a cockroach.'

'Survive anything?'

'Pretty much.'

'The drug thing you had with Machete and Viaspa— you got any idea why they would be agitated about it now?'

'Keep going over it in my head. Can't think of a reason, except if he needs the money and still thinks we're hiding it.'

'But you said he let you go because you stuck to your story.'

Stuart shrugged. 'That's what we thought. But who knows?'

My phone rang and I answered automatically. 'Yes.'

'Tara?'

'Hoshi?' I wanted to cry with relief at the sound of his voice. 'Hey!'

'Been following that fellow. Not looking so good for his missus.'

I waved a finger at Stuart, excusing myself, and walked over to the other side of the room. 'You think he's sleeping with her?'

'Can't see through walls, you know. But we tagged him at her place three times this week.'

'How long was he there each time?'

'One hour the first time, then half an hour.'

'Where did he go when he left?'

'Work.'

'Where did he park?'

'On the street. Then he went down the side of the house and through the back door.'

'Anything else?'

'Last time he stopped at the ATM and took money out 'fore he visited the woman.'

'Crap!' Belle's blackmailing him for sex was my first thought.

'You want me to do more?'

'No, Hoshi. That's enough. I'm coming home tomorrow. I'll take it from there. How did Cass work out?'

'That girl's as psychic as a plank of wood but she's street smart. I'd pick her on my team.'

'I thought she would be. What about Wal? You find out anything?'

'I asked around. He's sure gone to ground. Word is he's not even here.'

'Not where? Perth?'

'Not in the state. Other word is … he's in deep this time.'

I swallowed. It wasn't what I wanted to hear at the start of what was shaping up to be the longest day of my life.

'Hoshi,' I whispered, 'I'm…' Scared? Freaked?

'You're a smart girl, Tara. Trust yourself. Trust your gift.'

'Thanks.' I turned my back on Stuart and cupped my hand around my mouth so my voice was muffled. 'Have you heard of a biker called Bon Ames?'

'Not so much. I stay away from those guys.'

'Can you find out his reputation for me?'

'Say the name again?'

'Bon Ames—he's sergeant-at-arms for the West Coast Cheaters in Perth. See if he has any connection to Johnny Viaspa.'

'I'll see,' he said, and hung up.

I stared at the watercolour on the wall in front of me. It was a yacht on a river. You could just make out the red life jackets and windblown hair of the two people sailing it. Why couldn't I be one of them?

'What's wrong?' asked Stuart.

I returned to my chair by the window. 'Sure. Just some stuff going on at home while I'm away.'

'You think Bon might be connected to Johnny Viaspa?' he asked.

'Oh, you heard that. Well, maybe, but not in a bad way. He can't stand Viaspa, I know that. I just wanted to know a bit more about his background.'

'Can we trust him? Should I cut him loose?'

I shook my head.

There was a brief, heavy knock at the door.

'That'll be him now.' I got up and looked through the peephole. Bon Ames through a fish-eye lens at 7.30 AM was a more unpleasant sight than I expected. I opened the door quickly.

Today he was wearing leather, the first time I'd seen him out of denim. He also had on his dark glasses and a pair of work boots. His aura rolled energetically around his body and the colour seemed more intense than normal.

'Dressed to kill,' I said lightly, and instantly regretted it.

'Morning, Bon,' said Stuart. 'We're just planning the day.'

Bon took my seat without apology, letting his legs sprawl out and his belly flow over the chair arms.

I rolled the desk chair over and perched on it. Now that I was awake and my brain was firing, I wanted to move. Sitting here felt wrong, like I was wasting time.

'Problems last night?' asked Bon.

'Nope.' I wanted to ask him where he'd been and why he'd left so abruptly but I wasn't game. 'All quiet.'

He nodded. 'Well, that's something.'

'You expecting trouble?'

He shot me a suspicious look. 'You aren't?'

'Well… I thought we should talk about yesterday with Stuart. You and I were both followed. Your guy was sent by Johnny Viaspa and Ash Machete. You got any clues what that might mean?' I neglected to add that Bon had pulverised his guy and I wasn't sure he hadn't committed murder.

He didn't answer me but gave Stuart a stare. At least, I think he did—he still had his sunnies on. 'You got some old shit going on with Viaspa?'

Stuart sighed. 'Maybe. Though nothing's been said to me directly.'

'I'm bringing in some help for the gig tonight. In case

Viaspa brings it on.'

'Who?' I asked bluntly.

'Brothers in arms,' he said noncommittally.

'Thanks for the offer, but I can't afford to pay for more protection,' said Stuart. 'I was thinking of going to the police, maybe saying we'd had a death threat or something to get them watching the place.'

'No police,' said Bon. 'We'll do the job as a favour.'

Brothers in arms. Yikes. 'Don't you think it's time you shared information?'

Bon looked at me like I'd grown a second head.

'Do you think the guy following me was working for Viaspa as well?' I asked.

He shrugged. 'Maybe.'

Frustration welled up in me. The kind of annoyance that usually only faded when I played a game of basketball or went for a run. Bon Ames knew something and he wasn't talking.

Breathe. Breathe. You can't get into it with this guy. You'll lose. 'Okay. Well, extra security would be good.'

He nodded.

Stuart nodded.

We fell to talking about times and methods of transport. Slim had a sound check and rehearsal just before lunch followed by a few free hours before the gig.

'Count me out of the security detail,' I said. 'I've got to attend to other business.'

Bon curled his lip in an unimpressed manner but Stuart

came to my rescue. 'I've asked Tara to do something for me.'

'Who's keeping the crazy fucker under control then?' asked Bon, jerking his thumb at the bedroom door.

'Juanita,' said Stuart. 'She'll be here soon.'

'He'll be fine,' I said. 'Chilled out as—'

'Aaaaarghhhh!' The scream that emanated from Slim's bedroom cut me dead. I leaped from my chair and beat Stuart across the room by a nose.

Slim was half off the bed, his arms working like paddles as he dived onto the floor. But Dickle held one of his feet in a death grip, stopping him.

The door to the adjoining room was open. How the hell did she get hold of the key to that?

'Let go!' I bellowed.

'I—just—want—him—to—sign—my—CD.' Her mouth was puckered with peevish determination.

Without a thought to the consequences, I threw myself at her. My tackle tumbled us both into the bedside table.

'Owwww!' she cried. 'Help! Help!'

Peripheral vision told me that Slim was in the foetal position by the bottom of the bed. Stuart was bending over him, making awkward soothing noises.

'Get him out of here,' I called.

My concern for Slim cost me. Dickle blindsided me with a punch.

'Bitch!' she screamed in my ear. Her hair had come out of its bun and her t-shirt had ridden up high, revealing a wealth of flesh.

Death by boobs flashed through my mind.

I circled my arms around her and managed to pin her underneath me. 'Who let you in here?' I shouted in her face. 'Who?'

'Bitch!' she squealed again.

I raised my fist and aimed it at her face.

Her expression filled with fear. 'Don't touch my nose. I'm getting married soon.'

Married? A shadow appeared over my shoulder.

'Coming, Fran!' Dickle's tall, skinny boyfriend fell on my back, arms pumping like a windmill on speed.

I let go of Fran and rolled sideways, kicking him in the knackers for the second time. He crumpled into a ball. While Dickle tried to comfort him, I grabbed the bedside phone from the floor to ring security.

'Already done!' said Bon. He was leaning against the opposite doorway with his mobile in his hand. 'Speed dial.'

Before I could comment, hotel security charged into the room. In a matter of minutes, after some stern words, Dickle and her crumpled-over fiancé had been marched out. The staff relocked the offending door behind them with profuse apologies and an offer of a complimentary banquet breakfast.

I sagged back onto the bed, holding the side of my face. 'Thanks for the help,' I snapped at Bon, not caring right now that he was much bigger and scarier than the pair I'd just wrestled.

'Never get into it when women are fighting,' he said.

'What was that guy then? Dog meat?'

'Him? Looked pretty girlie to me. Quit whining. You can handle yourself.' He walked back into the other room.

If he meant it as a compliment, I wasn't feeling it.

It took a few minutes to get my head together. I straightened the bedside lamp and the bed sheets, washed my face in the ensuite and finally re-joined the others.

Slim was still shivering, his hands cupped around a mug of tea.

Stuart stood next to him with a look of near-despair on his face. 'Juanita's nearly here.'

'Where's Bon?'

'In the corridor.'

I kneeled in front of Slim. His aura was lumpy and shredded as though it might fall apart. He raised his head from his hands to look at me and the terror was still there.

'It's okay, Slim.'

'Tara?'

'They've gone. Bon Ames is bringing in extra security for the rest of the Brisbane tour.'

His eyes shimmered with unshed tears and his breathing was tight. What on earth had happened to this guy that contact with strangers terrified him so?

'Can't do this,' he said.

'They won't hurt you, Slim. Even if they get close, we'll always be there to stop them.'

'Nooooo,' he moaned.

I quashed my impatience and kept my tone gentle. 'What are you afraid of? What do you think they'll do?'

He began to rock back and forth. 'You don't know what it's like being touched by them. They don' see me. They see a thing. Meat.'

I took another tack. 'How long have you been rapping for?'

It was a while before he answered, as though he was accessing a distant memory. 'Since I could talk,' he said eventually.

'You still love the music?'

He nodded like a child being asked if he liked riding his bike.

'You going to let a crazy dropkick like Fran Dickle stop you from being the best at what you love? You going to let her stop you from doing the right thing by your aunt and your cousin?'

He lifted his chin.

'Jeez, Slim, where's your pride, man?'

He stiffened and his aura solidified a little. 'I got pride.'

'Bullshit you have.'

This time he really sparked. 'Don't go speakin' to me like that, bitch.'

I grinned. 'Never thought I'd be happy to hear you call me that.'

He paused, his aura positively bristling, and then suddenly grinned back at me. He glanced over at Stuart. 'I'm hungry, man. Need me some of your Ossie hotcakes.'

Stuart let out the breath he'd been holding. 'Already on their way, Slim.'

The rapper nodded his approval. 'I'll go grab a shower.' He got up and left the room, his swagger and his aura restored.

'Good job,' Stuart said to me when the bathroom door closed and we could hear the shower running.

'Don't let him get the self-pity happening. He's got to move on from the past.' Not quite sure when I turned into Dr Phil, but I was flying on instinct and auras, and it felt right.

Stuart nodded. 'I'll tell Juanita as well.'

His phone belted out a line from a Slim Sledge song and he fished it out of his pocket to read the message. When he'd read it, he held it out for me.

The Frankston, Kingsford Smith Drive. 1 PM. Sofia. x

I raised my eyebrows in query.

'It's a boutique hotel on the way to the airport,' Stuart explained. 'Low-key but expensive.'

'How long to get there?'

'Fifteen, twenty minutes by taxi, depending on traffic.'

'I'll go soon then. Find a way in before they set up.'

Stuart took his phone back and pursed his lips.

'What?' I asked.

He pressed his forehead with his thumb. 'I know I'm paying you, Tara, but this could be dangerous. I mean, someone tried to burn down my home. Who knows what else they're planning?'

I wasn't going to let him wimp out on this now. 'Listen, Stuart, Wal's in a bad place, you're in a bad place, Slim's in a—well, God knows where he is, but it isn't a place I'd want to be. Johnny Viaspa's involved, which means at some point he'll come after me as well. I couldn't walk away from this if I wanted to.'

He took a deep breath and nodded. 'Alright. But if anything looks dangerous, call the cops. Promise?'

'Promise,' I said. 'And you promise me something.'

'Sure.'

'Don't tell Bon Ames where I've gone.'

'Okay. Why?'

'Just promise.'

He nodded. 'I booked your flight. It's leaving at eight tomorrow morning.'

'Thanks. I'm heading back to Inigo's for a shower and change and then I'll get over to the Frankston. Keep Slim busy today and I'll see you at the venue tonight, early.'

'How am I going to do that?'

'I dunno,' I said. 'Do what everyone else does with tourists. Take him to see the koalas.'

Chapter 19

Inigo was lying in wait for me, her coffee table laden with candles, little containers of liquid and strewn with petals. She was sitting cross-legged on the floor, eyes closed as if meditating.

'Inigo, hi,' I said, and kept on walking. 'In a rush.'

'Sit or die,' she commanded.

I stopped in my tracks. 'Beg pardon?'

'You must be cleansed or you will die.'

Man, I did not have time for this kind of crazy shit. At least with Dickle I could kick her arse. 'I'm not going to die, Inigo, and I have somewhere important to go right now.'

Her eyes snapped open. 'You will sit or I will call the police about the assault yesterday! They will tie you up in interviews.'

Damn. I sighed and sat in front of her. 'Look, I appreciate your interest in my safety but can we make it—'

She made a hissing noise and I shut my mouth.

Satisfied that I was finally compliant, she got up and walked a slow circle around me. She picked up a bowl of liquid and flicked some onto my head and shoulders with her fingertips. It smelled of lavender; nice, but it reminded me of my grandmother's underwear drawer. Then Inigo began to chant. That went on forever, chanting and occasional scented-water flicking, while I resisted checking my phone for messages. Finally, her chanting worked up into a peak of short, staccato words and then a long and eerie shriek that made the hairs on my body stiffen.

To finish her ritual, she put her hand on the back of my neck. I felt a charge of cold energy and my flesh goose-pimpled as if I'd jumped into a cold swimming pool on a hot day.

'And relax...' she said.

She removed her hand and the feeling faded, leaving my brain feeling fresh, as though I'd woken from a long, rejuvenating sleep.

'What the hell was that?' I asked.

She returned to her position on the floor in front of me. 'For one with such a strong gift you have so little belief.'

'Belief in what?'

Her only answer was a reproachful, weary stare. 'When you are ready to believe, to be honest, you will need me.'

'It's been very kind of you to have me to stay, Inigo, but I'm going home tomorrow.'

'That is irrelevant,' she said in her direct manner. 'In time, you will need me. I will be here.'

'Oh.' I wasn't sure what else to say. 'Thank you. I'd best get ready.'

'I'll prepare you some food.'

'No need—'

But she was already up and on her way to the kitchen.

I'd never met anyone as forthright and indefatigable. Inigo would intimidate my mother. Speaking of whom, I really needed to ring her back.

I thought about that and a bunch of other things while I had a shower and got changed. I couldn't do anything about Smitty and Henry until I got home. And to help Wal (and by default Liv) and Stuart (and Slim), I had to get through today.

The last of my clean clothes were crumpled but I wasn't in the mood to iron, plus it was already after nine. I had to move. Jeans, t-shirt, trainers and a cap—Tara Sharp business wear. I stuck the cap in my bag and donned the rest.

I tossed everything else in my suitcase and zipped it up, knowing today was going to be long and I might not get a chance to pack later. My flight was leaving early.

Inigo waited with a paper bag in her hand and a small flask of liquid. 'Corn cakes for energy, a special tea for clarity.'

'Thank you again. But I really—'

She silenced me with a look and I took the proffered food like a good girl, planning to dump it somewhere down the road.

'I'll be back to get my case sometime. And I'll see you at the concert tonight.'

'Yes. You will need me.'

'I will?'

'Blessed be, Tara,' she said, using the Wiccan farewell.

I gulped. 'Blessed be, Inigo.'

I managed to catch a cab almost outside the front door and asked them to drop me a block away from the Frankston. Less than ten minutes later I was standing on the side of busy Kingsford Smith Drive debating the best way to approach the hotel. In the end, I decided to go down one of the side streets and approach from the back.

The street I chose had a café halfway along with a decent view of the back of the Frankston. I sat down at a table, ordered a glass of iced chocolate and watched for a while. The delivery entry seemed to be my best bet. Small trucks were coming and going regularly. I just had to talk my way in.

The drink fortified my sugar levels, and the cold breeze still blowing through my mind from Inigo's cleansing seemed to have made me more detached than usual. The task ahead of me was clear: get in, find the meeting room and a way to listen, or at least identify who the other investors were.

As I devised this brilliant plan, a dark sedan cruised down the road and pulled up behind the delivery truck bay. Four sharply dressed individuals got out; two headed to the front of the building, two strolled up to the delivery entrance.

A few minutes later a troop carrier came from the other direction and parked across the road. This time three guys got out and dispersed to different points of the hotel. I recognised Andreas's office assistant, Fubulo, as he disappeared around the corner heading to the main entry. The hotel employee at the delivery entry was suddenly surrounded by men wanting to talk to him.

I scrabbled in my bag for the Reverb Promotions ID I'd used at the film shoot and pinned it to my shirt, letting my hair out to obscure the lettering. At a glance, it looked like any official badge. Close up, it was definitely the wrong official badge. I put on my cap and pulled it down low.

My mind stayed cold and fresh as I walked the hundred metres to the group of men. As I approached, I caught snippets of their conversation. They were arguing about their right to sweep the staff section of the hotel for listening devices. They stopped and stared at me as I walked up. One of them wolf-whistled and I lifted my chin.

The hotel guy glanced at my badge.

'I'm with Fubulo Giannoukakis,' I said before he asked

to inspect my ID.

He groaned. 'Look. Everyone wait here while I get our security officer. I'm not authorised to admit anyone.'

'Make it quick,' said one of the guys.

As he hustled inside, a van pulled up, blocking off the entry altogether. More security.

The guys that got out of this van made me sweat. I'd jogged enough early mornings along Swanbourne Beach to recognise ex-SAS. The SAS barracks were just over the sandhills from the water and they used to sprint up and down the dunes as their warm-up. SAS guys moved differently to everyone else.

I should have run screaming right then but Inigo's mind-wash helped me keep my nerve. Some of the men I was standing next to could have done with Inigo's help.

'Fuck,' said one of Andreas's boys. 'Look who.'

While all their attention was on the approaching security guards, I drifted back and slipped inside. The back of the freight bay led straight into a wide corridor with numerous doors leading from it. I heard what sounded like kitchen noises on one side, so I chose a door at random on the opposite side. It was a huge cleaning-supplies room lined with shelves of detergents and mobile vacuum cleaners stacked like little robots. I stuffed my cap in my pocket, removed the badge and slung a vac on my back.

A peek into the corridor told me the coast was clear so I marched onward as though I belonged. The first person

I saw was a cleaner with a two-way radio pinned to her uniform.

'Hey, what floor is this special meeting on? I've been told they need another vac.'

She frowned at me. 'Ask Kristine, I've finished. Who are you, anyway?'

'Jane. My first day. Kristine told me where to pick up a vac, but she didn't tell me where to get my radio or uniform.' I acted nervous and a bit fraught and she seemed to buy it.

'She's such a bitch. I had to start early to set up, and now she's telling you to vac it again.'

'I don't think she knew what else to do with me. She seemed kinda harassed.'

She sighed. 'Come on, I'll show you.'

We went back into the storage room and she flicked on the light. Down past the detergents was another door, which she unlocked with one of her fistful of keys. Inside were cleaners' uniforms on hangers and a cabinet with the radios in it. Another of her keys unlocked the latter. She passed me one of the radios and I selected the biggest uniform I could find.

'Thanks heaps.'

'No problem. I'm heading home. Had enough of this place for one day.' We retired into separate cubicles and I didn't come out until I heard her leave.

I tied my hair up, then bundled my clothes into a ball and stuffed them in a corner out near the vacs so I could retrieve them again quickly. A few seconds' fumbling with the radio got it switched on but all I could hear was the odd bit of static.

As I stepped back out into the corridor, the delivery entry guy and a security guard hurried past me without a hint of recognition. That left me free to peer in open doors. Those with name plates I left alone, though one caused me to stop and stare. Hristos Giannoukakis, Operations Manager. Now that couldn't be a coincidence. I swallowed. It had to be Andreas's brother.

A staff member entered the corridor from the other end, forcing me to move on. This time I didn't stop until I found the staff-only lift. I stood there for a few moments, wondering how the hell I'd get it to open. Then it pinged and a guy pushing a room-service cart exited.

'What floor is this special meeting on?' I asked.

He glanced over his shoulder at me. 'Are you new?'

'Yeah, first day. Been sent to vac—'

Both our radios blared into life before I could finish my sentence. 'All male staff please report immediately to the delivery bay. Immediately.'

'What's that about?' he said to me.

'Something to do with the meeting. There're security guys crawling all over the place.'

He rolled his eyes. 'That must be what's happening in the Elizabeth Room. No one would say what it was about, except that they were in real estate or something. Had to take a trolley of mugs up there for their coffee—

they didn't want cups. Better go. Nice to meet you.'

'Back atcha,' I said jumping into the lift.

The door shut and I scanned the buttons. There were no names listed next to the floor numbers, so I took a guess. Function rooms were usually either on the first floor or the top floor.

When I stepped out on the first, there was a brass sign opposite me. The Elizabeth Room was on the left, and inside it I could see a lot of activity. I slipped in among the staff who were spreading white linen tablecloths on side tables and arranging glasses and jugs of water on the large boardroom table that filled the centre of the room.

At one end, a podium stood in front of a white projection screen. At the other, was a small door that I guessed led to the AV area that serviced this room and maybe the one behind it. I switched on my vac and cleaned my way in that direction.

When I was just about at the door, a woman in a suit and high heels with a shiny staff badge that said Senior Housekeeper—Kristine Akros accidentally knocked a glass off a table and signalled for me to come and clean it up.

As I hurried to get it done, all the staff began to leave until only the woman and I were left.

'Hurry up,' she said. 'They'll be here soon.'

She tottered over to the main door to greet them. As she swung the door open I saw Andreas Giannoukakis standing outside waiting to come in.

I bolted around the table and slipped into a small adjoining room filled with stacked chairs and desks, some outdated projector equipment and a handful of computer screens. Through the two-way mirror, I could see the housekeeper looking around for me. She made a beeline for the room I was in.

I ditched the vac in a cupboard and folded myself under a desk, curling up as small as I could. A moment later the air conditioning sucked in as she opened the door and paused. I held my breath until she shut it again. Then I heard the lock click.

Shit.

I waited a little before I crawled out. Not daring to try the door handle yet, I sat on the desk and watched through the mirror. The room was filling up slowly and the housekeeper was back at the door greeting newcomers. A couple of wait staff arrived and started offering pastries around.

My two-way radio crackled and I nearly jumped out of my shoes. I fumbled to turn it off quickly and kept studying the people in the room.

Andreas was looking uncomfortable as hell, tugging at his tie and collar and licking his lips. More people entered and two of them sent a tingle right through me: Johnny Viaspa and Ash Machete. In their uniforms of tight black chinos, white shirts and polished Italian shoes they looked like high-end waiters. If they were part of this development deal, then my money was on them, not Andreas, having sent the arsonist to Stuart's house.

The room was almost full now, about twelve guys seated around the table, leaving spaces between themselves and their fellow investors.

The door opened one last time and the housekeeper exited, taking the wait staff with her. Through the open door, I caught a glimpse of security guys outside. But it was the four men who entered late then closed the door after themselves who caught my attention. At least, one of them did.

Bon Ames.

My heart pounded so hard it shot pins and needles through my fingers and toes. What the hell was he doing here? The guys he accompanied were obviously bikers as well, more formally dressed than him, but each wearing something connecting them with their gang. One of them had the Hells Angels insignia on the back of his leather dress jacket and another had Rebels embroidered in white and black on his long-sleeved shirt. No wonder there'd been so much private muscle outside.

Everyone at the table shook hands, then a small, nervous-looking man in a suit got up from the table and dimmed the lights. I picked him straight away for a public servant.

He began talking but the storage room was soundproofed and I couldn't hear what he was saying. He activated a slideshow from his laptop, which was set up on the podium at the front of the room.

From this distance, the graphs he showed looked very simple but I couldn't tell what they were representing. Then he flicked onto a series of slides that showed a 3D model similar to the one I'd seen in Giannoukakis's office, except bigger. Looked like it wasn't just Stuart's little street they were planning to bulldoze.

At the end of the slideshow he picked up a red marker from the table and wrote a date on the board, which he then circled. Next to that he wrote a dollar figure that I had to read several times to make sure I'd got it right.

That much?

Even more troubling was the date, which was only two days away. Monday.

Ten minutes later, the presentation was over, the lights went back on and the public servant left. The rest of the men at the table took a vote over something and then the meeting seemed to take on an informal tone which, from my perch in the storage room, seemed increasingly tense. Their auras buffeted each other in a mess of sulphur-streaked colours. I'd never seen so much harmful energy in one place.

Viaspa and Machete had shifted their chairs closer together, the bikers hunkered in another cluster, while Andreas—who was sweating like a marathon runner— sat with a guy who had to be his brother. The rest, who were down the opposite end but facing me directly, were unfamiliar. The four men were dressed casually, and one of them had red marks on his face like he'd been hit with a …

Duck beak! He was one of the thugs who'd attacked me. I studied the other three with him. The style of their clothes and shoes weren't local. They were all American, I guessed, except Mr Peking Barbeque Duck.

One of the Americans got up and pounded the table a few times. I tried lip-reading and caught the odd phrase: Our money… Who are they… Bring them to us… If we do business again…

The speaker left the table and prowled around the room, coming to rest just in front of the two-way mirror—facing me, his back to the room.

I noticed two things almost simultaneously: he had a tattoo with what looked like the initials KA on his hand, and he was disguising the fact he was pressing numbers on his mobile phone.

Before I could process what I'd seen, the three security guys from outside the door burst into the room with pistols drawn.

Shit! My instinct was to duck but I settled for drawing my knees up under me, ready to leap in any direction off the table. I doubted the two-way mirror was bulletproof.

The guys put their guns to Ash Machete's and Johnny Viaspa's heads. Part of me freaked at seeing such a bald, unvarnished threat. Part of me hoped they'd pull the triggers.

Andreas turned pale enough to faint and I didn't blame him one little bit. Dots were bouncing around before my eyes too. Bon, on the other hand, seemed faintly entertained, like he was enjoying the sight of Viaspa feeling the heat.

Mr Tattoo turned away from the mirror and walked over to the table. He was cementing his position of power now, jabbing his finger at Machete and Viaspa, jutting out his jaw and making a point.

With a gun close to his head, Viaspa's normally pus-yellow aura had diluted to something almost colourless. Ash Machete, though, never even altered his rate of breathing and his aura stayed rock solid. The guy had nerve.

With a final gesture at the whiteboard, Mr Tattoo turned and left the room. His friends, including the guy I had duck-attacked, followed quickly.

As soon as they'd gone, Ash Machete leaped up and began speaking in short, emphatic sentences, punching the air in front of him with his fist.

When he'd finished, Bon and the other bikers had some curt words to say as well. I couldn't work out who they were talking about, but by all the nodding, they seemed to reach an agreement of sorts.

Andreas was the next to leave, his aura bled almost white and spinning crazily with agitation. I imagined him running into the first toilet he could find and heaving into it. Something told me the promoter was in over his head.

Conversation went on between the final seven for

what seemed like hours. So long that I had to wiggle blood into my toes and shift position a few times to stop my legs cramping. From time to time they became agitated and Machete once knocked over a jug in a fit of anger. The water pooled on the table and began to drip onto the floor. No one made any attempt to clean it up.

By the time Bon Ames and the others finally left, I was contemplating the fact that my bladder might burst.

The final two waited in silence until they were sure the others had gone, then Machete took hold of Viaspa by the shirt and pulled him close, enunciating his words so clearly that this time I had no trouble lip-reading them.

Kill him tonight.

Chapter 20

Kill who? It had to be Stuart.

I sat still for ages after the pair left the room, worrying over what I'd seen and too scared to move in case they came back.

Shit! was the only thing that came to mind for a long while.

From what I could tell, a bunch of different organised crime groups (except, perhaps, for Andreas, who was acting as some kind of frontman) were looking to develop a big chunk of real estate in Fortitude Valley. They'd paid off a minister—in advance—and things were ready to go forward, except there was a problem between the Americans and Machete/Viaspa. Perhaps the date was when the money was due.

It was nothing new for organised crime syndicates to invest in real estate—that was often how they legitimised their illegal earnings—but why would an American west coast gang have a finger in this particular pie? Seemed ridiculous and unlikely. According to what I'd read, their rivalries were all about race, territory and local drug boundaries. Why would they be involved in a venture thousands of miles from home? Unless they already had some kind of network here that they needed to support legitimately…

I had to make some urgent calls but my phone was tucked in my jeans pocket in the cleaners' room. Which meant… I really had to get out of here.

The door handle wouldn't budge, so I got out the radio and turned it on. 'Can someone help me? I don't know where I am,' I said in a lost, frail voice. It wasn't such a stretch really.

'Who's this?' came the crackling reply.

'It's Jane. I'm locked in a room filled with projectors and stuff. I can see into another room with a big table and chairs and a picture of the Queen on the wall.'

'That's the Elizabeth Room. What are you doing in there?'

'I don't know. But I hate small spaces! Please help me…. I can't breathe in here.' I banged the microphone end of the two-way against the desk like I was thrashing around and added an aaargggh for good measure.

Housekeeping and hotel security made it to me in record time, running past the overturned chairs to unlock the door.

I was ready for them, hyperventilating, my hair messed up and my uniform unbuttoned a bit, shoes in my hand.

Stumbling out into the light as if disorientated, I covered my face with my free hand.

'Oh thank God,' I muttered, over and over again.

The security guy poured me a glass of water while the housekeeper, Kristine, stared at me suspiciously. 'You were vacuuming in here then you disappeared. I searched for you in that room.'

'Was I?' I said, continuing the confused act. 'I don't remember.'

'What do you mean you don't remember?' she demanded.

'I'm so sorry. Oh my God... Look, this is a bit embarrassing, but I've been taking pills to help me with insomnia. I think I may have been sleepwalking.'

The security guard looked amused while the housekeeper narrowed her eyes. 'Why would you be taking sleeping pills during the day?'

I ran my hand through my dishevelled hair. 'I've had a bad few nights, just needed to sleep, but I took them a bit late.'

'When did you start here? I haven't seen you before today. No one's mentioned a new staff member.'

'I'm Mr Giannoukakis's niece, remember?' I said.

'Go easy, Kristine, she's looking pretty rough,' said the security guard.

The housekeeper ignored him, her steely gaze fixed on me. 'Mr Giannoukakis or not, there was a private meeting in here. Did you hear anything?'

I shook my head. 'I passed out under the table. Maybe that's why you didn't see me. I don't remember anything except waking up a few minutes ago on the floor. I'm staying at a house in Ascot while I find somewhere to live.'

'This hotel's in Ascot,' said the guard.

'I must have sleepwalked here,' I said, looking down at what I was wearing. 'But where are my clothes?'

'Niece or not, I'm taking you to see Hristos,' said the housekeeper. 'This won't do at all.'

'No one has to know.' I gave the guard a pleading look and he went to bat for me.

'Come on, Krissie,' he said. 'She hasn't done anything wrong.'

Kristine didn't look convinced. She took the two-way radio from me. 'This way.'

The three of us marched out to the lift. As we got in, a couple of staff got out and headed to the Elizabeth Room to clean up. Fortunately, none of them was the guy I'd seen earlier.

Once we reached the staffroom, it didn't take long for me to accidentally stumble over my clothes. I took them to the change cubicle while Kristine and the guard moved outside to have a whispered argument.

I knew I had to get out of there quickly but I called Stuart while I was wriggling into my jeans.

'Tara? Where have you been? I've been trying to ring you.'

'Got caught up,' I said. 'Listen, be extra careful

tonight. I think Viaspa might be coming after you. I'll meet you at Paolo's soon.'

'I feel so much better for talking to you,' he said in a strange voice, which suggested people were listening. I knew he was being sarcastic; I hoped they didn't.

I hung up.

'Jane,' called the guard. 'You ready?'

'Just coming,' I sang out.

They led me back into the corridor and Kristine informed me again that we were going to see Hristos to clear this up.

'Fine,' I said. 'But can I just use the ladies first? I'm busting.'

We turned into a side corridor and Kristine pointed to the staff toilets. 'Please don't take too long,' she said. 'I'm very busy.'

'I won't,' I said, going in the door, giving the toilet a longing sideways glance (I really did need to go badly), searching around for a window or ceiling hatch. Even better, I discovered a second entrance which led me into the kitchen, where I apologised for taking a wrong turn and asked how to get back to the lobby.

A young guy in a stained apron showed me back out to the staff lift, and keyed it open for me. I hit the button to go up to the ground floor and walked straight out through the lobby as though I was a guest.

As soon as I'd rounded the corner off Kingsford Smith Drive, I bolted down past the hotel delivery bay to the café. I quickly used their loo then hurried to the end of the street where I turned right and entered a small park. There I called a cab and gave them directions to the nearest cross street. It was unlikely Kristine and the guard would bother looking for me outside the hotel. I'd gone and that would be it, most likely. It wasn't like I'd stolen anything.

I found a swing to sit on and watched some toddlers hitting each other with plastic buckets in the sandpit. Their mothers gave me curious looks and I smiled reassuringly to let them know that I wasn't a kid-snatcher. Even so, they collected their kids and set off up the road.

I took a very deep breath and made a call I hoped I wasn't going to regret.

'Senior Constable Bligh speaking,' said a voice.

'Fiona, it's Tara Sharp. Can you spare a minute or two?'

'Seeing as you're not one for social calls... What's up?'

A minute or two turned into fifteen as I gave her an abridged version of what I'd stumbled across: the planned development on a heritage site, the meeting today and the kill order I'd witnessed. I left out other bits that might incriminate me or Wal or Stuart, like their history with Viaspa and how I'd got the information on the site development.

She was very quiet while I spoke.

'You still there?' I asked.

'What do you want from me?'

'Look, I know this is way off your turf, but do you have a friend you could ask if it's possible an American gang might be involved?'

'No. You should go to the federal police.'

'Of course,' I said. 'I plan to. As soon as I hang up. But that'll take time and long explanations. I'm worried someone is in danger tonight.'

'I can't disclose police business to you,' she said sharply.

'I'm not asking you to. But … hypothetically … do you know someone you could ask?'

'NO! But while I have you on the line, has Wallace Grominsky been in contact with you?'

'No. Why?'

'His, er, friend—your aunt—has filed a missing person report and we know you have ties with him. In fact, we'd like to interview you when you return. When will you be back?'

'Tomorrow. If you can help me out here, Senior Constable, I'll make sure you're my first stop.'

'Are you attempting to bargain with me, Sharp?'

'I'd call it assisting the police.'

She made an irritated noise and then sighed. 'Alright.'

'You'll get back to me soon?'

'As soon as I can.'

'Today.'

'Yes, today. And Sharp…'

'Constable?'

'Senior Constable. Next time you have a problem like this…'

'Yes?'

'Call someone else.'

'You don't really mean that,' I said.

'I do.'

'Bye, Fiona.'

'I wish.'

She sounded pissed but I knew enough about Fiona Bligh to guess that her curiosity was piqued. Bligh was as straight as they come but she was also ambitious. I admired that. Her partner, Bill Barnes, was far less hardline and far less interested in anything beyond his next meal and his kids' next footy match. He was a good foil for Bligh when she got a bit too officious.

The taxi beeped its horn and I hurried over.

'Brunswick Street Mall in the Valley, please,' I told the cabbie.

By the time I reached the Valley it was dark. Two hours until the gig started and I hadn't eaten or drunk anything since this morning. I hunkered down in a corner of Ric's Bar and ordered a toastie, water and coffee. The table rocked when I rested my elbows on it, so I leaned back in my chair. The clarity I'd felt after Inigo's cleansing had faded and my mind was heavy with fatigue and fear.

Who had Machete ordered the kill on? It had to be Stuart. He was the one standing in the way of the development by refusing to sell. If that was the case, then maybe Machete and Viaspa weren't chasing Stuart and Wal over the drug thing after all.

On impulse, I rang Nick Tozzi, just to hear his voice. When he answered, I knew right away he was drunk.

'Starting early,' I said lightly.

'Tara?'

'The one and only.'

'When are you coming home?' he said.

'Tomorrow. I'm on an early flight.'

'I'll meet you at the airport. There's something I need to tell you.'

I thought about my promise to Fiona Bligh. 'No, don't do that. Tonight is going to be a long one and the flight takes forever. I'll call you as soon as I've caught up on some sleep. What's so important anyway?'

'Face to face is best,' he said heavily.

'Alright. Is everything okay? No one died?'

'No one died,' he affirmed. 'Not really.'

'Not really?'

'No.' He wasn't slurring but his voice was thick and slow and delicious. I imagined his tawny aura flowing like honey around his tall, broad body and a sigh escaped my lips.

'What about you?' he asked. 'How's the job going?'

'Messy,' I said.

He laughed. 'That's my girl.'

I didn't know what to say to that. He sounded different—drunk, sure—but different. 'Well, I'd better be going.'

'Was there something you wanted?' he said softly.

'Nothing really … just saying hello.'

There was a long pause and neither of us spoke.

Then the waiter slapped my bill down on the table, sending it rocking on its wonky leg.

'I'll see you soon then,' I said, the spell broken.

'Soon,' he echoed.

It sounded like a promise.

Rather than giving me the comfort I'd been looking for, the call made me more unsettled. Why was Tozzi being so … nice?

Focus. Hoshi's voice echoed through me. I couldn't let Nick distract me.

I paid the bill and walked back down the mall. Saturday night meant the crowds were bigger than usual and I eased my way through them, trying to think calmly.

Surely Viaspa couldn't be planning something during the show—it was too public. It would most likely be afterwards, on the way back to the hotel.

I couldn't count on Bon Ames now, either. In fact, I was guessing he'd probably taken the job to get close to Stuart. He must have been stunned when I rang and asked him to help out. My own ignorance had put Stuart in more danger, not less. Crap.

I reached for my phone to ring Ed and tell him not to come tonight. The last thing I needed was him caught in any crossfire—figurative or literal.

Stop being dramatic! I berated myself silently. There will be no shootout! This is Australia!

But what about a shooting drive-by? They happened just recently on the Gold Coast.

Crap!

As I took one step towards the police booth, a hand grabbed my arm and swung me around. It was Ed, smiling and handsome.

'Hey,' I said.

'Hey, you.' He leaned into me and gave me a wet, warm kiss.

I wanted to grab his hand, run off to a hotel somewhere and not come out for a month. By then this thing would all be done and dusted—one way or another.

'You going in there?' he asked when I drew back.

I looked around at the police booth. The cop behind the counter was scowling at us. He probably had other places he'd rather be on a Saturday night, like home with his girlfriend or wife. I suddenly realised how I'd sound going in there and telling him that I thought my music promoter client was about to be murdered by interstate criminals.

'No,' I said. 'Just looking around before the gig starts. It's been a long day, I needed to wind down.'

Ed slung his arm over my shoulder and we walked towards Little Paolo's.

I stopped a little away from the door. There was already a queue outside the club, curling back down into Ann Street, and I didn't want anyone overhearing me. 'Ed, if I asked you not to come tonight, would you be offended?'

He looked at me. 'Explain.'

'It's just that I think some stuff might be going down and I don't want you caught in it.'

'What stuff?'

I stared at him unhappily. 'You know I can't say.'

'Is that why you were standing in front of the police kiosk?' he asked. 'Tara, you never go to the police. Is it that bad?'

I bit my lip. 'Please...'

He took a deep breath. 'Under no circumstances am I leaving you here alone if "stuff" is going on.'

I should have protested more or, better still, told him that I'd changed my mind about us and had another date for the night. But the truth was I didn't have the courage to do either. I needed him there.

'Well, at least promise me that if anything does happen, you'll stay out of it.'

'As long as you're safe, it's a deal.'

Chapter 21

I showed the doorman my Reverb Promotions badge and told him Ed was with me. Ben Bower, the book guy, popped into my head, so I gave his name plus one as well.

The doorman grunted about too many freebies but put Ben's name on the list on his iPad. He let us in and shut the door quickly behind us.

We walked up the stairs and into the club. The sliding doors were pulled back leaving a bare dance floor that could fit upward of five hundred people. Little Paolo was over at the bar talking to the bar staff and I waved at him and Brendan. Brendan waved back.

'I'm going to do a sweep of the room,' I told Ed, feeling restless. 'Introduce yourself to the guy who just waved at me. His name is Brendan and he's cool. I'll catch you there in a bit.'

'You don't want company?'

I smiled at him and pushed him towards the bar. 'Not for this.'

I was over by the stage scoping out the DJ—Slim didn't have a backing band on his tour, just a guy who ran the music and cued the sound effects—when my phone rang. It was Stuart.

'We're here,' he said. 'Coming up the back stairs.'

'There are back stairs? Why didn't I know this?'

'Paolo keeps it quiet. You have to enter through another building. They're near his office.'

I glanced over at the bar. Paolo was on the move in that direction, so I gave Ed a reassuring wave and fell in behind the club boss.

He grunted, 'Evening, lesbo' at me as I caught up with him. I scowled.

We walked past his office and went through a narrow open door to the left. It was nothing more than a small corridor with another door at the end. It had been locked when Bon and I were here before and I'd assumed it just led into another room, not a tiny passage and a back door. I wondered why Paolo hadn't offered us entry that way for the media visit.

Paolo reached into his baggy duds without speaking a word to me and brought out a fistful of keys. He chose one, keyed some numbers into the burglar alarm pad winking on the doorjamb, and stuck the key in the lock.

Stuart, Juanita, Bon, Slim and an enormous dude I'd never seen before piled in, forcing me to back up into the main corridor.

'Hey, baby girl,' said Slim, knuckle-fiving me.

'Looking good, man,' I replied.

And he was. Favouring black tonight, except for a white fedora and some gold bling, he looked so like the real deal I was semi turned on.

'Sledge, would you care to follow me?' said Little Paolo.

'Hey, big guy,' said Slim and followed Paolo through to the performer dressing room. The rest of us tramped after them.

Juanita and Stuart both gave me strained smiles and nods which I returned. Juanita was doing rock chic with jeans, a choker, leather jacket and wedge heels that brought her up to my eye level. Stuart was doing this morning's crumpled clothes.

'Good you could make it,' said Bon sarcastically as he shouldered past me. 'This is Dragstrip. I got some boys on the front door as well.'

'Hi, I'm Tara,' I said, holding out my hand to the behemoth trailing Bon.

Dragstrip gave me an unnervingly gappy grin, and returned my handshake. His hand pulverised mine.

He positioned himself outside Slim's dressing room while Bon walked me out into the bar. Punters had been let in and the bar staff were already run off their feet. I couldn't see Ed, but just knowing he was here somewhere made me feel better.

The DJ was working the room up with some rap and I recognised Bliss n Eso and Drapht numbers. The audience looked like they were going to be surprisingly diverse; some older, straighter types among the caps, hoodies and baggies. Slim had been around for enough years that some of his fans had grown up.

'What's goin' on?' said Bon.

It was exactly the question I felt like asking him. 'Not much. Haven't seen Dickle and her lot yet.'

I sure spoke too soon on that one. The obsessed fan entered a moment later, surrounded by her band of believers. We locked eyes across the room and her lip curled.

Bon saw the exchange and smiled.

Suddenly, I couldn't stand being next to him. 'I'm going up on the side of the stage where I can see the room properly.'

I left him and scooted past the club security near the stage, climbed the stairs and settled into a position alongside the speakers and behind the DJ. From there, I could see all parts of the room; more importantly, it looked like a good place from which to keep an eye on Slim and Stuart.

I sent the latter a text and told him to lock himself in Slim's dressing room for the duration.

Can't do that, he replied. Will be on the floor with the punters.

Crap.

An expectant vibe filled the club as more and more people arrived. There was no seating here, standing room only capped at around five hundred people, though I expected Paolo wasn't one to worry too much about fire and safety regulations.

Looking for people I knew became harder and harder. The lights dimmed and faces blurred. I texted Ed and told him to stay by the bar, that I'd come and find him later.

Little Paolo was up on the stage now and the DJ had wound down the latest Pitbull song so that it was a murmur in the background. Paolo waited there—experienced at milking the crowd, knowing how to build their anticipation. I took a few breaths to calm myself and let my eyes lose focus. An echo of Inigo's clarity came to me as I relaxed. It helped me examine the aura blur in the room. Mostly it was the usual energy you'd expect. But with this many people, it was intermingled with slivers and flashes of all kinds of colours. My head began to hurt and I suddenly grew incredibly tired. I needed coffee—or…

Reaching into my bag, I pulled out the small flask of 'special' tea Inigo had given me that morning. Without hesitation, I drank it down, grimacing at the vinegary flavour.

Within seconds, a cold wind was blowing through my mind and my senses sharpened. The crowd's aura was a mass of red, like a particularly bloody sunrise. I concentrated on searching out dark spots or any virulent yellow.

There were a few areas marring the general vibe: one

to the right of the stage, another close to the front, and one to the left, halfway in. I decided to go right first, as it was closer to where Slim would be … was.

Just as I decided to move, Slim came by me, threading his way past the speakers at the back of the stage to make an understated entry.

We exchanged glances. He looked terrified and excited so I gave him a confident grin and a flexed bicep. He nodded to me and took his place on the stage next to Paolo.

The crowd went nuts at the sight of him and the line of club bouncers in front of the stage endured the first push of the night as they surged forward.

In that moment, I totally understood all Slim's fears— so much adulation and desire that was not really about him but about what, or who, they thought he was.

I climbed down from the side of the stage and made my way to the bouncers. They let me walk behind them after I flashed my pass. Rap audiences generally didn't do mosh pits but this was Australia, anything could happen. The young guys at the front were already jumping up and down in unison, arms linked.

Paolo's intro was over, the music started and Slim was making eyes at his fans. I climbed under the barricade and pushed into the crowd.

Sweat, heat and energy hit me. I clung to the sight of the black spot against the crowd's aura brilliance. Moving in the wrong direction against them was tough, but my gnawing anxiety drove me forward. Stopping a few people short of the dark shadow, I tried to get a glimpse of who it was.

Slim started his first song and the audience raised their hands in homage. I had to push closer to my target than I wanted in order to see. Ash Machete and Johnny Viaspa stood there, cocooned by a bunch of their henchmen. Viaspa spotted me and started talking quickly in Machete's ear.

People around us began to jump on the spot and I backed away. Immediately punters took my spot. I changed direction and banged straight into a small guy, knocking him over. Automatically, I stopped to help him up. Familiar eyes blinked at me from under a rapper's cap.

'Harvey?'

'Tara?'

'Are you watching Johnny Viaspa?' I asked.

He gave me a blank stare and we both staggered as the crowd pushed forward again. 'Who?'

I glanced over my shoulder, expecting one of Viaspa's bodyguards to grab me at any moment. 'Listen, don't bullshit me,' I hissed in his ear. 'I know you're working for the feds and that you're watching these guys. I think someone's going after my client, Stuart Cooper, Sledge's promoter, tonight.'

The expression in his eyes went from blank to focused in an instant. 'What makes you think that?'

'I was at the hotel today where I saw them meeting.'

'Impossible,' he said.

I glanced over my shoulder again and saw one of the thugs pushing through the crowd.

'Gotta go!' I shoved Harvey in front of the guy and dived forward again. My shoving had a ripple effect and within seconds a fight had broken out. I kept moving until I reached the middle of the room.

When a hand tapped my shoulder, I turned around swinging. Luckily, the person was so small that my fist kissed air. 'Inigo? Where's Stuart?'

'Come with me.' She grabbed my hand and hauled me along until we reached a wall. From there she pointed across to the back of the room. She looked so out of place here with her flyaway hair and black clothes, her face a study in determination. 'He's near the bar. Be careful, the spirit plane is agitated.'

No shit!

As I plunged back into the crowd and pushed in that direction, Slim was in full voice. The room became a single unit of movement as he rapped out his classics 'Kill a Boy' and 'Mama Said No'.

The crowd at the bar was five deep but I was taller than most and could see Ed in a corner on a stool. Stuart was next to him.

It took me two songs to get to them. When I did, I gave Ed a quick kiss and pulled Stuart close.

'Viaspa and Machete are here.'

'Here? In the club?'

'In the club with muscle.'

He stared at me, the smile on his face fading. 'You think they're here for me?'

I nodded. 'Not during the show, though. It'll be after. We have to get you out of here before they make their move.'

'Are you sure?' he said.

'Yep. And I'm pretty sure they'll try and get me too, to save trouble later.'

'You got a plan then?'

'Working on it,' I said.

I stayed near Stuart for the rest of the show. If my mind hadn't been so overwrought and my senses strained, I would have had a blast. Slim gave his best and the crowd ate him up. His encore was his version of an old Flo Rida song that sent everyone home yelling, singing, fist-pumping, high-fiving and crumping like it was the last night on earth.

Despite everything that was going on, Stuart wore a flush of satisfaction and elation.

Ed was grinning like a madman and hugging me off and on. 'Awesome, Tara. Awesome.'

I wanted to join their celebration but my back-brain wouldn't stop fretting. When would they strike? How would they strike? How could I stop them?

After the last encore, Slim disappeared to the back of

the stage and Little Paolo took the microphone, thanking his patrons and reminding them that the bar was now closed and not to drink and drive.

He got a sarcastic cheer all of his own for that.

The DJ put on 'Closing Time' by Semisonic and after more cheers and some rowdy singing along, the crowd began to trickle out.

I told Ed that I had work to do and I'd meet him back at his hotel. He left me with a lingering kiss and a promise that I wanted him to keep.

When he'd gone, I stuck like a limpet to Stuart while he wended through the remnants of the crowd, talking to people, accepting many pats on the back and congratulations on the great gig. A music journo cornered him for a few minutes, and the guy's photographer took some happy snaps.

Finally, Stuart and I headed up the stairs near the bar which led to the VIP box. Sofia and someone who had to be her sister were sitting on a couch, nursing rum and Cokes. Behind them was a circle of men drinking beer and being thoroughly entertained by Juanita. I didn't know any of them except the guys from the Hilltop Hoods, but she had them mesmerised. If I ever needed a publicist, I'd be sure to call her.

While I hovered at the door, edgy, Stuart joined the schmoozing. From the VIP box window, I could see Viaspa and Machete still standing at the edge of the dance floor with their protection detail.

Bon Ames was also watching them from his position between the door and the stage. Dragstrip, the other biker, had probably taken Slim back to his room.

What if Viaspa and Machete waited until everyone left and then just took Stuart by force? Would Bon Ames help us? Would anyone call the police except me?

I walked over to where Stuart was talking softly to Sofia.

'We have to go,' I said. 'Now, before the club empties.'

He glanced up and saw where I was looking. 'Okay.' He kissed Sofia gently on the cheek. She gave him a nervous look and me a quick nod. I wondered how much Stuart had told her.

'Thanks for coming,' Stuart said to his VIPs. 'We're on a strict curfew here at Paolo's, but we'd like to show you how much we appreciate your support by offering you a small gift, which you can collect from the bar.'

His statement was met with approval, and the VIPs picked up their drinks and traipsed downstairs behind Juanita.

'The Pied Piper had nothing on her,' I said in Stuart's ear.

'She's the best there is,' he agreed.

By the time Stuart and I caught up, Juanita had distributed the gift bags containing Slim's new single and signed pictures of the rapper. She shooed the VIPs to the door and signalled for a bouncer to escort them out. Now only the bar staff, three other bouncers, Bon and the Viaspa–Machete crew remained.

'What transport have you arranged?' I asked Stuart.

'We've got a limo booked for Slim.' He checked his watch. 'Be here in about twenty minutes.' Now that Sofia had gone, so had Stuart's composure. Sweat beaded his forehead. I steered him over to the bar.

'You okay, man?' said Brendan, who was wiping down the drip tray.

'Water,' croaked Stuart.

'They can't do anything in here,' I whispered. 'Still too many witnesses. We have to get you back to the Stamford.'

'They'll just come at me another way—tomorrow or the next day.'

'I'm not so sure about that.'

He sipped his water and stared at me. 'I know why Grom likes working for you.'

'What?' I said, keeping one eye on Viaspa's lot.

'You'd never bail on someone, would you?' said Stuart.

To be honest, I felt like bailing right now. Other than on the plane I hadn't been this physically close to Johnny Viaspa in a while. This was the guy who'd set a hit man on me. I felt torn between wanting to gouge his eyes out and wanting to run for my life.

Bon walked by them on his way towards us. He didn't look at Viaspa and Machete and they didn't look at him. My hand tightened on the back of a bar stool and I turned my head so no one could see my lips but Stuart.

'Listen, tell Bon the limo will be out the back in twenty minutes and that you want him to go and wait there in case Dickle and co try to get access. Tell Juanita to take Slim back to the hotel with Bon and that you and I'll leave early and catch a taxi from the rank down near the police booth.'

'Will Slim be alright?'

'It's you they're after,' I said.

Stuart gulped the rest of his water and raised his hand in greeting to the approaching biker.

Bon didn't like being told to wait by the back door, I could tell. But Stuart was quietly insistent. 'Collect Slim and Dragstrip from the dressing room and we'll meet you there soon.'

'You okay with that?' Bon said to me, nodding towards the Viaspa and Machete crew.

'All good,' I said.

He gave me a strange look, part disbelief, part curiosity, then shrugged and headed across the floor to the back offices.

Stuart beckoned Juanita from the door while I turned around and went over to speak to Brendan. 'Hey, I need a favour,' I said. 'Can you take a couple of the club bouncers over to those guys there and run some interference while Stuart and I leave?' I indicated Machete and Viaspa.

Brendan had finished his cleaning and was leaning back against the drink fridge, stretching his shoulders. 'Everything ok?'

'It will be if you can help me,' I said.

'I'll see what I can do.' He grinned. 'Might be that someone saw them selling speed to the punters. We'll have a chat with them about it.'

He ducked through the gap under the bar and whistled the door bouncers over. After a quick discussion, the three of them and Brendan sauntered over to Viaspa's group. As soon as they blocked the direct eye line to us, I grabbed Stuart's arm. 'Let's go!'

We hustled to the exit and down the stairs, bursting out onto the mall.

People milled everywhere, those still talking and celebrating the gig mingling with normal Valley traffic wandering from club to club.

I shoved Stuart ahead of me, hurrying him to the end of the mall. We passed by the police booth, which was manned by four cops now. It gave me some small peace of mind as we stopped at the taxi rank. Unbelievably, though, the rank was empty.

'There'll be one here in a minute,' I assured Stuart. 'It's Saturday night.'

My phone rang. It was Fiona Bligh.

'Fiona, I'm just in the middle of some—'

'Listen!' she said, cutting across me. 'This is strictly off the record, you understand?'

'Uh?'

'The feds have got a joint operation going with our local spooks. There's been some kind of push by US organised crime—a west coast gang called the KAs—to buy up property in Australia, and they're keeping an eye on it.'

'Why would a US gang want property in Australia?'

'The taskforce think they're trying to get a foothold in here but our local players—guys like Viaspa—don't want outside interests competing with them. They've got enough trouble with the Triads and others.'

'So it is possible that I saw US bangers at the land developers meeting?'

'It's possible, yes. It's been flagged that something was going down in Brisbane this weekend. The spooks have got people on the ground.'

'Anything else?'

'There's some background to it you should know. Narcotics intercepted a big cache of drugs eighteen months ago in South Australia. The drugs were being distributed by Viaspa and Ash Machete.'

'Oh?'

'But they think the supplier was actually the KAs. These guys have had a dry run at working together before.'

'I don't get it. At the meeting the KAs had guns on Viaspa and Machete. They didn't look much like happy business partners.'

'That's where it gets grey for us too. Maybe they've fallen out over something. Happens all the time. You're talking about a high level of paranoia and mistrust here. Maybe one owes the other money from that drug haul?'

'Listen, thanks… I owe you for this. I promise I'll take this information to my grave.'

'Let's hope it doesn't come to that, Sharp. I'd advise you to get home. I've passed on your information—as an anonymous source. Let the spooks and feds take care of it. Don't complicate things.'

'On the plane in the morning.'

'Well, I'll see you straight after you land, so we can talk about Grominsky.'

'Deal.' I hung up and turned back to Stuart.

His phone beeped before he could ask me what was going on and he quickly read the text. 'Fuck.'

'What?'

'It's Juanita. She can't find Slim.'

'What do you mean she can't find him? How about Bon Ames and Dragstrip?'

Stuart called her and fired off a bunch of questions. I could hear the near-scream in her voice from where I was standing.

'Stay cool, we're coming.'

'What?' I demanded.

'She went to Slim's dressing room but he'd gone.'

'Where was Dragstrip?'

'At the back door with Bon Ames. Little Paolo had

told him Ames wanted to see him.'

'Little Paolo?'

'Yeah. According to Dragstrip, he came back to the dressing room when the gig finished. He and Slim were in there alone and then Paolo came and told Dragstrip to go see Bon Ames. But when Juanita got to the dressing room there was no one there. Do you think they've just gone to get a coffee or have a drink next door maybe?'

Something dark and terrible gripped my stomach and twisted so hard I thought I was going to be sick. KAs. Could that stand for Kings and Aces, the gang that Slim used to run with?

If I was right and Machete and Viaspa had decided they wanted to sever their business relationship with the KAs, what better way to declare war than by assassinating the KAs' greatest success?

'Tara, what is it?' Stuart demanded. 'You look awful.'

'It's not you,' I whispered.

'It's not me what?'

'It's not you who's in danger. It's Slim.'

'What do you mean?'

'Come on!'

I turned and ran up the mall as fast as the crowd would allow. The door to the club was closed and Viaspa and Machete were standing outside, still flanked by their boys.

'Tara Sharp,' called out Viaspa. 'Everything alright?'

His aura glowed its usual unpleasant luminescent

yellow around him and his smile was pure and utter evil. He knew I was on to him, I could see it in his face. His hand gesture was almost invisible but it was all his boys needed to come for me. Three of them, hands loose by their sides.

I took them by surprise, running straight at them, bowling them apart like they were oversized skittles. They catapulted into their employers as I bolted up to the door, calling to Stuart to follow me. I hammered desperately to be let in. Brendan unlocked the door and stood aside as Stuart and I pelted up the stairs.

'Lock it quickly!' I yelled at Brendan.

'What the hell...?' I heard him saying.

I didn't stop for a confab, nor did I stop to talk to Juanita, who stood outside the empty dressing room. I ran right down the corridor to Paolo's office.

It was locked, so I peeled a fire extinguisher off the wall and began smashing the door handle.

'Whoa, whoa,' shouted Brendan from behind me. 'I'll go get the keys, if you tell me what's going on.'

'No ... time,' I panted.

'Sharp!' bellowed Bon. He shouldered past Juanita, Brendan and Stuart. 'What the fuck?'

I held the extinguisher high as though I was going to take a swipe at him. 'Stuart, take the others back into the club. Now!'

They mustn't have liked the look of Bon's tensed back, because they did as I asked without protest.

As soon as they'd gone from earshot, I said, 'Paolo's taken Slim.'

'How do you know that?'

'He's working for Viaspa and they want to piss the KAs off.' I got up in Bon's face. 'Listen, I know why you're really here in Brisbane, and frankly I don't give a shit. But you will help me find Slim or I'll spill everything I know to the feds.'

His normal mask of disinterested calm flickered. 'What do you know?'

'I was in the hotel today, in the AV room. I heard everything that was said at the meeting. I've recorded it and it's ready to go straight to the cops if anything happens to me.' I'd tried this bluff once before with Viaspa and it had worked. It would always work because the other party had no way of knowing if it was truth or lie.

'You'd go to the cops about what?' he hissed.

'About the minister you're paying off so your land development can go ahead...I'm guessing you guys want the KAs on board for this little venture, but I'm telling you, if Viaspa kills Slim, the gloves are off.'

He drew in a breath. 'You're messing with trouble, Sharp. You know that?'

I put on my most stubborn face. 'And you're messing with my clients. Like I said, I don't care about your plans to launder drug money and get rich, but you will not do it at the expense of my client.'

He stared at me for a long, awful moment and I saw my life hanging in the balance as he weighed the pros and cons.

Then he wrenched the extinguisher from my hands and lifted it into the air. I covered my head as he brought it down. It swished past my ear and broke the handle clean off the door.

Shit. I pushed it open and ran in, frantically searching for any clue to tell me where Paolo had taken Slim.

I quickly noticed an overpowering smell of rubber and petrol. I pulled out my phone and called Inigo.

'Tara?'

'I can smell rubber and petrol.'

'That is to be expected,' she said serenely. 'Your reading told me that.'

'I know, but what does it mean? Is it real?'

'What you can smell is your psychic senses attuning to your destiny. You need to work this out. I can do no more at this point.' She hung up.

My instinct was to throw my phone against the wall. Instead I looked at Bon. 'If I said rubber and petrol to you what would you think of around here?'

He looked at me as if I was crazy. I brushed past him and ran down the corridor onto the dance floor where Brendan, Juanita and Stuart had gathered.

'Guys, if I said rubber and petrol to you, meaning a place close to here, what would you think of?'

They stared blankly for an instant then started flinging

ideas at me.

'Wickham Street traffic lights,' said Stuart. 'Cars are always dragging each other off there.'

'The servo down the other end of Brunswick Street,' said Juanita. 'There's a tyre shop next door.'

'McWhirters,' said Brendan.

I stared at him. 'I know that name. What is it?'

'It's a car park in the next street. It always stinks of burned rubber and petrol fumes.'

'Does Paolo park there?' I asked.

'Sometimes,' he said.

'Take me there quickly.'

'But I've got to finish up,' Brendan protested.

'Now!' I pleaded. 'For Slim. Please!'

He glanced around. 'Okay. The back door is quicker.'

'Fine.' That meant we didn't have to go past Viaspa again.

Stuart tried to convince Juanita to go home but she was having none of it, so the five of us hurried into the alley. One direction led to a wall with a warehouse-like door.

Brendan explained, 'We keep that door locked so people can't hang around outside the back door. It exits onto Wickham.'

'This way' turned out to be a crooked lane wide enough to fit one car.

'We came along here in the taxi,' said Juanita.

Brendan led as we hurried along until we hit the traffic

on Wickham, where we turned right, then right again towards McWhirters. The converted nightclub next door had a queue outside and the bouncers were busy rubber-stamping arms for pass-outs.

The clock on the club turret said it was after midnight as we rounded into the car park building. Only a few cars were left on the lower level.

'Let's split the floors,' I said. 'Bon and I'll take the top floor. Stuart and Juanita take the first floor, Brendan take the ground floor and basement. Keep your phones handy.'

'I don't have your number,' said Brendan.

I quickly gave it to him and then we split up.

Bon stared at me as the lift took us up. 'Were you really there today?'

I nodded, feeling wary, wishing I'd brought some pepper spray to Brisbane. The only thing I could think of in my handbag that might be good as a weapon was Inigo's thermos flask.

'You saw something you shouldn't have, Tara. Not gonna lie to you.'

I shrugged. 'Not the first time.'

He bared his teeth but I bolded him out.

'Like I said, Bon, I don't really care what you and yours are planning as long as you leave me and my clients out of it. I'm not going screaming to the cops unless I have to. It's not my style.'

'What is your style, Sharp?'

I gave it some fake consideration, hoping the distraction of the conversation would last until we got out of the lift. I reckoned I could outrun him, but at close quarters, I was a goner. 'Simple. I do the right thing by the people who hire me.'

His scowl faded a little. 'I'll have to remember that.'

The door pinged and I was out of there quicker than a lightning strike. It only took a few minutes to determine that Slim and Paolo weren't on that floor. Only a half dozen cars were parked over on the Ann Street side; other than that, the level was deserted.

Brendan rang just then. 'Nothing here except a couple making out in their car.'

'Listen, thanks. Go home or back to the club if you have to. Really appreciate your help.'

'Nah. If Slim's in trouble, I might hang around. He's a good guy.'

'Fine. Can you watch the exit down there?'

'Sure.'

He hung up and Juanita rang. 'Nothing,' she said.

'Can you go down and wait with Brendan?' I asked. 'We're still looking.'

'Be careful, Tara.'

'Always.'

'We're still looking at what?' said Bon as I slipped my phone back in my pocket.

'There.' I pointed to a gate that led to a narrow overpass leading into the building on the other side of the street. The gate was chained up. 'What's that?'

'Dunno,' said Bon. 'Not my city.'

I called Stuart and asked him.

'McWhirters used to be a department store that spread over two blocks. It's joined by that overpass.'

'What's on the other side?'

'Yuppie apartments.'

'Thanks.'

I walked over to the gate and rattled the chain. The padlock fell open. It had been left open either deliberately or by accident because someone was in a hurry.

My sense of urgency escalated. 'Come on!'

I pushed past the gate, sprinted across the enclosed bridge and into the darkened landing on the other side.

The only light was the exit sign over the emergency stairs. It was enough to illuminate Paolo and Slim; Slim was bent back over the railing, about to fall or be dropped. He was gagged and his arms were tied. His moans of terror were like a knife in my gut.

'Stop!' I shouted.

Bon pulled up alongside me, sucking in noisy breaths. 'Let—him—go—arsehole!'

But Paolo was well past backing down. 'Piss off or I'll do you next.'

It was then I saw the pistol in his free hand.

'You really think the cops won't know you've committed murder?' I asked. 'They'll be all over you.'

'He's not gonna talk. Which only leaves you.'

'Bon?' I said.

'He's right about that, Sharp. I don't talk to cops.'

'But this is murder. You can't keep that a secret.'

Bon didn't reply.

'This is Ash Machete's call, isn't it? He and Viaspa want to send a message to the KAs to get out of town?'

'You know a lot for a lesbo,' said Paolo. He was breathing so heavily it was like he'd sucked all the oxygen from the air. 'Guess it'll be two for the price of one.'

Out of the corner of my eye, I spied a shadow— creeping up the stairs and instinctively I knew I had to keep Paolo looking my way. 'Ames won't let you do this. His people want the property deal to go ahead. They want the KAs here.' I didn't know that for a fact, but I was guessing the bikers knew Viaspa and Machete might be stacking the deck in their favour. Maybe that's why Ames had agreed to be bodyguard. Keep an eye on Stuart as well.

'You think I'm gonna talk our business with you, bitch? Or that biker fuck?'

What was with everyone calling me 'bitch'? And Bon Ames didn't much like being called a 'biker fuck', either. He growled like a bloody great bear.

'She's right, you fat bastard,' said the biker. 'Don't wreck our deal.'

'You want those Yankee scum here on our turf?' said Paolo incredulously.

'They got connections we need. Machete knows it.

He's trying to choke them out so we all have to use his supplier.'

Little Paolo levelled the pistol at us and then lifted Slim with his other hand, ready to drop him down three flights. 'Who knew a dumb cheater could be so smart? Too fucking late. This prick's gonna have a nasty accident. And lesbo's gonna die trying to save him.'

The shadow that had been creeping up the stairs suddenly hurled forward, taking out Paolo's gun arm. I moved a second later, diving for Slim.

Paolo let go of the rapper to fight off his attacker but I already had hold of Slim by his shirt.

He teetered against the railing and began to slip over.

'Bon!' I gasped. 'Help!'

The biker shot out one huge paw and wrapped it around Slim's wrist. Together we hauled him back from the brink.

The shadow, though a third the size of Little Paolo, went to work and in seconds had the club owner face-down, tying his hands with something.

I got to my feet and found the light switch in the stairwell.

'Wal!' I'd never been so glad to see someone in my life. He was looking rough and unshaved, his face half-hidden by a beanie.

'Grom?' said Bon.

My security chief gave us both a wink. 'Call the cops, Tara. See you on the flip flop.'

With that he ran down the stairs and disappeared.

A noise at my feet grabbed my attention. Slim was writhing against my leg. I bent down and untied the gag and then his hands. He was shaking so hard I thought he might puke, so I put my arm around him.

With the other hand, I rang Stuart. 'Get the police. We're on the landing of the building across the road. You can access it through the overpass on level three.'

'Slim?' he asked.

I looked at the tears streaming down the rapper's face and the way he was shaking. 'He's … safe.'

Chapter 22

By the time the police had taken statements and told Bon and me that we were free to go it was nearly 4 AM. Stuart and Juanita had taken Slim back to the hotel and called a doctor in to give him a sedative.

'You knew this might happen, didn't you?' I said to Bon.

'It fell to me to protect our interests. Once Machete set a tail on me, we figured they were planning something.' He wasn't going to say more than that and I knew it. 'And a word to the wise, Sharp—stay out of Viaspa's way for a while.'

Hadn't I come here to do just that? 'So you don't think the police will be able to pin this on him? Paolo's good for a stretch.'

'Not a hope in hell,' he said. He walked off, talking into his phone, and I called a taxi.

I had to catch a plane in a few hours and I didn't fancy spending my last few hours in Brisbane at Inigo's, so

I called Ed.

'Tara? You alright? I waited up.'

'Sorry,' I said hoarsely. 'Can I come over?'

'Now?'

'Yes.'

He barely hesitated. 'Call me again when you arrive. I'll come down and get you.'

The cool air of Ed's hotel sent every muscle in my legs cramping and I almost collapsed in the foyer. The night receptionist gave me a strange look as I hobbled over to the lift and waited.

Ed came down quickly, wearing a thin cotton dressing gown over his boxers. He took one look at me and hooked his arm under my shoulders. We barely spoke while he got me to his room and ran me a bath.

I sank into the warmth and shivered for a while, letting the shock of seeing Slim almost thrown to his death slowly settle.

'Food's here,' Ed called out.

The bath water had started to cool so I dragged myself out and put on the hotel dressing gown he'd left for me.

'Ordered you an all-day breakfast,' he said.

The sight of scrambled eggs, bacon, croissants and a pot of tea made me want to go down on one knee to him. 'I think I want to marry you.'

He suddenly looked shy and a bit awkward.

'Joke,' I said. 'Rough night. What I mean is … thank you. It's just what I needed.'

He sat on the end of the bed and watched me wolf down the food, speaking only to suggest I slow down or I'd give myself indigestion. Naturally I didn't listen to him.

'What happened after I left?' he said as I lay back against the bed head propped up by four fat pillows.

'Paolo, the owner of the club, tried to throw Slim down a stairwell. We stopped him in time.'

'Shit.'

'Yeah. The police are all over it now.'

'You saved Slim's life.'

'Joint effort actually.'

'Can I ask what it was about?'

'Officially it will be something along the lines of Paolo and Slim getting into an argument about fees. Unofficially, it's a crime turf war. But I can't say any more. And honestly, Ed, you don't want to know.'

'If I was Wal, would you confide in me?'

I thought of my security chief appearing from the darkness like a ninja to save the day. 'Wal knows things. But he's made choices in his life a long time ago. You don't want the history he has. Believe me.'

Ed looked down at his hands and curled his fists. 'I want you though.'

My heart liquefied into treacle. 'Our timing hasn't been good.'

'I don't just mean sex, Tara. I want you. To go out with you properly—not the hit-and-miss way things have been going.'

My treacly heart almost slowed to a stop. I leaned over and put the tray out of the way then I drew my knees up. It was time he knew the truth.

'Ed, you're younger than me and you're astonishingly beautiful—inside and out. It can't work. My life is … chaos; your career is about to take off. Soon you'll meet some gorgeous model or actor or producer and you'll be off to Hollywood or the catwalks of Paris. I'm not really in the market for that sort of broken heart.'

He listened to me with a serious expression. 'I can't read the future, Tara. But I know what I want now, and that's you. You're not like anyone else. You have this … energy in you that's irresistible. Whenever I'm close to you, I just want to live. You're so much more than just beautiful, Tara.'

I didn't think anyone had ever said anything so sweet to me before. I was a little less weary.

Nick Tozzi flashed into my mind but I banished him. The only time Tozzi had made advances towards me had been when he'd wanted to have his cake and eat it. Wife and one-night stand.

'Well…' I said slowly. 'I suppose we could give it a go.'

'Exclusive?'

'No point otherwise,' I said.

He got on his hands and knees and crawled up the bed towards me. As his weight descended on me, I felt the rest of my fatigue vanish in a surge of desire.

I rolled him over on his back and sat astride him. If there was one thing I knew how to do well, it was this, and Ed was going to get my best performance.

I pulled his dressing gown open and started by putting my lips to his ridiculously toned abs. The whole world disappeared.

I was a girl on the best kind of mission.

The taxi took me via Inigo's to pick up my bag. I left her key on the kitchen table along with a posy of flowers I'd bought from the flower barrow outside Ed's hotel. Her bedroom door was shut and I didn't feel like an odd goodbye, so I left quietly and got back into the waiting cab.

I dreamed my way to the airport and most of the flight home; mushy, girlie thoughts about the last few hours with Ed and the possibilities of a future with him. After the meal, I dozed for a bit, which proved to be less pleasant— dreams of Slim screaming and Bon Ames strangling me. I woke with a jolt, scaring the gentleman next to me, and told myself proper sleep could wait until I was alone and free to have nightmares.

I drank tea and coffee for the rest of the trip home and was on my seventeenth wind by the time I picked up my luggage from the carousel and went outside to hail a taxi.

As the driver loaded my case into the boot, a figure carrying a small backpack sauntered up and got into the back seat.

'Oi!' said the driver.

'It's okay,' I said. 'He's with me.' I got in next to Wal Grominsky and leaned over to give him a peck on the cheek.

'Boss!' he said in an admonishing tone.

The taxi driver got in the front. 'Where to?'

'Euccy Grove police station, please,' I said.

Wal frowned.

'Liv reported you as a missing person. I promised Bligh I'd come in for an interview about it. Best if she sees you in the flesh.'

He sighed, nodded, put his head back on the seat and went to sleep.

Thankfully the taxi driver didn't make conversation, so I listened to the radio and thought over the Brisbane trip. Slim was safe now at least, and with all the media attention around the attempted murder, Stuart would be too hot to go near for a while without raising all sorts of flags. The problem of his house being in the way of organised crime groups' land development still remained, though. Or did it?

'Could you please turn up the radio?' I asked.

The cabbie obliged and I caught the end of the news item.

'…attempt on a Brisbane minister's life last night was foiled by a homeless man. Antonio Messo, the victim, was set upon in his own home by a criminal who tried to cut his throat.

'The homeless man, hearing screams, went in to help Queensland's Environment Minister and together they fought off the attacker. Messo has been helping federal police with an investigation into a land development deal thought to involve an area of heritage-listed properties. According to sources, Messo's wife moved out of their home last week when he came under investigation. The homeless man could not be found for comment.'

'Shit,' I said softly. I'd been saying it a lot lately.

'Homeless man, eh?' said Wal enigmatically, his eyes still closed. 'Would never have picked Harvey T. as homeless.'

I leaned back on the seat and took a deep breath. Wal and I needed to have a long talk. The details could wait until later but there were some things I had to know now.

'So why did you disappear and how the hell did you turn up like that?' I asked.

'I thought Viaspa was coming for me over some past history.'

'The Adelaide road trip?'

I got a sideways glance. 'Stu fill you in?'

'Uh-huh.'

'Yeah, well I figured there'd be a reason for it coming up now, and wondered if Stuart's problems were connected.'

'You knew all that before I went!' I admonished him.

His mouth twisted into something that might have been a sly grin, but it was hard to tell with Wal. 'Had always planned to come over and keep an eye on you. Just thought I'd do it from a distance. In case I had it wrong.'

'So you've been following me ever since I got here?'

'Pretty much. Took the next flight after you. Saw Harvey T. outside the club after that press thing you had. Knew then some big shit was going down.'

I lowered my voice. 'So he does work for ASIO?'

He shrugged. 'Or something like it. Sussed that back when we used to come to those groups of yours.'

'You never said.'

'You never asked.'

I thought about that for a bit. 'So was your road trip with Stu and the land development in Fortitude Valley connected?'

'In a way,' he said, lowering his voice as well. 'That shipment we "lost" had been supplied by the KAs. Machete and Viaspa were trying to do business with them. Things went pretty sour when it disappeared. KAs wanted their money, blah blah. Fast forward a year and a bit and now they wouldn't spit on each other in a fire. Machete didn't want them in on the land deal.'

'Whew. That's one tangled web.'

He lifted his shoulders in indifference and laid his head

back on the seat again.

That reminded me to switch my phone back on. Messages beeped in fast and furiously. There was a long text from Stuart saying Slim was surprisingly okay and that the reviews on the gig were so good he'd had two enquiries already about adding new dates to the tour. He'd see me in a few days as the Perth winery had confirmed. Thanks, Tara, from the bottom of my heart, the message finished. Slim says he wants to book you for his US tour when he goes back.

God, no!

The next was a hysterical voice message from Liv. I cut that one short and curtly told Wal to ring her. He feigned sleep, ignoring me.

The next was from Smitty, as hysterical as Liv and threatening to throw herself off the Cottesloe groyne for the sharks to eat if I didn't tell her something today. I texted her back and said I would be at her house in an hour.

The phone rang and I answered without thinking.

'Sharp?'

'Constable Bligh. I'm in the taxi on the way to Euccy Grove station as promised,' I said.

'Look, don't come in now, something's come up. I'll call you with another time.'

'Someone here you should speak to.' I shoved my phone under Wal's ear. 'Talk to the good constable.'

Several short exchanges later, he handed me back the

phone. 'Sorted. No longer a missing person.'

I told the taxi driver we wanted to change destination and he punched Liv's address into his GPS. When we arrived, Wal got out without a word and gave me a finger-roll wave.

'See you tomorrow for a full debrief,' I said, not envying him the next few hours. My aunt was gorgeous and charming but she was more ferocious than my mother when she got riled.

'Where to now?' my unimpressed taxi driver asked. With a sinking heart, I gave him Smitty's address.

Between Liv's and Smitty's I checked in with Mr Hara.

'You back, Tara?'

'Back and tired.'

'You go well?' he asked.

'Kinda. Just heading over to Smitts' place. Any change in status?'

'Not much. Not looking so good for Mrs Smitty though.'

'Okay, thanks. I'll call you tomorrow.'

'Make sure you do.'

Walking up Smitty's drive after I'd paid the taxi driver was one of the worst feelings I'd had in a long time; worse than being locked in a room next to a bunch of violent criminals, as bad as seeing Slim dangling in the air.

I dragged my feet as I tried to work out a plan. Get Henry alone, give him a piece of my fury, and then insist that he lies to Smitts was the best I could come up with. Oh, and tell him I'd have Wal chop him into little bits if he ever went near Belle Bussey again.

Henry answered the door when I knocked. 'Sharpy,' he said. 'Come on in. How was Brissie?'

My plan came undone right about then and all the frustration and fear and anger of the last week exploded out of me. I punched him fair in the mouth.

Henry was neither robust nor a fighter, nor was he expecting to be king hit by one of his best friends. He went down like a demolished house.

'How could you!' I bellowed down at his shocked face.

As I lined up for a walloping great kick Smitty ran down the corridor towards us.

'T! T! Stop!'

I stared blankly at her. 'What?'

She stepped over Henry and shoved her hand in my face. I was almost blinded by a sparkling diamond the size of a sugar plum.

'Uh?' I managed.

'It's my anniversary present. Henny just gave it to me. He got it imported especially. And guess who from? Belle Bussey. You remember her from school? Well, she has connections in the Kimberley mines. Henny didn't want to use her because he knows how I feel about her, but she's the best wholesaler around. He wanted the best for me.'

'Oh,' I said. 'Hen, are you alright?'

He was holding his jaw, which was hanging at a funny angle. 'I fink is bwoken.'

Suddenly the kids were on us.

'Tara broke Daddy's jaw,' squealed Xavier.

'I told you she'd beat Daddy in a fight,' said Jo.

'Dad will sue you for this,' said Claire gravely.

Smitty stared at me helplessly.

'Crap,' I said.

The trip to the hospital and ensuing hours were filled with much guilt and apologising and totally inappropriate fits of the giggles, the latter had by Smitty and me as Henry was wheeled off to surgery to have his jaw pinned. Then came the tears and the waiting for the news that the surgery had gone well and, finally, somewhere around dinner time, I got to go home.

I cheeped at the birds as I staggered down the driveway and they cheeped back, pleased to see me.

As soon as I got in the door, I locked the world out and flopped on my bed. It took a while for my head to stop spinning, but eventually I fixed on the few hours Ed and I had spent together, and let myself feel happy that things in my love life were at least sorting themselves out.

I was almost asleep when my phone rang. I nearly didn't answer it but then I saw it was Tozzi. Whatever he wanted to tell me must be important. I hoped his mum wasn't sick.

''Lo,' I whispered.

'Tara, are you home? Are you ok?'

'Yes. And yes. Just beat. I was going to ring you after I had a nap.'

'I know,' he said thickly. 'But I just had to hear your voice.'

I raised myself up on my elbows. 'Nick, what's wrong?'

'Nothing's wrong, and everything's right.'

'I don't understand.'

'I wanted to say this in person but I can't wait any longer. You have to know.'

'Know what?'

'Antonia and I have separated. I've left her because … because… Tara, I want you in my life.'

Crap!

Acknowledgements

A big thanks to Jud Campbell aka Sheldon D'Arc who let me bribe him with beer to talk about all things musical. To Ian Amos for all those great contacts. Thanks also to my sons Ivan, Marcus and Jules who find their mother's eclectic tastes inexplicable but love me despite them.

Australia's Marianne Delacourt delivers the laughs and action with her sassy, unorthodox PI Tara Sharp in her novel Sharp Turn.
– THE HERALD SUN

Sharp Turn is suspenseful, hilarious and absolutely impossible to put down! This book left me desperate to know what happens next. A must-read!
– AUTHOR, NANSI KUNZE

Delacourt has invented a Stephanie Plum character who is just as ballsy and loveable but this one lives in Perth and has 2 pet Galahs instead of a hamster. An easy read with multiple story layers, Sharp Turn will keep you guessing till the end, pick it up this summer if you like Janet Evanovich and Val McDermid's, Blue Genes.
– SHE SAID MAGAZINE

Sharp Edge

Also by Marianne Delacourt
Book 4 in the Tara Sharp series
Coming Soon!

Dead bodies at the beach, a complicated love life, and a conflict between the local drug cartels have Tara scrambling to stay ahead of the game.

Chapter 1

You are what you've been. I heard or read that somewhere. It popped into my head as I lay on my bed, contemplating the mess on the floor. Strewn clothes, gnarly pizza crusts and a half-eaten packet of Tim Tams were definitely where I'd been.

And what did that say about me?

It said that my life was in disarray, and I had no one to blame but myself. I mean, I'd chosen to become a psychic investigator. And because of that, I'd crossed John Viaspa, the drug lord who was set on fitting me with a pair of concrete boots. But worst of all… I'd chosen not to marry some nice well-to-do boy and condemned my mother to eternal despair.

The latter problem was my current vexation for recently two presentable and divine (and I mean divine) men had indicated that they'd like to court me. The world had turned inside out. The sky had fallen. White was black. Blue was pink.

I reached for the Tim Tams. Chocolate for breakfast clearly the only solution.

As I sucked the chocolate coating off the biscuity goodness, my phone rang. It was one of my best friends, Bok the Beautiful, aka Martin Longbok, fashion magazine publisher.

''Lo,' I glugged through my chocolate.

'Tara! Are you sucking on a Tim Tam? What's wrong?'

'Nothing.' Sheesh, the guy had superpowers!

'Tara!'

'Alright … it's just … I mean … oh everything's wrong!'

Bok took a long slow breath, as if he might be about to meditate. 'OK, I have a Skype meeting with Sydney soon. So give me the quick version.'

I rolled over on my back and noticed there was the beginning of a prettily patterned mould stain on the ceiling.

'Tar-ah!' he said impatiently.

'I broke Henry's nose.'

'You broke Henry's nose?'

'I did it because I thought he was cheating on Smitts?'

Smitts was our other best friend. The three of us were tighter than a plate of unopened oysters.

'But he wasn't?' asked Bok.

'No,' I said mournfully.

'Awkward,' said Bok. (I just knew he was biting the inside of his cheeks to stop laughing.) 'He was always one to hold a grudge too.'

'That's not all. I agreed to … you know … go out with Ed.'

'Out … like be his girlfriend? You? Thought you'd sworn off that kind of thing since the last one stole your furniture.'

'Ed was in Brisbane on a job while I was there. And we … hooked up. Like … properly hooked up.'

'The old boom chikka, eh. But that's good news? Right?'

'Well it might have been, but something else happened.'

'There's a third thing?' asked Bok.

'Tozzi's left Antonia … for me.'

'Oh my fucking cheeseburger! You mean rich, rugged, man-mountain, Tozzi?'

'You know exactly who I mean,' I said miserably. 'Bok, what the hell am I going to do? I'm never the girl who gets to choose.'

'Time to convene the tribunal.'

'But Henry won't let Smits talk to me on account—'

'—of the broken nose?'

'Yeah. That.'

Smitty aka Jane Smith was petite and perfect in every way, and married to a guy we'd known all our life. Henry'd always been pretty tolerant of our close relationship and some of my more dubious pastimes. But punching him in the nose for thinking he'd cheated on her kinda crossed a line. Smitts had texted me to say she'd had to hose him down from pressing charges.

In my defence, Smitts had wound me up a bit on the whole thing. She'd got green-eyed about a woman from their past and asked me to spy on her husband. It hadn't looked too good for Henny after we'd done some surveillance, and I kind of flipped my wig when I next saw him. I mean, she is my bestie.

'For crap's sake, doesn't he realise you were defending her honour? He should be pleased you popped him. It shows you care,' said Bok.

I perked up a bit. 'You think?'

'I do. Not. You broke his nose Tara. What were you thinking?'

'I'd do the same for you,' I said, my mood deflating quickly again.

Bok sighed in a way that told me he was about to do me a big favour. 'Let me talk to him. I'll smooth things over and set up a time with Smitts. What's good for you?'

'Sooner the better. After dinner tonight.'

'Fine. I'll get back to you. And T…'

'What?'

'Don't do anything until we've talked.'

'Roger that.'

I hung up and continued wall-staring for a bit. That didn't make me feel any better at all. Perhaps I should go for a run, or hit the gym? Exercise was my default mood-changer. It was a habit leftover from having played so much sport when I was younger. But somehow, I still couldn't get my butt moving.

If only Cass was here. She'd want to go to the bakery for breakfast. But my runaway sixteen-year-old flatmate had left early for her part-time job at the deli. She wouldn't be back 'til late afternoon.

My phone beeped incoming messages and rescued me from my paralysis.

Call me ASAP!

It was from Garth Wilmot, my ex-fiancée and current accountant. Garth was a supercilious, uptight, know-it-all guy who I loved to hate. He was also dependable—above and beyond—and honest.

I was immediately intrigued. I'd known Garth for more than ten years and he'd never, ever sent me a message like that.

I rolled back onto my stomach, and hit his name in my contacts list.

He answered in an uncharacteristically high-pitched voice. 'Tar-ah?'

'What's up, Garth? Sock go missing? Coat hanger round the wrong way?' My standard dig at his OCD didn't elicit the response I was expecting.

'Can you come over right now?'

'Sure. I guess.'

'No ... wait ... they might be watching. Meet me at Sable's as soon as you can.'

'Who might be watching?'

'Just meet me, okay?' He sounded downright panicky.

'What's the time now?' I asked him.

'4PM'

'Give me twenty minutes,' I said crisply. 'I'll see you there.'

'Thank you.' The relief in his voice was so out of character, it gave me goosebumps.

I sprang up, suddenly energised, and grabbed clean knickers, a t-shirt and shorts from my sorting bench, aka the couch, on the way to the shower. Confusing and unwelcome love-life dilemmas melted away under the drill of the hot water, and were replaced by investigative curiosity. What did Garth want? Was he in trouble? He had to be in trouble? It'd be the only reason he'd need me.

I thought back to our relationship and brief engagement. JoBob—Joanna and Bob, my parents—had been thrilled to bits with Garth being both an accountant and a Wilmot. The Wilmot's were a large well-to-do family name with roots in Canberra politics. Garth had two uncles well-placed in the Liberal party and several cousins working at Parliament House. This brought him seemingly unending respectability as far as my mother was concerned, no matter how much I argued that I didn't vote Liberal and that politics was as dirty as organised crime. Or, in fact, maybe it was just organised crime in spectacles.

But Joanna had grown up with an old-fashioned awe for local two-party politics and the monarchy, and had been devastated when I broke off the engagement.

Why Tara? Why? Rang in my ears for weeks.

In fact, the Wilmots and the Sharps had taken it far

worse than either Garth or me. By then we'd worked out that we drove each other crazy.

Funny thing, though, was that I trusted him nearly as much as I trusted Bok and Smitts. Garth still did my tax for free, and I was his date when he had to go to work soirees and boring accountants' balls. We had the rules worked out these days. We were friends who couldn't see too much of each other on account of the fact that we got quickly annoyed by each other's irritating habits.

One thing Garth NEVER did was ring me in panic demanding to see me. Also, he'd picked Sable's, my cousin's bar in North Fremantle, to meet. It was a little out of the way for both of us, and not a place he'd normally go. When Garth did go out, he liked the after-work bars in the city where the women could afford to buy him drinks.

Adrenalin shivered me alive. Something was wrong. And now, it wasn't just my love-life.

I cut short the shower, donned my clothes, grabbed a bag and car keys and scooted down the driveway of my parents' house out to my car.

My dad was in the front garden leaning over an azalea bush with a pair of secateurs in his hand.

I waved and pulled a face at him.

He pulled an equally tragic face back.

Dad hated gardening. That's why they had a gardener who came in once a fortnight to weed and prune. These days, he only picked up the pruning shears when he was doing penance for something, or if Joanna was planning a soiree.

I hoped to hell it was the former. Joanna's soirees were impossible to dodge and usually involved her trying to set me up with an alcohol-soaked investment banker. Bok sometimes ran interference for me, pretending to be my boyfriend—until JoBob cottoned on to my ploy and had banned him.

'Soiree?' I mouthed at him.

His nod was curt.

I unlocked my car door and leapt in. It was official—I couldn't go home for at least a week.

About the Author

Marianne Delacourt is the pseudonym of a successful Australian sci-fi fantasy author who is sold throughout the world. Sharp Shooter and Sharp Turn are set in Perth, where the author grew up. Too Sharp, book three in the Tara Sharp series, is set in Brisbane where Marianne now lives with her husband and three sons..

Also from *deadlines*

Deadlines is the crime imprint of the award-winning Twelfth Planet Press specialty small press. We aim to promote quality, fun writing in fresh, exciting projects that seeks to raise the awareness of women's voices, and demonstrate the depth and breadth of Australian fiction to a broader audience.

Tara Sharp 2016

Sharp Shooter

Sharp Turn

Coming in 2017

Too Sharp

Sharp Edge

Café La Femme
by Livia Day

A Trifle Dead

The Blackmail Blend

Drowned Vanilla

Keep Calm & Kill the Chef (coming soon!)

Sharp Shooter

Tara Sharp Book One

Marianne Delacourt

Availiable in paperback and ebook

Tara Sharp should be just another unemployable, twenty-something, ex-private schoolgirl ... but she has the gift—or curse as she sees it—of reading people's auras. The trouble is, auras sometimes tell you things about people they don't want you to know.

When a family friend recommends Mr Hara's Paralanguage School, Tara decides to give it a whirl - and graduates with flying colours. So when Mr Hara picks up passes on a job for a hot-shot lawyer she jumps at the chance despite some of his less-than-salubrious clients.

Tara should know better than to get involved when she learns the job involves mob boss Johnny Vogue. But she's broke and the magic words 'retainer' and 'bonus' have been mentioned. Soon Tara finds herself sucked into an underworld 'situation' that has her running for her life.

Winner of the Davitt Award for Best Crime Novel and nominated for a Ned Kelly Award for Best First Crime novel.
Killer Nashville Silver Falchion Finalist

Sharp Turn

Tara Sharp Book Two

Marianne Delacourt

Availiable in paperback and ebook

Tara's quirky PI business is attracting some even quirkier customers. She's not sure how Madame Vine's Escort Agency got her number. And then there's the eccentric motorcycle racing team owner, Bolo Ignatius. Both these clients want to Tara to investigate suspicious circumstances that turn up dead bodies. That can only mean one thing in this town: John Viaspa. Tara goes in for round two with the local crime boss, while balancing the tight rope of her deliciously complicated love life.

Tara Sharp's life can only be describe as furious fun.

Book 1 in *The Café La Femme* series
Livia Day

Availiable in paperback and ebook

Tabitha Darling has always had a dab hand for pastry and a knack for getting into trouble. Which was fine when she was a tearaway teen, but not so useful now she's trying to run a hipster urban cafe, invent the perfect trendy dessert, and stop feeding the many (oh so unfashionable) policemen in her life.

When a dead muso is found in the flat upstairs, Tabitha does her best (honestly) not to interfere with the investigation, despite the cute Scottish blogger who keeps angling for her help. Her superpower is gossip, not solving murder mysteries, and those are totally not the same thing, right?

But as that strange death turns into a string of random crimes across the city of Hobart, Tabitha can't shake the unsettling feeling that maybe, for once, it really is ALL ABOUT HER.

And maybe she's figured out the deadly truth a trifle late…

Shortlisted for Best Debut Book, Davitt Award for Australian Women's Crime Writing

Killer Nashville Silver Falchion Finalist